Port of
No Return

A NOVEL

MICHELLE SAFTICH

ODYSSEY
BOOKS

Published by Odyssey Books in 2015
ISBN 978-1-922200-28-0

www.odysseybooks.com.au

A Cataloguing-in-Publication entry is available from the
National Library of Australia

ISBN: 978-1-922200-28-0 (pbk)
ISBN: 978-1-922200-29-7 (ebook)

This is a work of historical fiction, inspired by real-life persons and
events. Names, characters and incidents have been changed for
dramatic purposes. All characters and events in this story—even
those based on real people and happenings—are entirely fictional.

Cover image courtesy of Wikimedia Commons

For my father, Mauro, and in memory of his family.

Also, for my husband, Rene, and sons Louis and Jimi who inspire me to write about family and love.

Chapter one

January 1944
Fiume, Italy

'Finally, he sleeps,' Ettore grumbled as he dipped a chunk of hardened bread into a shallow dish of olive oil. His arms rested upon the wooden kitchen tabletop. A lit candle cast no warmth and only enough light to reach his callused hands. The oil caught the flame's reflection and glowed; he gazed past the golden orb, unseeing.

'He's exhausted,' Contessa replied. She sat opposite, a shadowy figure in the pre-dawn darkness.

'Aren't we all?' Ettore shook his head. Breakfast done, he scraped back his chair and reached for his coat. The thought of leaving to work on the docks, damp and chilly from the harbour mist, was not appealing, but work he must.

'I know. I'm sorry. I don't know what to do. My milk only upsets him,' Contessa despaired, not for the first time. She had left their three-month-old baby asleep in a bassinette in their bedroom, lying still—too still for her liking. His scrawny, closed fists flanked pale cheeks and his eyelashes had become mere clumps of moist spears attached to red and swollen lids that had borne too many tears and an unrelenting torrent of squalls and wails, keeping them awake all night, every night. But for now he slept.

'There's something we can try,' came a husky voice from the darkness. Contessa's mother, Rosa, the family's revered Nonna, was desperate to raise the parents' hopes. Coming out of her bedroom wrapped in a woollen shawl, she had caught her daughter's last words. She lit another candle, a larger one, and carried it towards them, chasing away the shadows.

Nonna was a tall, broad woman, olive skinned and robust, with long, coarse, black hair often caught in a crocheted net at the nape of her sturdy neck. This early, however, it hung like a curtain down the full length of her back. She had never been beautiful, but was handsome and well respected in their north Italian neighbourhood.

'I've tried everything,' moaned Contessa, exhaustion making it difficult to believe in solutions. Like her baby, she too was losing weight—though in her case it was from long hours on her feet nursing, cradling, and comforting her irritable son, while she sacrificed the greater portions of their meagre food supplies to her other children. Occasionally, Nonna would give her a break, but the baby only wanted his mother and remained unsettled in her arms.

Contessa's wool dress was covered in milky sick-ups, her hair—fairer and finer than her mother's—was frizzy and hard to pin back. She had not tended to it in days, leaving it spongy as fairy floss. The tendrils surrounded an almond-shaped face, drawn and weary, and her dark brown eyes struggled to keep open.

'Ah, but you haven't tried everything. You haven't tried my minestrone soup …'

'Minestrone!' Contessa was incredulous.

Despite his glum expression, Ettore smiled, squeezing his wife's tense and bony shoulders. 'You should listen to your mother. She knows …' he said. 'Now I best leave before the kids wake up and make me late.' He kissed Contessa on the cheek, but she couldn't smile.

'I don't know about soup … too rich for him. He'll bring up red sick everywhere.'

'Let me try,' insisted Nonna.

'Let her try,' Ettore agreed.

As much as she wanted to, Contessa didn't have the energy to argue. 'Okay, we'll try it.' She stood and kissed her husband on both cheeks. 'Ciao and keep safe,' she whispered.

Ettore wanted to heed her words, but these were not peaceful times. The war had brought years of devastation to Italy, and to Europe. For Ettore, it meant having to work for the Germans who had taken over their city in Italy's north-east. They lived in Fiume, a city the Germans had wanted for its strategically placed seaport. The city had also provided the Germans with many industries to support their war effort, including the oil refinery, torpedo factory and shipbuilding facilities. In the face of the occupation, the residents of Fiume had only one choice— to serve the heavily armed Germans.

Keep safe—and serve, Ettore thought sourly.

'Ciao,' he replied. He closed the door gently on his household of sleeping children. Apart from the sleeping baby, tucked up in their beds were six-year-old Taddeo, three-year-old Nardo and Marietta, aged two.

Rubbing sleep from bloodshot eyes, Ettore ambled down the familiar front steps and onto the cobblestone street, before making the steep and foggy descent to the port. The sun was rising, and he welcomed the light filtering through the mist. He thrust his frozen hands into his coat pockets and hunched his shoulders forward to cut through the icy air. Occasionally he peered through the window of an empty shop or a closed boutique or a boarded up school. On one corner was a century-old administration building that had been cracked apart and left to crumble away, the result of a bomb dropped from the sky a few months ago. The closer he got to port the more destruction he saw. War had come to this beautiful city—a city rich in Hungarian architecture, and old enough to boast ancient relics including an arched Roman gate. The presence of German troops had ensured that Fiume, its port and facilities, had become the target of deadly Anglo-American air raids—dozens of them.

His purposeful stride soon brought the port into view. Majestic four- and five-storey buildings fronted the harbour, including a grand old dame of a palace built by a Hungarian shipping company. It now overlooked a hectic display of vast, towering warships and raised submarines. German and Italian soldiers patrolled the decks of the ships and marched in unison down on the quays. For a moment, Ettore looked back at the city, where hills dotted with houses loomed—along these hilltops a line of cannons pointed towards the sky. Would they need them again? He prayed not.

He was early to work, preferred to be, for the Germans were strict when it came to clocking in. It was his job to help pressure test the submarines, find leaks and repair them. Not a bad job, but once the fully operational submarines left, crammed with men destined for naval combat, he did not like to dwell upon the poor bastards' futures. It was not a good way to die.

When he reached his station that morning, he did not even get a chance to clock in. The emergency sirens erupted, their shrill warning blaring across the entire city. Instantly, soldiers and workers were running in opposite directions. While those in uniforms raced to take up arms to defend the port, unarmed men scurried single-mindedly to the safety of bomb shelters. The words 'keep safe' rang in Ettore's ears, but he was no longer thinking of himself. Instead, he pictured his baby Martino at home, peaceful in exhausted slumber. He thought of his other three children, and of his weary but lovely Contessa and dependable Nonna. They would be hearing the sirens too. No baby could sleep through that racket.

'Keep safe,' he mouthed, almost out loud, but he was gripped by a sense of dread that would not leave him. 'Keep safe.'

* * *

Contessa had been standing at her second-storey window looking down on their front drive, where two petrol bowsers sat collecting dust. It marked the entry to her husband's workshop, where he had toiled for many years as a mechanic. Once a hive of activity, the business was deserted. It had been abandoned when Ettore had been conscripted into the Italian war effort. She remembered how nice it had been to have him downstairs, chatting to regular customers, bringing in enough money to buy fresh foods and small luxuries. They used to have a good, relaxed lifestyle—lazy mornings and late nights with friends. Back then her babies had suckled well and slept soundly. Laughter and feisty conversations had filled the house.

Contessa lifted her gaze. The early morning mist had evaporated to reveal clear skies; she could not help but notice that it was a perfect day for bombing. She tensed with apprehension and instantly regretted the gloomy thought. It would be a nice day, she assured herself. Contessa did not know what had drawn her to that spot, to look upon their cobblestone street, their neglected shopfront, to remember times before the war. From the window she could see the harbour—a bluish grey mirror reflecting sky and ships—and she wondered, with a sense of unease, what Ettore was doing. As she gazed out, she felt sadness weigh her down. The lack of sleep perhaps? And yet it felt stronger than just fatigue, closer to fresh grief—as if she was about to experience a deep loss. Looking back, it was as though she knew it would be the last time she would take in that view.

The sound of her children squabbling brought her away from the window and into the kitchen.

'I was here first,' six-year-old Taddeo whined.

'You had it yesterday,' cried Nardo.

The brothers were wrestling, their fair-skinned limbs entangled in a purposeful struggle. The subject of their battle was a chair. Its position close to the cast iron stove had made it popular.

Marietta, the youngest of the trio, stayed out of it, sitting the farthest from the stove but content to be eating her torn-off piece of oil-moistened bread.

'Stop pushing,' Nonna said sternly. Stirring the soup, she feared the boys might knock over the pot and spill its simmering contents on themselves. She had wanted to make minestrone, but it had turned out to be a very thin version—just canned tomatoes, water and a pinch of salt. Thanks to the war food was scare, and their measly rations could only be supplemented with what they could find on the black market.

'Can't you see this is hot?' Nonna admonished.

'But I was sitting here …'

Contessa swept into the room. 'Stop it, both of you! Taddeo, sit over there. Now! It's Nardo's turn.'

'But Mama …' Taddeo started.

'I've told you. Now move. All this fighting will wake Martino. How many times have I told you not to make too much noise when …'

Her call for quiet was ironically and comprehensively drowned out by the shrill blast of sirens. Fear and dread clutched at her already strained nerves. Her baby son awoke instantly with a piercing cry that matched the siren's intensity.

'Martino,' she shouted, bolting to her bedroom. From there she called back to her other children. 'Taddeo, Nardo, Marietta—grab your coats.'

By the time she had gathered up her baby and reached the front door, her other children were assembled, coats in hand.

'Put them on,' she instructed.

They did not need to be told twice. Despite their young ages, the children knew the drill and understood the importance of reaching the dugout shelter quickly. They were afraid, but didn't cry. The baby was crying enough for all of them.

'Nonna,' Contessa called.

The older woman rounded the corner with a glass baby bottle full of hot soup. She took her full-length coat from the rack by the door and slipped into it, then handed Contessa hers. While the day was fine, it was bitterly cold and they would need the protection of their woollen overgarments. Rugged up, they hurried outside.

'Nardo, stay with me,' ordered Taddeo, taking hold of his younger brother's hand. Their fight over the chair was completely forgotten.

Nardo gratefully clutched the hand that had wrapped around his, relieved to be guided through the chaos that the sirens had created. The two brothers kept their eyes on Nonna, who led little Marietta across the mossy cobblestones towards the church, three blocks away. The streets were overcrowded with people, all hurrying in the same direction, all with the same stern expression on their faces. Once in the churchyard, the boys followed their mother and Nonna into the shelter and joined the other families, mostly women and children, piling inside.

It was dark and musty in the dugout, but no one complained. Martino was still crying—a pathetic, hungry and urgent wail that did not help to settle the panic-stricken people bunkering down. Desperately, Nonna took the baby from Contessa's arms and put the bottle of cooling soup to his lips. She prayed he and his frail little body would accept it. He took a suck ... and another and another. He was silenced—at last. Content to be sucking on the sweet, warm juice he'd been offered, he was finally in a rare and blissful state—awake and quiet, simultaneously. Nonna looked at Contessa, whose brown eyes held tears of relief.

'It will be all right, Mama,' Taddeo said, misreading his mother's tears.

'I know, darling. I know,' she said, cupping his tiny face in her hands and planting a kiss on his lips. 'Thanks for looking after your little brother.'

She looked at Nardo, who was tall for his three years. His dark eyes were shining, but he emitted a calmness that even she could draw strength from. 'My brave Nardo,' she mouthed to him.

Across from her, clinging to her Nonna's coat, was Marietta, a chubby-cheeked girl with a head full of black curls and a prominent beak-like nose. Fear had rendered her still and silent.

Beyond the siren, they could hear the planes approach—a distant buzzing, which quickly grew into an alarmingly loud roar. Then the bombs started ... one, then soon after another, and another.

Oh God, thought Contessa as the ground trembled. *So close.*

There was a collective gasp among the women as the bombs fell again—too near. Contessa looked to Nonna, but her eyes were shut. Being Roman Catholic by faith, she sought solace through a murmured Lord's Prayer. 'And forgive us our trespasses as we forgive those who trespass against us ...'

More bombs ... their world was shaking, the blasts above loud and violent. It was the worst air raid to date and Contessa was terrified. Her boys sat closer, pressing their trembling bodies against her own. *Please stop*, she thought. How she wished Ettore was with them—it would be better to be together if anything should happen.

At last, the thunderous roar of the planes subsided, gradually fading until the sound was a distant hum. All was still. The sirens ceased. Someone in the shelter was crying—a frail, wrinkled old woman dressed in black, overcome by emotion. It added to the communal sense of despair. Whatever awaited them outside could not be good. They knew their part of town had not been spared this time. They waited, longer than perhaps was necessary, but shock had rendered them immobile. Eventually a few families ventured out.

'Come,' Contessa croaked to Marietta and the boys. They leapt to their feet, eager to follow their mother.

Nonna stood too, pressing the whimpering baby against her chest.

After so long in darkness, they emerged, quiet and still in the bright light. Even baby Martino had gone silent. Blinking, they became aware of the full extent of the surrounding damage. They shuffled home, their eyes wide with disbelief as they took in crushed houses, blackened and cratered yards and crumbled stone walls—occasionally a body could be seen beneath rubble and a wail of a loved one echoed in the distance. An old man was being helped away from the wreckage, blood gushing down his face.

Contessa buried Marietta's face against her coat in attempt to shield the toddler from the worst of it. She looked behind and saw her sons holding hands, their heads down, watching only their Nonna's feet as she walked in front. They had already seen enough to not want to look.

Such devastation! Contessa had not expected it to be in such a scale. Fear for her house, her neighbours and friends set in. She picked up her pace, Marietta stumbling alongside as they picked their way around houses and walls that had slid into the street. Plumes of dust scratched their eyes and stung the backs of their throats. Everywhere there were sharp, jutting objects to be avoided. Away from the bulk of the debris, their feet manoeuvred around uneven concrete and brick blocks, shattered glass, fallen street lamps and broken clay pots, window shutters and cracked roof tiles.

Home for Contessa was pegged by a strong, lean figure, simply clad in grey coat and trousers, standing, head bowed, where once a house had stood. He was in his thirty-fourth year of life and should have been reaping all he had sown. Instead, the man appeared crushed, defeated. On hearing their approach, he turned.

'Ettore ...' Contessa exhaled, her parched throat struggling to cry out her husband's name. He saw them and his eyes darted from face to face, accounting for each member of his family—only then could his legs find enough strength to stumble over. He picked up Marietta, whose black curls were littered with bits of paper and dust, and he noticed her cheeks were moist from tears, accompanied by frightening silence. He embraced the child, held her tightly and planted a kiss on her dark head, before plunking her safely on his shoulders. He ran his hand affectionately and roughly through his boys' thick hair. Then his eyes rested on the baby, at peace in his Nonna's arms. Relief that his family had escaped to the shelter momentarily replaced the devastation of finding his home, his business, all he had worked for, gone. There was nothing left. Nothing. Unlike other houses, theirs had disintegrated. No doubt the petrol bowsers and grease-filled workshop had fuelled the utter destruction.

'Where will we live now?' Nardo asked. His small voice quavered.

No one answered, but his father reached out and pulled him against his side.

Contessa surveyed the blackened hole in the ground then closed her eyes to it. *What will become of us?* she thought. *We've lost everything.*

Chapter two

The Coletta family lived at the foot of a hill on the outskirts of Fiume, a short walk from the end of the tramline. They had a farmhouse with chickens and goats, as well as a productive bee-hive and vines of luscious tomatoes.

In the past, their cellar had held the fruits of their labours: cheeses and cream made from goats' milk, jars of honey and stewed tomatoes and cartons of eggs - until the Germans took over the city. Soldiers quickly became regular, uninvited visitors, demanding they hand over their stores to feed the troops.

'You want to support the war effort, don't you?' they challenged. 'Come on then. Make a contribution and make it generous.'

Even after their generous contribution, the Germans would help themselves to three or four of their precious chickens as well.

The last time the soldiers visited there were only two sickly chickens to be found.

'They are all we have left,' Lisa told them mournfully.

They took them anyway. In truth, Lisa's husband had staked a lookout for the Germans. On seeing them approach, he had walked three strong goats up into the hills and carted away a large crate of healthy chickens. He had stayed hidden until the Germans were long gone.

'It worked,' Lisa told him happily on his return. 'They searched the cellar and didn't find anything. They searched the storage house—nothing again. They didn't like the look of those chickens and I told them they were our last.'

'Good. Hopefully they'll take us off their list and leave us alone.'

The soldiers returned one more time, but again, they hid their chickens and goats up the hill and the Germans left empty-handed. That had been four months ago.

It was mid-afternoon, and Lisa was sitting outside, plucking the feathers of a large waterfowl bird that her husband had caught by chance that morning. Head bowed in concentration, she was surprised to hear the front gate squeak, followed by the scraping of light footsteps. The knock on the front door was not the usual brisk, hard sound of the Germans' pounding so she did not believe she had soldiers on her doorstep, but she was not expecting guests. She was nervous, but intrigued.

Could it be a telegram? Her nineteen-year-old son, Marco, was away fighting, and a tragic delivery was always a possibility. But she had heard several footsteps.

Could it be her youngest son, Cappi, with comrades? He had run off with the Yugoslav Partisans, deciding it was better than being called up to fight for the Germans. When the Germans took over Fiume, they had rounded up all the young Italian men not yet at war, and sent them straight to the front line and almost certain death. Fearing such a fate, her son had fled into the hills and left it to his family to spread the false tale that he had become a commercial fisherman and left for sea. He had returned once, looking for food and warmer clothes.

Her husband, Dino, was at the markets and their sixteen-year-old daughter Lena was at work in the city and not expected back until dark.

Lisa took a deep breath and walked down the side of the house to peer around the corner suspiciously. Two women and a few children were huddled on the doorstep, a bedraggled lot, with tousled hair and long dusty coats.

'Can I help you?' she called, no longer harbouring any fear of her guests.

The younger woman turned and Lisa recognised her instantly—Contessa Saforo.

'Contessa!' Lisa cried, hurrying towards her friend, who only managed to return a wan smile in greeting. The sad-eyed woman held a baby, and around her were three tired children and her formidable mother.

'What has happened?' she asked, her voice thick with concern. Because of the war, she had not seen her friend in over a year.

Contessa, even with a grubby face and tangled hair and in obvious distress, was still a picture of loveliness, as she had always been.

Lisa envied her friend her gentle beauty and grace. Unlike Contessa, Lisa was somewhat brisk and bustling in her manner. At thirty-five, she was six years older than Contessa, but had started her family much earlier, giving birth to her first child at age sixteen. A strong, buxom woman, she had worked hard on their farm, especially during the war. Although the hard labour, hot sun and deep angst over her sons at war had toughened her skin, beneath it still laid a soft heart.

When her friend hesitated, Lisa waved her hand. 'Please come in.'

The dazed family shuffled inside and Lisa stifled an urge to wrap her arms around them all. 'Come sit down.'

She ushered them into a spacious room, which featured stone walls and floor, and a high ceiling with exposed oak beams. Black cloth hung from the windows for use as blackout curtains; the windows were taped up—a necessary precaution given the bombings. Along the left wall was a massive stone hearth. The children sat before it on a large, woven rug and Contessa and Nonna sat on a soft, but rather worn yellow sofa.

'It was the bombing …' Contessa began, wanting to explain their uninvited intrusion.

'Ettore … is he all right? He is not with you?'

'He is safe. He is at work.' She hesitated. 'But everything else, the house, our life, it is gone,' she said, tears in her eyes. She paused to compose herself, and then continued. 'We have nowhere to go. My sister is in Bergamo. We have no other family here. My mother, as you know, lives with us. We lost everything.'

Lisa's heart went out to her. 'You did right to come to us. We have plenty of room. Please don't worry. You are all welcome to stay ... until the war is over.'

Her last words revealed a generosity of such magnitude that Contessa could no longer contain her emotion. 'Oh no, Lisa. You are much too kind,' she said, wiping at tears that kept flowing. 'We couldn't stay long,' she sniffled. 'I only came to ask for one night's stay.'

'One night—and then what? Ask another friend and another? Moving your children and baby from house to house so as not to overstay your welcome? Don't be crazy! You must stay here until you have a real plan.'

• 'But we are a big family ...'

'Which is why you must accept my offer.' Lisa was adamant.

Contessa felt Marietta tugging on her dress and looked down.

'Please Mama. I like it here. They have goats.'

Lisa smiled broadly. 'You remember my goats. Bless you child but it's been a year and many months since you last visited. They must have made an impression on you. We still have three.'

'Do you have the one called Milksha?' the girl asked, flicking her black curls out of her eyes.

'Yes. She is the playful one. Why don't you children go out in the yard and see? Just remember to keep the gate shut.'

Marietta danced towards the door. 'Come on,' she said to her brothers.

Taddeo looked up at his mother. 'Is it all right if we go out-side?' he asked solemnly. The boys had been quiet and troubled since the bombing.

'Of course. Go see what else you can find,' their mother urged, wiping her damp hands on her dress, rimmed with ash from the burnt-out rubble.

'There are chickens. But keep away from the bees,' Lisa advised.

'I remember the bees,' Taddeo said with a smirk, having been stung at the last visit after venturing too close on a dare from his brother.

'They won't bother you if you don't bother them.'

'I won't,' Taddeo assured her.

Marietta bounded outside while her brothers followed slowly.

'The boys are feeling the shock, but Marietta is too young to understand,' Nonna said, once the children were out of earshot.

'War is no place for children,' Lisa said, understanding. 'The boys are young and strong. They will recover in time. Let them stay here. There is the small stone house out back ...'

'But that is for your stores,' Contessa said, not wanting to cause any disruption.

Lisa shook her head and lowered her voice. 'Up until two weeks ago, we were hiding a Jewish family in there,' she confided.

'Jews!' Nonna gasped, her voice barely above a whisper. 'You took such a risk!'

'They were our friends and we couldn't let them be loaded on the trains. There was a risk, but the Germans have been leaving us alone and we always had someone on lookout. They've now escaped, heading for southern Italy. I pray they got there. So, the point is—the house is ready and comfortable. It has a fireplace, which you can use for warmth and cooking. We have plenty of firewood.'

Contessa looked to Nonna who nodded her head.

'We would love to stay,' Contessa said, and her heart lifted with relief.

'It is only right that you do. I could never turn you away. Now come and I will show you the house. It's small, but it has two rooms and is clean and dry.'

The women inspected the house and were very pleased with its simple but comfortable furnishings. As they looked over the cups and plates in a small cupboard, Martino started to cry.

'We have only one baby bottle,' Contessa said.

Nonna held up the empty glass bottle that she had been carrying in her coat pocket since they left the house the day before.

'He does not take the breast?' Lisa inquired, knowing that her friend had breast-fed all her previous children.

'He won't take milk,' Contessa said, in a sigh that revealed some of her exasperation.

'Tomato soup ...' Nonna cut in.

Lisa smiled. 'Tomato soup! Mercy! This baby likes it sweet, hey? Luckily, we've plenty of tomatoes—though the jars are hidden.'

'The Germans ...?'

Lisa nodded. 'Let's get that hungry baby fed,' she said as Martino's cries increased in volume.

Contessa nursed the baby to keep his cries under control while the other two went to work in the kitchen. Soon, they had enough tomato soup to keep the baby fed for two days. Martino was silenced. Peace had returned. With the highest priority sorted, they then turned their attention to freshening up the storehouse and helping Lisa prepare that night's meal. Nonna put her talents in the kitchen to good use. Excited to be working with more ingredients than she had seen in a long while, the older woman set about making stuffing for the bird and preparing a tomato-flavoured gravy to accompany it.

When Lisa came into the kitchen, she was pleasantly surprised.

'You can stay as long as you like,' she enthused, inhaling the savoury aroma. 'Look at that! I can't wait to serve this up to Dino.'

'How is your husband? It has been—what, four years since we last saw him?' Nonna inquired.

Their families used to get together regularly, but once the war had broken out, they had not socialised—night curfews, blackouts, raids, food shortages and late work shifts had not made it practical to make the journey across town for a dinner party. Lisa and Contessa had still managed to meet up during the day but even those visits had become less frequent.

'He is well. Tired of the war, but well enough.'

'That is good to hear. I would change for dinner but we have only the clothes we have arrived in. The children have only their coats and bed clothes.'

'I can lend you some clothes for now. Though tomorrow we should visit the local church. I know they are helping families to replace clothes and other things,' Lisa said. 'It's a short walk from here.'

'Thank you. I think we'll have to ask for a handout from the parish,' Nonna said, feeling embarrassed. 'I have often given.'

'Then it is your turn to be helped.'

Lisa's husband Dino arrived home an hour after the sun had set. Ettore arrived about ten minutes later. They had caught the same tram, yet not seen each other, and it had taken Ettore longer to recall the way to the house, having last visited it several years ago.

Contessa had assured her husband they would be able to stay at the farm for at least one night and had arranged to meet there come nightfall, but she was delighted to inform him they could stay as long as they needed.

'Are you sure?' he pressed, surprised at such open hospitality.

'I'm sure. Lisa would not let me refuse!'

Dino was also surprised but proud of his wife for taking in the homeless family. He found her in the kitchen, looking happy yet flushed from the heat of the fire burning in the stove.

'We've only just farewelled the Jews, now it's your school friend,' he whispered to her good-naturedly, while she stirred Nonna's thickening sauce. 'You have a soft heart.'

He kissed her moist cheek. 'Dinner smells incredible,' he said, trying to see what was simmering. His cheeky face and ready smile were trying to charm her into an early sample.

'Just wait. Go wash your hands,' Lisa told him. 'We are serving up in minutes.'

The short, dark-skinned man chuckled as he reluctantly retreated from the kitchen. As instructed, he washed his hands then ducked out on the porch, despite the chilly night. He waved at Ettore to follow him.

'Here,' Dino handed his friend a cigarette. He had acquired a packet on the black market early that morning. Cigarettes were hard to come by. He had been looking forward to smoking one all day and would enjoy it even more in being able to share the moment with an old friend.

'Light up,' he said giving him a matchbox.

Ettore was impressed. A cigarette! A rarity! He smoked it and smiled.

Dino struck the match proudly. 'One of the few joys left to us these days,' he muttered, lighting up and inhaling deeply. 'Ah.'

'We take what we can,' Ettore agreed.

'Damn war.' Dino recalled Ettore had had a fine house on a hill and a large workshop beneath a floor of three bedrooms. It was hard to imagine it was no longer there. He recalled many a good meal enjoyed in their kitchen served with Nonna's home-made liqueurs, but that was a long time ago.

'Your children—Marco, Lena and Cappi—how are they?' Ettore asked. The last time he had seen Lena she was twelve years old. 'Your daughter must be what—sixteen now?'

'She works all day at the torpedo factory and then does a night shift. She won't be home until after midnight.'

Ettore was not surprised. It was common for the young ones to work two jobs, but he was sad to hear that the young woman worked in such a dangerous place—a key target of the air raids. She was a nice girl and kind to his children. He knew they were looking forward to seeing her.

'That is no good,' he told his friend. 'I pray she keeps safe. And how is the farm?'

'It has its challenges. With food rations the way they are we are lucky to have the extra food and we do well at trading on the black market. But our honey draws German soldiers faster than flies.'

Dino took a long drag on the cigarette. 'And my son Cappi is still with the Yugoslav Partisans. They are killing off the odd German and Italian soldier. Cappi has managed to stay out of it—for now. If it comes to full-scale battle ...'

'When it comes to battle,' Ettore observed.

'You are right. When the Germans weaken, the Yugoslavs will make a grab for our city and then my Cappi will have to come home.'

'The Partisans are not organised though.'

'No. But they will be.'

The men considered what a Yugoslav assault would mean to Fiume and shuddered in the chill of the night. The majority of the city's population, more than eighty per cent, were Italian, though the surrounding suburbs and a nearby town were Croatian.

Fiume had once been ruled by Hungary, but with the collapse of the Austro-Hungarian monarchy at the end of World War I, it had become a city under dispute, with both Italy and Yugoslavia putting in a claim. After a period of strife and intense diplomatic negotiations, a peace treaty eventually assigned its governance to Italy. However, the Yugoslav neighbours had never taken their eyes from the prize, and another chance was looming.

'Any news of Marco? He is away fighting?'

'No news. No news is good news.'

The cigarettes were finished. The men stood silent in the dark, their thoughts even darker.

'Time to go in,' Dino said at last—the aroma of garlic and tomatoes too enticing to ignore any longer.

The meal was the best the Saforo family had consumed in a long time. Even Lisa and Dino were elated to have a different and flavoursome meal before them. Slices of roast bird were served alongside mushroom and goat cheese stuffed tomatoes.

'Yummy,' Marietta said, sauce spread from cheek to cheek. The bird was similar to chicken, its skin crisp and its meat juicy.

Afterwards, the families shared the warmth of the fireplace and took turns telling the children stories. Their stomachs were full, their faces flushed, and the joy of good company put them all in good spirits. It was just what Contessa had needed.

* * *

While her family relaxed by the fire, sixteen-year-old Lena was hard at work, polishing the torpedoes until they shone, using one hand and then the other, until both wrists felt strained. But on that night, it was not just her hands giving her cause for pain. She had a bad toothache—one that was becoming harder and harder to ignore.

Lena had dreamed of being a dressmaker, and had been learning the trade when the war broke out. After the Germans occupied Fiume, she was rounded up with the other young people and assigned work. Her task was to shine weapons that would then be loaded on to trains, destined for Trieste, where they were transported to Germany for use in the war. As she polished, she wondered how many lives, how many ships they would destroy. Sometimes, she would catch her own reflection on the shiny casing and be surprised at the depth of the sorrow she would see in her eyes.

After a long day in the factory, she had to attend to her night work and walk to a large hall, not far from the port, to help serve food for up to one thousand workers, finishing their late shifts across various city posts. It was exhausting, even for a girl of her age.

It was eleven o'clock at night and her shift wouldn't end for another hour. Lena was now in sheer agony. She clutched at her jaw, trying to press down on the throbbing, unrelenting ache, her face contorted in pain. Her obvious discomfort eventually caught the eye of her matronly supervisor—an Italian nonna, who made no secret of the fact that she felt sorry for all her young charges.

'What is wrong?' she asked of the tall, slim girl, whose green-flecked eyes were wide and troubled.

'My tooth,' she replied, hardly able to speak.

The matron, whose hair was plastered against her forehead from hours spent sweating over bubbling pots, wiped her brow and glanced up at the clock. 'Why don't you go home now? We can finish up here all right.'

'Thank you,' the serving girl managed to mumble through her clenched jaw. The pain was such that Lena, after pulling on her coat, chose to wrap her woollen scarf around her head and beneath her chin to apply pressure to the tender site. She caught the second last tram and disembarked at the end of the line. Home was only a short walk away.

It was close to midnight, and her blistered feet scurried along the street, eager to be home. However, as she turned the corner, two uniformed men came into view. It was dark and no one else was about. Usually when she caught the last tram, it would be crowded with workers finishing the late shift and she would walk home with a few others heading in the same direction. Catching the earlier tram had meant alighting by herself. She slowed her pace and pulled her scarf tighter around her face, hoping to hide her youth and prettiness from their prying eyes. In the low light, she was unable to tell if they were German or Partisan, and she felt her skin crawl with apprehension.

'You there! Where are you going at such an hour?' they demanded to know in Yugoslav, which set her heart pounding fearfully. She did not understand them, but knew they were questioning her. The German soldiers had been ordered not to harm women, but the Yugoslav Partisans were under no such policy.

'I'm sick,' she said in Italian, then again in German, hoping they would understand one of the languages.

They studied her for a long moment and talked between themselves.

As they conversed, her fear grew. Despite her long legs, she did not think she could flee or outrun the men. Trembling, she kept her face lowered and waited.

'Take off your scarf,' one of the men said.

She looked at them helplessly, not understanding.

The gruff, thick-necked man strutted over and wretched the knitted item away from her, so they could get a full view of her face.

'She's very pretty,' he said admiringly, his dark eyes squinting.

'A pretty girl alone at night must be looking for something,' the taller one said, licking his fat bottom lip and gawking at her breasts.

Lena felt their eyes raking over her body. She crossed her arms and tried to take a step forward, away from them.

The tall man grabbed her roughly by the arm and she let out a small yelp of pain and panic.

A voice, strong and forceful, boomed across the street.

'Unhand her.' The command was given in Italian. The Communist soldiers, unshaven and uncouth, turned, ready to knock down whoever had dared to interrupt their play. They never saw him. The short man went down first—a thick staff of wood slammed into the back of his head and, with a bone-chilling crack, he slumped to the ground, unconscious. The other watched his comrade collapse and, not wanting to take on such a capable foe, fled. He released the girl and ran into the darkness, his boots crunching on gravel in the distance.

'Not so brave now,' the Italian commented. Lena glanced at the man who had come to her aid so swiftly. He looked familiar, but it was dark and she couldn't make out his face. She gathered that he was about the same age as her father, perhaps a few years younger. He wore a nice coat and the outline of his features reminded her of Humphrey Bogart, the famous actor—whose poster had been in the window of the city cinema.

'Thank you. Thank you,' she breathed. Her tooth shot a stab of pain through her jaw and her hand flew to it.

'Are you hurt? Did he hit you?'

'No. My tooth.'

The man smiled kindly, picked up her scarf and handed it to her. 'Come. We best get moving before he wakes up. I'll walk you home,' he turned her in the direction of her house and they started to walk briskly.

'You know where I live ... and I know you,' she said, wincing as she spoke.

'Yes. My name's Ettore. I haven't seen you for a few years. My family is staying in your farm's storehouse. You are lucky I couldn't sleep. Our fire had burned low and I came down this way to search for more firewood.'

He waved the wooden staff that he had used as a weapon, indicating it was meant for the fire.

'Ettore ... you are Contessa's husband! I know you. Ouch.'

'Stop talking. We will get that tooth looked at. Nonna should know just the trick for easing your pain.'

Lena smiled as best she could. 'You went the wrong way for firewood.'

'Lucky for you.'

* * *

The next morning, right on sunrise, Ettore awoke. He was alone on the mattress. Where was everyone? Why hadn't Contessa woken him?

He splashed icy water on his face from a full bucket by the door, dressed hurriedly in his work clothes and went to the main house in search of his family. He found them seated at the large wooden table in the kitchen. Marietta was seated on Lena's lap, who helped the toddler to dip her spoon into a cracked boiled egg. Nardo and Taddeo had finished their eggs and were guzzling a glass of milk. Contessa had offered Martino a sample of warmed goat's milk and, if the glow in his cheeks was anything to go by, he seemed to be enjoying it. Even Contessa appeared more radiant, having washed and brushed her hair—not to mention having had a decent night's sleep. With Martino feeding well, he was now sleeping well—right through the night, allowing everyone else to slumber in peace.

'Good morning,' Nonna sang out to Ettore as he appeared. 'There is an egg for you keeping warm beneath the apron.'

'Thank you.' He lifted the cloth, found the egg and cracked it open. It was golden yellow in the centre and he plucked the plump yolk out hungrily. Still tired from the previous night's events, he sank into a spare chair at the table.

'I heard about your night,' Contessa said softly to him. 'Lisa told me.'

'Yes, Lisa met us when we came in and helped Lena with her sore tooth. How is it feeling this morning?' he asked the teenage girl. A giggling Marietta was being bounced on her knee.

'It is so much better,' she said, smiling happily.

'Glad to hear it.'

'It was an infection of the gum,' Nonna informed them. 'The salt pack and warm water has got it under control now. Keep up with the salt,' she instructed the girl.

'Yes, I will.'

With breakfast over, Ettore, feeling somewhat embarrassed about the role he had played in coming to the girl's aid, hurried from the warm and cosy kitchen, pausing on his way out to kiss the top of Nardo's head. He then went in search of his boots, which he found on the porch where he had left them. There, hunched over with cold, he found Dino, having a cigarette. Dino looked up and brightened on seeing Ettore.

'You're awake,' Dino stated and in three strides was before his friend, embracing him. 'Lena told her mother everything. I can't thank you enough. I can't repay you enough. If not for you … here, take it,' he said, thrusting the packet of cigarettes at him. 'Take them all.'

'Don't be crazy. You keep them,' Ettore pushed the packet back at his friend. 'We are already in your debt for letting us stay here.'

'Now I am in your debt—a debt I could never repay if you stayed here a thousand nights.'

'I could not stand by and do nothing.'

'Lena said you were out looking for firewood,' Dino put to him, raising a questioning brow. There was plenty of wood by the storehouse. It was hard to miss it.

Ettore smiled knowingly and sat down on a wooden bench to pull on his boots.

'Actually, I went to the outhouse, it was then I saw the Partisans walk down your street towards the tram line. They were armed and acting suspicious. I wanted to see what they were up to. I knew your girl must be coming home soon, so I armed myself with that stick of wood I found in your front yard and followed them.'

'We often see the guards around here. They are patrolling the outskirts to make sure men don't desert or people don't try to leave the city without a pass. They don't usually accost our women but they are getting more hostile towards the Italians. From now on, I'll meet her at the station.'

'You could try reporting them to the Italian authorities,' Ettore suggested.

'They are powerless to do anything.'

'For now, perhaps.' Ettore had his boots on and he stood. 'At least one of them has a large bump to his head.'

Dino smirked. 'I'm glad of it.'

'I best get off to work. I'll see Contessa first.'

'Thanks again, Ettore,' Dino said, his voice cracking with sincerity as he shoved a cigarette into his coat pocket. 'For later, yes?'

'Tonight, yes. Thanks.'

Ettore found Contessa in the living room, putting the baby down on the rug. Martino smiled and gave a squeal of delight on seeing his father approach.

'It is good to see you not crying, little one,' Ettore commented.

On hearing his voice, Contessa came to her feet. 'What you did last night …' she started.

'Was the right thing.'

'Was risky and …'

'I couldn't stand by and watch the girl be harmed—the daughter of the man who has taken in my family and put a roof over our heads and given us more food than we have seen in months.'

Contessa closed her mouth. Then said more softly, pleadingly, 'No more risks.'

'There is a war on.'

Contessa took a deep breath. 'I know. We all know that. We just had our house bombed.' The tears were in her eyes again.

Ettore wrapped his arms around her and kissed her wet cheeks. 'Tessa, Tess … these happenings are out of our control. We will have another house. Let's just see the war out. Let's wait and see. We are all alive. The baby has never been happier.'

She smiled grudgingly and wiped her eyes. She was much less tense since Martino started taking the soup, and now he was keeping down goat's milk too. 'I'm sorry. I don't want you to be late for work. You should go and catch your tram.'

They kissed briefly and he was gone, back to report to the Germans.

When is the war going to end? she thought, kneeling down next to Martino. The baby looked at her searchingly, then gave her a joyful smile. *For him, the world is still peaceful and safe. He will not even remember the war,* she realised. How she envied him that.

Chapter three

The Saforo family were feeling much more settled. They had made the stone storehouse into a homely space, filling it with cushions, rugs and knitted blankets. They used boxes for cupboard drawers, which the children were encouraged to brighten with crayons.

Winter eventually gave way to spring—a busy time at the farmhouse for planting, pruning and trimming. Always looking for a way to repay the Coletta family's hospitality, Contessa and Nonna threw themselves into the work. They were often seen wearing gloves, with turban-like scarves around their heads— turning the soil, clipping branches and removing diseased stems that had struggled to thrive through the winter.

For Contessa the work was very satisfying, and helped to take her mind off worries about the war and their future. In fact, at the farmhouse they were very much protected from the worst of it and her fears lessened. She also enjoyed Lisa's company enormously.

One sunny Sunday, Lisa decided they should have a picnic outside. With breezes still keeping the house cold, the idea of lunching in the sun was well received, and the women went to work, cutting slices of bread and cheese and cracking nuts. Once done, they congregated around the food, sitting on wooden chairs, crates or the grass, as they helped themselves to the large plates. Sunday was a rare day when they were all at home and the men and Lena didn't have to rush off early to work.

Once the food had been devoured, Lena stood and walked over to where her mother and father were seated on old wooden crates.

'Papa, Mama … I have something to tell you,' Lena announced tentatively. 'I've met a young man. His name is Rico. He is studying mechanical engineering at college during the day, and at night he works as a fireman for the Germans. He has asked me to marry him. He wants to meet you, Papa, to ask your permission.'

Lisa and Dino were stunned, to be sure. They had not known she was seeing anyone.

'How long have you known him?' her mother asked.

'We have known each other only ten weeks, but it is enough. We love each other.'

At that, both parents started to smile. The war had intensified every part of their lives, even love, apparently.

'Bring him home at once. We can't wait to meet him,' Dino declared. 'Everyone, raise your glasses …' They were only drinking water but everyone did as he said.

'May a husband keep my daughter safe and happy.'

'Happy in love,' added Ettore. Lisa, Contessa and Nonna applauded. They all drank deeply.

'Surely I have a bottle of wine somewhere in the cellar for such an occasion,' Dino said, already wandering off in search of it.

'Save it for the wedding,' his wife shouted after him.

But he did not heed her and returned with a dusty bottle, filling their glasses with a thick, dark syrup—a wine as black as olives. It kept the smiles on their lips and in their eyes. While they sipped, they took it in turns to barrage the poor girl with questions until, laughing, she put up her hand in defence.

'Enough. You just have to wait to meet him. I can tell you no more,' Lena said.

'But I thought you were going to marry me,' Nardo suddenly piped up, his tone serious.

No one had noticed the brooding boy, splitting blades of grass into a small green pile at his feet.

Ettore laughed good-naturedly. 'You have good taste my boy. But you are too young. There will be another girl for you.'

'I don't want another girl,' he said solemnly and then ran off, wanting to put the many sympathetic smiles behind him.

* * *

Looking back, Contessa saw that spring as a happy time. They were very much a part of the small but joyous wedding that followed. Held at the farmhouse, Lena's family and friends joined with her husband's large family and friends from college and the fire station to bless Lena and Rico, wishing them a long life together. Rico turned out to be a handsome man—fair haired and blue eyed. He wasn't as tall as Ettore, but he was broad and strong, and bright as well. Dino and Lisa welcomed him into the family with open arms. Wine was sourced from the black market and filled many a glass. The accordion played, and the guests danced and sang until close to dawn.

Lena was sorry that her brothers had been absent, but somehow Cappi had sent a written message wishing her well.

Little Nardo had come around to accepting the union on seeing that Rico was indeed a good match for his lovely Lena. He took comfort in the thought that a worthy opponent had bested him.

Such occasions were made all the more special in their isolation—for the war dominated their way of life and gave them little to celebrate.

Soon after, Lena fell pregnant. Once confirmed, she could give up her work duties and cease her daily shift at the torpedo factory. Her parents and Rico slept easier, knowing she was no longer working in such a high-risk area. The bombs still fell though, and each time the siren sounded, Lena found herself struggling a hundred metres uphill to a bomb shelter, a trip that grew harder the more advanced her pregnancy became.

Hers was not the only pregnancy, even in such difficult times. On the day before Christmas Eve, Contessa told everyone that she was pregnant with her fifth child. To mark the occasion, Nonna wanted to cook up a treat and sent Ettore off with a shopping list of ingredients that could only be sourced from the black market.

He returned to find Contessa waiting for him on the front porch. She held the door open and followed him into the kitchen, peering into the box as he placed it on the table.

'Next time we should send Dino,' Contessa teased, smiling as she took jars and packets out of the box. 'I don't recognise any of these items from the list.'

Ettore turned and wrapped his arms around his wife, drawing her near. 'Dino would've done no better. These were the best foods the market had to offer today.'

'Then they'll have to do,' she said, gazing into her husband's eyes and rubbing her hands along his arms.

'So, after losing so much, now we have a baby on the way,' he said, glancing down at her stomach.

'Do you want a boy or girl this time?'

'Well, we have three boys. It's time to give Marietta a sister, I think.'

They both smiled, imagining Marietta's happiness on being presented with a sister.

'The boys will want another brother,' Contessa noted.

'A sister will be just as loved. They are good boys. His hands slid down his wife's hips and spanned her belly. 'What shall we name her?'

Contessa pressed her lips together, considering. 'I named Martino. It is your turn. What name do you like?'

He thought for a moment. 'How about my mother's name?'

Contessa met his serious eyes. His mother had died before the war began. 'Yes. If it is a girl …' she agreed readily, and he kissed her long and hard.

It was fortunate that Nonna was an excellent cook. Later that afternoon, using honey instead of sugar, she turned out a rich and moist Venetian style carrot cake—a wonderful treat indeed. She put it aside and served it up to both families after dinner as a special dessert. After every cake crumb was licked from their fingers, they sat in the living room by the fire, Contessa basking in Ettore's adoring gaze. She was the happiest she'd been in a long while.

That Christmas would be the last of the family celebrations to be held at the farmhouse. Dark days were ahead and a miserable winter descended. Life might have been stirring within Contessa's belly—but outside, guerrilla-style attacks by the Yugoslavs were increasing, resulting in more Italian and German deaths. They heard the military was carrying out reprisal attacks on surrounding Croatian villages, which only served to fuel more intense hatred and violence. Fiume's Italians were all too aware that their city was on borrowed time and they were becoming apprehensive that, as the world war appeared to be winding up, the local threat was escalating.

One night in April, Ettore returned home from work, his mood pensive and troubled. Contessa watched him uneasily. Lost in his thoughts, he frowned and muttered under his breath, keeping to himself and hardly eating a thing at dinner, which wasn't like him at all. Disturbed, she still did not attempt to find out what ailed him until they were alone in bed, the children asleep.

'What is it?' she asked.

They were in each other's arms. The room was dark except for the low light that filtered in from the front room, where a low fire crackled.

'I overhead talk—two German officers, high in rank. I understood parts of it and what I didn't understand, I had confirmed from other men, Italians, who had also overheard bits and pieces.'

'What?' She was intrigued but frightened. She knew it had to be bad news.

There was no easy way to tell her so Ettore launched into the dreadful truth. Hearing it in the dark made it all the more sinister for Contessa.

'Are you sure?' she gasped. She had known it would eventually happen but now that it was, she didn't want to believe it.

'Yes, there is no doubt. Yugoslav troops are on the way—thousands, tens of thousands, perhaps hundreds of thousands.'

'But the Germans will fight?' she pressed nervously.

'The Germans are amassing around the city in an arc—to the east and north—and geographically they have the advantage, but the Yugoslavs are a mighty force and strong under Tito's command. They will be hard to defeat.'

Contessa rested her hand on her husband's chest. 'If the Communists win … if they take Fiume …' She could not finish.

'It is possible. We have to consider it. If they come—we'll have to get out.'

'How? The authorities won't let us leave.'

'We'll have to find a way,' he said firmly.

Contessa put a hand beneath her breasts where her skin was stretched taut and round. She was afraid the panic fluttering in her stomach would upset her unborn child. Stay calm, she told herself. The Germans may hold them back.

On April 20th, the attack began. The 4th Army, along with several Partisan divisions, marched forth to meet stiff German resistance. However, the Germans were clearly outnumbered and early reports told of a large, brutal battle being waged.

A solemn mood settled over Fiume. It was like a sea of dark clouds had rolled in overhead and every eye was watching and waiting. The threat of occupation was imminent—it was a storm that had to come.

Contessa attended church and prayed for their city not to be seized. Spare us, she begged on her knees. It had already been a long war, and she was weary. She craved peace.

At the farmhouse, for the sake of the children, Ettore and Contessa kept up a brave front and did not let their children know how perilous their situation had become. So much hinged on the outcome of the battle.

On Sunday night, Lena and her husband Rico, who now lived in an apartment in the city, came to visit for dinner. Lisa baked a mushroom omelette and served it with stewed tomatoes. Martino sat at the table on a seat made high with cushions. He could now tolerate a range of foods and loved the soft fluffy egg, which his mother was now spooning into his mouth.

'Good boy,' Ettore praised. He still rejoiced in watching his young son eat. The first few months of his life, when he was rejecting milk and losing weight, had worried Ettore more than he had let on. Still a scrawny child, every mouthful of food he consumed was a blessing to his parents, and they longed to fatten him up, always pushing seconds on him—a push met with stubborn resistance.

'He eats like a sparrow,' Nonna was fond of saying.

At least he is eating, Ettore thought.

'More salt,' Lisa said, passing the shaker to Rico.

'Mama—if his eggs were any saltier they'd taste like clams!' Lena cried.

'He likes them salted,' Lisa said defensively.

'Salted, not preserved,' her daughter laughed.

'Thank you. My eggs are cooked to perfection,' Rico assured his new mother-in-law. Lisa smiled at him then turned to Lena.

'See, he likes them.'

Contessa smiled, amused by the exchange. She lifted the

spoon to feed some more egg to Martino and in doing so glanced over his shoulder. There, in the kitchen doorway, she spied a strange figure—a young, wiry man with a dark, rough beard and unblinking eyes. He was clothed in black and held a rifle at his side. His entrance had been stealthy—his sudden appearance and the shocking sight of him brought a scream to her lips.

Everyone turned in the direction of her sight.

'It's okay, Contessa. It's my son Cappi.' Lisa was on her feet in an instant, rushing to embrace the son she had not seen in over a year, but he did not smile, and only returned the embrace briefly.

'I've come to warn you, father,' he said quickly and quietly. 'I must have a word with you and your friend, Ettore. We must talk quickly. Hurry!'

Ettore and Dino did not hesitate to heed his words, and followed him into the living room where the fire was blazing. They did not sit down.

'Your name is Ettore Saforo,' Cappi started.

'Yes.'

'I've seen your name on the list. They are coming for you. The Partisans.'

There was a gasp behind them and they turned to see Contessa, hand over her mouth. 'No,' she cried and ran to her husband's side, clutching his arm.

'I've heard Partisans are entering the suburbs looking for Italians known to be working with the Germans,' Ettore said coldly.

'What are they doing with them?' Contessa asked.

Cappi looked to Contessa's belly and saw that she was pregnant. He did not answer.

'Tessa, go back in the kitchen,' her husband said gently.

'No. Go on, say what you have to say—all of it,' she addressed Cappi, urging him not to spare her any details.

'They are on their way. They know you live here. They will come for you soon—within the hour. If you stay here another night, you will be taken by morning. Your name is on the list. I saw it with my own eyes.'

Now Lisa rushed into the room and ran to her son.

'Cappi, you should go. You risked much to give us this warning and bless you for it. But now go.' She put a cloth bundle of boiled eggs and cheese into his hand and kissed him hard on his unshaven cheek.

'I am safe, Mama. I am with a group of Partisans who understand my situation. You and Papa will be left unharmed. I have their word. But I cannot save your friend. He has worked in direct support of the Germans and it is well known.'

'You have helped more than could be expected,' Ettore told him, humbled by the risk the young man had taken.

'I can tell you if you run into the hills, staying to the west, you will be safe. Other Italians have taken refuge there—you will be in good company. But you must run now.'

Ettore looked at his wife. 'What about my family?'

There was a long, uncomfortable silence, as no one wanted to think the worst, but think they must.

'We'll watch over them,' Dino promised, his voice tight.

'They are not so interested in women and children, especially pregnant women,' Cappi said. 'You should go.'

'You too,' Lisa told her son, pushing against him. 'Go, both of you.'

Ettore fetched his coat by the front door.

'I'll pack you some clothes,' Contessa said, wanting her husband to escape, but worrying about how he'd manage.

'No time for that,' Cappi advised over his shoulder. His mother pushed him towards the back door. Before she could shove him out, he turned, and with his first smile of the night, called: 'Ciao Mama, Papa.' Then he was gone into the darkness as quietly and quickly as he had arrived.

'Tomorrow, I'll check in with Dante at the general store. We can exchange messages through him,' Ettore said, slipping into his coat. The local shopkeeper and his store were close to the tracks leading up to the hills.

'Yes. I'll pack clothes and food and leave the parcel for you at the store,' Contessa agreed calmly, though her eyes were glazed with fear.

'I'll keep safe,' he assured her. They kissed and then Contessa shoved him towards the back door. 'Go. Hurry. Before they come.'

At the door, he hesitated. 'First, one promise.'

'What is it?' she asked, fighting her exasperation.

'You go too. Get the children out of Fiume as soon as possible. I will find you.'

'How?'

'However, wherever … details don't matter. We must leave—all of us.'

'All right, all right. We will all leave. I promise I'll find a way. Now go.'

They kissed and Contessa felt her tears on their lips. She was desperately afraid for him. She didn't want to lose him, didn't want to let go, but knew she must.

As they parted, she wanted to pull him back, but she dared not. There was nothing more to say or do. She watched him as he ran along the grass past the storehouse, the beehive, around the chicken coup and up the slope in the soft moonlight, his swift form blending with the shadows of the trees. Above, the cold forest was silent—he would hide there in the dark.

He was gone.

What to do now?

She could not return to her meal. Her stomach was so tight, she thought she would be sick, but she could not give in to it. The Partisans would be coming in search of her husband within the hour. She had to tell them something, something that would buy him time. But what?

She hurried to the storehouse that had become their home and frantically started grabbing her husband's clothes in huge armfuls and shoving them into buckets. To hide the articles she placed baby cloth nappies on the top.

'What are you doing?' Nonna asked, entering the storehouse, her expression full of concern. 'What is happening?' Martino was on her hip, sucking his thumb with wide, tired eyes.

'I have to prepare ...'

Behind Nonna, the children appeared—Nardo, Marietta and Taddeo. They sensed trouble and were curious at this unusual activity.

'Where's Papa?' Nardo asked, looking around.

'Come in and shut the door,' Contessa snapped, rigid with fear.

The children came in and Taddeo closed the door. She looked at her children and marvelled at how tall her eldest son had grown. His hair had lightened and his kind eyes were full of concern. Nardo, chin raised, standing tall and proud and ready to help, stared at her expectantly.

'Papa's gone. Children, whatever happens ... do not say a single word. No matter what you see or hear, you let me do the talking and you agree with everything I say. Yes?'

'Who will you be talking to?' Taddeo asked.

'What's happening?' Nonna asked sharply. She walked over to the far corner of the room and put Martino down on a spread of cushions. He whimpered at being separated from his warm Nonna, but then picked up a cushion to cuddle.

'You should all go back to the kitchen ...' Contessa started to advise, but it was too late.

At that moment, they heard a loud, forceful rapping at the front door of the farmhouse. The four children and Nonna fixed their eyes on Contessa.

'Sit with your brother,' she commanded.

The children, picking up on the fear in their mother's voice, ran to join Martino on the cushions, without question. They sat close to each other and turned to face their mother.

'Let me do the talking,' she reminded them, taking a deep breath and preparing herself for the role of her life.

The door flung open.

Three heavily armed, heavily bearded Yugoslav Partisans barged in. They were tense and harried. Wearing brown coats, with lines of ammunition strapped across their chests, they easily filled the room, reeking of sweat and grime. The leader hastily checked his paper, containing the short list of names and addresses, and looked around.

'Ettore Saforo ... where is he?' he demanded, kicking over the chair and table, startling the women and upsetting the children. Nonna and Contessa moved to stand in front of the youngsters, shielding them from their unwelcome guests.

The Communists were clearly enraged that the man they sought did not appear to be at home.

'He left me ... the bastard ... left me with the children and took off,' Contessa spat, her heart pounding. She hoped she sounded convincing and glanced at the dark faces to see if they believed her. She could not let them think they were still amicably married or they might be inclined to kill her and the children or, at the very least, torture her to gain knowledge of her husband's whereabouts.

The leader, holding the paper, eyed her warily.

'He's run off with another woman—a whore!' Contessa exploded, warming to her story. 'He's run off with her ... he confessed it to me, then came by a few days ago for his clothes and then left. What are we to do now?' She broke into a convincing wail. 'All these children and another on the way ...'

The men took in Contessa's rounded belly.

'He left me like this ... how am I to provide for my baby?' she asked with shrill indignation. 'Tell me! How do I feed them … all of them?'

'All right, all right,' the Communist snapped, glaring at her. They were jumpy, their hands clenched tight around their rifles. 'He's not here … that I promise you. Look for yourself. See.' She threw open the cardboard drawers. 'His clothes gone. He's gone. If you find him, do me a favour and kill him for me,' Contessa demanded.

'These are his children?' The ominous question hung in the air for a few tense seconds.

'They are my children,' she stated defiantly. 'The minute he slept with that woman, he disowned them.'

Martino, still sucking on his thumb, peered around Nonna's skirt to look at the men who spoke so tersely. He was afraid of them and it showed on his face. But Nardo had no fear. He came to his feet and stood by his mother—staring at the men with defiance. They observed the four-year-old with obvious disdain and Contessa, fearing for her children, pulled the child back behind her, out of their sight.

'Come on,' one of the men urged. They had another home to search and their time was limited. They made a note on their paper and left abruptly, without a word.

As soon as the hostile visitors had left, Contessa collapsed to her knees and cried from sheer emotional exhaustion.

Nonna petted her hair, congratulating her on a believable performance. 'You did good. You did good,' she assured her.

The children gathered around, confused. Martino started to cry too and Nonna picked him up. She made soothing clucking sounds at him until he settled.

'Has Papa left us?' wide-eyed Taddeo asked.

'Only to hide from those dreadful men,' Contessa answered softly, wiping her eyes. 'But we can't stay here anymore. They will search for your father until they find him. We have to get out.'

'Out?' Nonna asked, stunned. 'Out of Fiume?' She had lived there for the past thirty years.

Contessa shared her anguish. She had lived here all her life. She knew the community, the church, the shops, the markets and had many friends—and yet, she would have to leave it all behind.

'Where will we go?' Marietta asked, in a voice so tiny it came out as a squeak.

'To Maria,' Nonna suggested firmly. Maria was her eldest daughter and Contessa's older sister.

Yes, of course, Contessa thought. She bent down to be at eye level with her children.

'My sister has a house. We could go to your Aunty Maria. She will take us in for a while. She lives in Bergamo where it is much safer. And you could see your cousins … so many of them.'

'Cousins? Yes, I think I met them once before. I'd like to see our cousins again,' Taddeo said. The other children looked interested.

At that moment, Dino and Lisa charged into the room.

'Everyone all right?' Dino asked. 'Sorry, we couldn't stop them. They kept a guard on us and wouldn't let us leave the house until they'd left.'

'We are sorry to put you through that. It is Ettore they want. The quicker we leave here, the safer you will be,' Contessa said apologetically.

'You stay as long as you want,' Dino said firmly.

'Thank you. But we will make our plans to leave. This cannot be our home anymore.'

Chapter four

Their heart-breaking decision to leave Fiume was a sound one, but Contessa knew it was not going to be easy. It was difficult to gain permission to leave the German-annexed city, and she was aware that many had been refused.

'There has to be a way to get papers,' she thought out loud. Then an idea struck her. 'Father Giovanni. He will know what to do.'

It seemed like an age had passed since the Partisans' visit, but it had been mere hours. The children were in bed, sleeping soundly, and Lisa and Dino were back in the farmhouse. Nonna and Contessa were sitting in front of the fire at their small table, righted after the intrusion.

'Yes, he has friends in city hall,' Nonna agreed.

'I will see him first thing in the morning.'

With this decided, Contessa and Nonna went to bed but neither could find comfort in sleep.

For Contessa, the mattress felt empty without Ettore by her side. She worried, wondering if he was out of reach of the Partisans who were known to wander the hills on patrols. She hoped he was warm, but she knew that, like her, he would not be asleep—not tonight.

Nonna stared at the ceiling, praying that Ettore would stay safe. She was also worrying about leaving the city. She longed to see her daughter in Bergamo; it had been a long time since she last visited, but her house was small and crammed with many children. They could not stay there long. She trusted that they would get to Bergamo, but then what? Could they return to Fiume? Sensing the answer, she sighed inwardly, her heart heavy.

The next morning, Contessa caught the first tram and journeyed across several suburbs, alighting within walking distance of the small, brick church. She had not attended its services since their house had been bombed, but she had been a faithful parishioner for many years, and Father Giovanni would hear her out.

At the church, despite the early hour, she found Father Giovanni in talks with a grieving widow. Contessa knew of the woman's loss and waited patiently in the pews. While there, she prayed her family would be delivered safely to her sister. At last, the priest blessed the widow and made his way over to her.

'You look upset, my dear,' he commented, as she got shakily to her feet.

'Father, it is not so good for us. The Partisans are looking for Ettore. It is not safe for us here. We must leave the city as soon as possible. But I don't know what to do …'

He nodded, wisely, not surprised. 'I see. Your story is not so uncommon. I have been telling some of my parishioners to seek out a friend of mine at the Italian consulate—he is a good man, a solicitor. He has helped quite a few families like yours escape. Go to him and make a strong case for evacuation.'

The priest took a notepad and pencil from his pocket and wrote down the name of the solicitor, passing it to Contessa with a smile.

'Thank you, Father. Thank you.' Contessa bowed her head with gratitude and respect. 'I will do everything as you say.'

'But Contessa … there is not much I can do to help your husband. The ones marked for Partisan arrest—those with strong links to the Germans—they will not be granted leave. Some are making it out illegally, getting themselves across the city's border, though it is very risky. I will add him to my prayers.'

'Thank you,' she whispered, trying to suppress a shudder at the thought of her husband's dire predicament.

Later that morning, Contessa visited the general store and approached the silver-haired proprietor, Dante. He had come to know her and Ettore over the past year as regular customers. Ettore had often traded with him, sharing a joke or two as they bartered over trifles. He was good-humoured but drove a hard and fair bargain.

'I have something for you. Something I'd have you keep for Ettore,' she said softly.

'I see,' he said. Surprise and sadness flashed in his eyes. 'Not a problem.' He winked. 'Whatever it is, I can keep it here for him.'

Contessa handed him a note and a parcel. He took the items and placed them swiftly behind the counter.

The note read:

My dear Ettore,

I will apply at once to the Italian consulate for passage out of Fiume. I will take the children and Nonna to my sister's house in Bergamo. You must meet us there as soon as you are able. Keep safe.

Love, Contessa

She had kept the note short and without reference to his situation in case it fell into the wrong hands.

'Thank you.' As Contessa turned to leave, the shopkeeper called out her name. She peered back.

'Good luck to you. You and Ettore,' he said. His wise eyes were moist, his expression gentle.

'Thank you,' she said again and left.

Straight from the store, Contessa headed to the consulate office in the city; a grand building marked by the two-headed eagle engraved in stone over the entrance. She trotted up the steps in her flat heels and through a pair of magnificent carved wooden doors. At a reception desk, she asked for a viewing with the solicitor whose name Father Giovanni had given her. There was no time to lose; she had to spend every moment wisely.

An agonising two hours later, she was led to a desk, dwarfed by huge filing cabinets lining the back wall. It was completely covered in documents, paper trays and a pile of books. Behind it was the legal man, dressed in a slightly creased grey suit and muted green tie. He listened to her sympathetically, as she was forced to once again recount her story.

'My husband has left me. I cannot possibly support my children if I stay here,' she sobbed.

Another consulate officer, who had a superior air about him and sported a more expensive suit, overheard her plight and wandered over to them. He pushed aside a paper tray and sat upon the overburdened desk. 'You know my dear, the state can provide for you,' he put to the weepy and obviously pregnant Contessa.

'For what—one or two days—weeks? What then? That is not enough. My sister in Bergamo has a big house,' she lied. 'She is well-off and can look after me and my children and my mother. Please take pity, have heart …' she wailed. 'I need my sister. She can help me. I have four young children. My mother, she is too old to help me …' Large, watery brown eyes lifted to the two men. 'Please, help me.'

* * *

Contessa departed the office with the documentation that would permit them to exit Fiume. Her heart was soaring with renewed hope. She had achieved an almost impossible task. As soon as she could manage it, she visited the general store to leave another note for Ettore, this time proudly telling him that she and the children and Nonna were assured a safe journey to her sister's house in Bergamo and would be leaving the next day. She also let him know she would not stop worrying until they were reunited. 'Please, please come to Bergamo as soon as you can,' the note ended.

That afternoon, she returned to the store in case he had left a reply. Whistling a tune, Dante casually took a brown paper bag and filled it with a scoop of nuts. He handed it to her with another one of his wise winks.

'My wife and I will miss you and your family,' he said quietly. 'It has been a pleasure trading with you and your husband. I hope your sons grow up big and strong like their Papa and that your daughter is as beautiful as you.'

'Thank you, Dante. And we will miss you more than you know,' she replied. 'Did you see him? Is he well?'

'Tired but well. We talked a little. He is hopeful …'

Dante cut his words short as a middle-aged man in white grease-flecked overalls approached the counter with a small box of goods.

'Ciao, Dante,' Contessa said.

'Safe journey.' He smiled wanly.

It wasn't until she was at home behind closed doors that she dared open the paper bag. Inside, beneath the nuts, there was a small slip of paper. It simply read: *See you in Bergamo.* She pressed the noted against her chest and hoped with all her heart that indeed she would.

The next day, with only a few belongings, Contessa, Nonna and the children left the farmhouse for the final time. Lisa, Dino, Lena and Rico followed them down the path to the gate.

'I still can't believe you're going. It feels like only yesterday that you arrived,' wept Lisa, wiping her eyes on her sleeve.

'I don't want to leave,' Contessa said, trembling with emotion.

The women embraced warmly.

A pick-up truck was already waiting. It was taking a few families to the city of Trieste and Contessa had arranged to travel with them. From Trieste, they could make their way to Bergamo.

Nonna and the children were helped into the back of the truck.

'Ciao dear friends. We can never repay you for all you've done for us,' Contessa said, hugging Lisa for a second time. She then climbed up and sat next to Nonna.

'Ciao,' the children shouted, waving excitedly from their high perches.

'Look after Lena,' Nardo called to Rico.

'I will.' The young husband saluted him.

Nardo nodded and let his eyes rest on Lena. He was missing her already.

Nonna wiped rare tears from her eyes and waved a white hanky at their dear friends. On seeing Nonna's sorrow, Lisa broke down and sobbed against Dino's shoulder, which only sent Contessa into a flood of tears. The truck pulled away. Lena ran alongside, waving at the children and when she gave up her chase, Marietta burst into tears and Taddeo hid his face in his hands.

'Look at us! We're not doing very well,' Nonna observed, handing her hanky to Marietta.

'Will we ever see them again?' Nardo asked.

'One day,' Contessa offered but did not know how it would be possible.

The truck travelled through Fiume's outer suburbs. Contessa kept her eyes on the winding, tree-lined road, knowing in her heart that she would never travel it again. Her friends and the city were lost to her. The war had taken away too much. It was time to start over, wherever the winds decided to take them.

* * *

The winds were not kind to Ettore; they enveloped him in icy drafts blasting down the hills from the snow-tipped mountains beyond.

After a week of traversing the broad, grassy slopes and forested hills to the north-west of Fiume, Ettore had come across and teamed up with a dozen Italians also hiding from Partisan arrest. They were cold, tired and hungry, desperate to leave the city that soon would be overrun by Yugoslavs. After a couple of days of trekking towards the city's border, they decided that they had drawn close enough to start mapping out their escape. Together, they brainstormed ideas to acquire a truck and travel as close to the city border as they dared, before dumping the vehicle and slipping out of the city on foot. They planned to go as soon as possible, knowing that at any time they could be discovered by Partisan or German patrols. However, they knew their best chance of escape would be under the cover of darkness, and so they waited.

They were blessed with a starless night. As agreed, four of the group left in search of a truck to steal, while the others waited in a forest clearing. It was no lighter there than in among the thick of the trees. In the darkness the men were like shadows, their voices as soft as the rustling leaves.

After a long while, Ettore walked away from the group, needing to stretch his legs and shake out the cramps brought on by the cold. He did not go far, simply moved to the clearing's edge where he could get a view of a wide dirt track at the bottom of a slope. The truck would come up along that path. He meant to be alone, but sensed someone behind him.

'They should be back by now,' Roberto complained to him, sniffling. He was a large, tubby man with wavy black hair. He coughed. He had a nasty case of flu and was chesty with it.

'They haven't been gone too long,' Ettore said calmly, feeling sorry for the fellow who, despite his size, was gentle and fearful by nature. 'Give them time.'

'We don't have time.'

'It's a good night for it. Doesn't get much darker, not even a moon behind all those clouds,' Ettore pointed out. He pulled his coat around him tightly, trying to keep out the biting wind.

'It's dark enough to rain. Whatever the weather, we can't hang around here forever. I'll die of flu if nothing else,' he said, coughing until he spewed out phlegm.

'Be patient.'

Ettore had learned that Roberto was a father of four and very much in love with his wife. A painter by trade, he had worked for the Germans, helping to load supplies on to the war ships. His constant hacking cough was making the men nervous. It would alert patrols a mile away.

'But what if they don't come back?'

'They will.'

'You are too sure.'

'It is better to be.'

Roberto fell quiet. Talking only made his cough worse. He rocked on his feet and listened to the other men whispering behind them, wondering what they were discussing. Another ten minutes went by in relative silence and then Ettore addressed his anxious companion, pointing down the slope.

'They're back,' he said, relief fuelling his excitement. 'See. Here they come.'

Other men, on hearing the announcement, joined them to gaze down. Sure enough, they saw the four returning, pushing a military truck ever so slowly along the path. They brought it to a halt at the bottom of the incline and the group hurried down to meet them.

'It was easy. The compound was unmanned,' Edrico informed the others proudly. 'Luck is on our side.'

Edrico was the unofficial leader of the group. Short and balding, he was not the strongest, but was clever and very persuasive. He had been a banker before the war and the Germans in Fiume had put him to use, helping to keep track of their expenses. It had been his idea to steal the truck.

'When should we go?' Roberto asked after clearing his throat loudly.

'Give it another hour. It will be after midnight then. Safer,' Edrico proposed.

'Yes. Another hour,' several men murmured in agreement.

Roberto didn't want to wait, but lacked the confidence to challenge the consensus. He coughed and moved away to go spit.

They parked the truck in a cluster of thick bushes on the hillside and wrapped blankets around its tyres. They sat behind it to be shielded from the winds and shivered anyway—partly with cold, partly with fear. When what felt like an hour had passed, they stood quietly and stretched out their cramps. At last, without any debate, it was deemed time to go. They were standing close together—a ring of thirteen. Some thought it unlucky but didn't say anything. After that night, who knew where they would end up? No doubt they would part ways, seek out families or friends, make their way to different Italian cities. It would be their last night in Fiume … if they were successful. They slapped each other on the arm or back, wishing each other luck, and then they set about their escape.

Ettore joined the men alongside to help push the truck noiselessly down the sloping trail and on to the dirt track. They did not want to start the engine if they could help it. For a hundred metres they pushed it along the downhill track, the vehicle steadily picking up speed. Men started to jump aboard. Ettore was about to follow suit and leap into the back when he heard shouts and explosive gunshots … then metallic strikes as bullets ricocheted off the truck's side.

Partisans! Damn. Where had they come from?

With a glance behind him, Ettore just managed to see Roberto, who had been pushing on the other side of the truck, fall to the ground. His motionless body did not get up.

They could not react. Still under pressure from gunfire, Ettore made a desperate leap into the back of the truck, but as his feet left the ground he felt a stab of pain searing through his right hip.

Twisting in agony, he landed awkwardly on his left side, bruising his shoulder on impact. Once righted on the floor of the truck, his hand sought out the pain in his hip, which was damp and sticky to touch. Edrico sailed into the truck, landing beside him. He was also clutching at a wound, one in his arm, and gritting his teeth. They pulled themselves into a sitting position as the remaining men threw themselves inside. All in, the truck's engine roared to life and the vehicle started rattling down the steep slope at an incredible speed. The men, especially those with bullet wounds, struggled to secure themselves against the aggressive jostling. The blankets around the tyres were torn to shreds as the truck hurtled along.

Ettore continued to hear gunshots, informing him that they were still being pursued. He wished he could do something, but the pain from where the bullet had sliced his skin was too much. One of the Italians seated not far from him, a short, quick-thinking lad in his late twenties, picked up an army pack he found on the truck's floor and scrambled over to the back where he tossed it out on to the road. The driver of the vehicle behind them was shocked to see a dark shape land on the road directly in front of them and swerved to miss it, believing it could be an explosive device. That defensive manoeuvre sent their vehicle catapulting over the edge of the ridge.

The fleeing Italians took ragged breaths of relief. Only the one vehicle had been following them. There were no more gunshots. They were alone and safe. Their driver cut the engine and soon the truck was gliding silently, closer and closer to the edge of the city.

Finally, it came to a stop and was parked off the trail, hidden among thick bushes of dark green foliage. They knew what to do. In pairs, they darted in different directions, scouting the terrain, searching for any armed patrols. Injured, Ettore and Edrico stayed by the truck. After ten minutes, they heard the first pair approach.

'See anyone?' Edrico asked. They shook their heads. The other scouts delivered the same heartening news. With the area deemed clear, they discussed possible routes and decided on an old, overgrown forest trail that involved a sharp decline but would offer them plenty of coverage from any roaming guards. It was a quick conference. Once the route was settled, they made haste. They didn't want to be hanging around the city's outskirts for too long … many men had lost their lives along those passages under the fire of patrols.

In pairs again, they took off, heading into the dark across the unknown, untamed landscape. Ettore and Edrico opted to pair up. Firstly, they tended to their injuries by tearing strips from their singlets. Ettore wrapped strips across his hip and around his upper thigh while Edrico hurriedly bandaged the searing wound in his arm. Both nursing injuries, they figured they would be travelling at about the same pace.

It was tough going for them. Ettore regularly lost his footing. Each time he slipped, the pain in his hip ripped through him, making another step seem impossible. But he took it anyway. It was so dark, they could not even see the ground and had no way of knowing if they were stepping on loose gravel, rocks, roots or in holes. Close up, they could see the outline of trees or branches, and their hands reached out for them to steady their steps. Their pace was frustratingly slow. They could no longer hear any of the group ahead. All they could hear were their own occasional grunts of pain as they upset their wounds. After an hour of stumbling down the old trail, which had fewer trees obstructing their direct path, they stopped for a brief rest.

'How much further do you think?' Ettore wheezed. He took a small container of water from his coat pocket and took a few gulps. Edrico did the same.

'Another half hour then we'll be certain to be out. We could be out already. This forest extends well over the city border.'

Ettore could not see the wound at his hip, but knew by touching it that his makeshift bandage was already saturated. Blood was still oozing out, drenching the leg of his trousers and leaving a trail wherever he trod. He tore the rest of his singlet out from beneath his clothing and wrapped it across his hip.

'Are you all right?' Edrico asked him.

'It's just a surface wound but I'm bleeding like a pig.'

'Damn. We must keep moving though. There's no other choice. We do this, we suffer this and then we're out. We'll find you a nice nurse in Trieste to fix that up.'

'Sure,' Ettore grunted. He held on to a tree branch above him and heaved himself up. 'How's your arm?'

'I don't want to talk or think about it.'

'All right. Let's go then.'

Ettore walked in agony. He was still bleeding profusely. Contessa … He kept his thoughts on her and the children. He would meet them in Bergamo. He would not allow pain or blood loss to weaken him. Not now.

All of a sudden he stepped where there was no ground. He fell away, sliding and slamming against upraised roots, stones and sharp branches. About thirty metres down the slope he came to a thudding halt against a sharp trunk of a pine tree.

His hip felt like it was on fire. He felt weak and battered. The last thing he heard were gunshots—two or three—he could not be sure. There was a flash of light overhead. Then he passed out.

Chapter five

Within the picturesque, medieval city of Bergamo, a small, gated house attempted to constrain all the noise and chaos of a big family.

Maria's husband had left for work, and she and her seven children were in the midst of their hectic morning routine when there was an unexpected knock at the door.

That's odd, the frazzled Italian mother thought.

She swung it open and, to her astonishment, saw well-loved faces she had not dreamed of seeing for a long, long time.

'Mercy be! Mama!' she cried. 'And little sister—Contessa!' Mother and daughter and then sisters embraced.

'My, how your children have grown! This must be little Martino …' she stared at the slight, pale boy whom she had not yet met. He was so thin, but his dark brown eyes were bright and shining.

'He has had his first birthday already,' Contessa said. 'And can you believe my eldest boy, Taddeo, is now seven!'

'Taddeo,' she exclaimed fondly. 'Your hair used to be dark. Now you're almost blond!' Then she took in the serious, dark-haired Nardo, such a strong, round face with straight teeth and a thin nose. She had an urge to squeeze his cheeks.

'Good boys and little Marietta—such curls! You were only a baby when last I saw you.'

Her gaze lifted to her sister. 'And you're pregnant again! Ettore is not with you?'

'We will talk inside,' Nonna said pointedly.

'Yes, yes,' Maria agreed, holding open the door for them. Maria was a straight-backed, proud woman with nut-brown eyes. She was taller than both her mother and sister and had her mother's long, thick hair and her sister's almond shaped face.

At the entry, seven children, dressed and ready for the day, had gathered. The eldest was twelve, the youngest just fourteen months.

'Hello beautiful children,' Contessa greeted them and they rushed into her outstretched arms where the aunt happily slapped kisses on both sides of several cheeks. The children then moved to greet their Nonna in the same way. Afterwards, Contessa conducted the lengthy introductions between cousins who were shyly sizing each other up. While the older ones had some memory of Taddeo, it had been a long time between visits and they were practically strangers.

'Have you had breakfast?' Maria inquired.

'Yes, we were given a tin of beans to share. We came by truck. It was a long, bumpy ride.'

'What an adventure,' she exclaimed, smiling at her three wide-eyed nephews and rather timid niece, who were transfixed by their cousins.

'Yes, it was,' Contessa agreed.

'We are here now,' Nonna rejoiced tiredly.

'Children, do you want to go outside and play?' Maria put to them.

Several of her children nodded, smiling. Martino just stared at her, unsure what she had in mind.

'Stella, you look after the little one,' Maria said to her eldest girl, indicating Martino.

A short, plump girl with budding breasts stepped forward with a warm smile and took the boy by the hand. 'Come along,' she encouraged.

The rest of the children followed Stella out the door to a tiny front courtyard. 'The gate to the street stays locked,' Maria told them. 'There's some chalk stones you can draw with on the pavers,' she suggested, before closing the door.

'They'll be shy for five minutes and then Heaven help us,' Maria said to her two travel-weary guests. 'Now come through to the kitchen and sit. I can make you a drink—it's not coffee but it is brown and hot.'

'Yes please,' Nonna said gratefully, wanting to be settled. Contessa nodded her agreement.

The women sat around the kitchen table, sipping from the sweetened, steaming hot brew. They talked about the battle between the Germans and the Yugoslavs. They worried together about Ettore and whether he would get out.

'He'll make it. I know he will. He'll take risks, but not without thinking it through,' Contessa said, her voice thin and strained. Her sister and mother readily agreed, if only to help keep her spirits high.

'Of course he'll make it. A stronger, more determined man I've never met,' Maria declared. 'He was born lucky that one.'

'He will need a lot of luck,' Contessa said and fell silent with her thoughts. What if the Germans lost the battle and he couldn't get out? Would he be killed, imprisoned or just disappear? Would she ever hear about his fate or would he just never meet her in Bergamo? Perhaps, she should have stayed behind and made sure of his escape ... could she have helped him more? Her head throbbed, and she rubbed her forehead.

'Well, you must stay here until he comes,' Maria said softly.

'I'm sorry to come here without warning. I know you don't have a lot of space ...' Contessa said.

Maria was starting to wonder where she would put them all and how they could spread the few blankets they had between them.

'... and we won't stay long,' Contessa continued. 'As soon as Ettore comes, we will arrange somewhere else to go.'

'I'm sorry it is not a bigger house,' her sister said. 'But please, stay until you have the baby.'

'That is too long! The baby is due in four months. Ettore will be with us long before that and we will make plans.'

'Of course he will be,' Maria said, pressing her lips together. *We must hope so*, she thought.

That night, they reorganised beds and put two to three children to a mattress, with Contessa sharing a bed with Martino and Marietta. Somehow they managed, but it was not a long-term solution.

In the morning, Maria, dressed in a plain black dress, approached her sister with a proposal.

'Some friends of mine, Lucas and Gina, have borrowed a car. They've invited us to join them for a drive to Milano to get some more supplies. You could come with us and visit the cinema there. It shows the latest newsreels—perhaps they will mention what is happening in Fiume,' she suggested.

'Do you really think they will?' Contessa asked. She longed to know the outcome of the Yugoslav attack, which would let her know what Ettore was up against.

'Can't hurt to go and see. Mama can mind the children. There is a park not far from here she can walk them to. It is safe there now.'

'The children would love that. Sounds good. Is Milano safe?'

'The resistance has been holding the city, but they say American troops are on the way. We may even see them arrive.'

Contessa was wide-eyed and curious. What would the American soldiers be like?

'I'm coming,' she decided.

Contessa dragged the brush through her rebellious hair, which was in need of a cut. Embarrassed by its unruliness, she borrowed a silk scarf from her sister and hid her hair beneath it. She wore a white blouse and straight short skirt with a jacket that had box-like shoulder pads. The jacket just covered the top curve of her rounded belly. Her practical, navy blue wedge sole shoes were in stark contrast to the lovely high heels that Maria chose to wear, but Contessa did not dare step out in heels for fear of taking a tumble in her expectant state.

Lucas and Gina beeped their horn out front to announce their arrival. With childlike excitement, Contessa followed her sister out to the footpath. She hadn't been in a private car for at least two years. She climbed on to the leather seat in the rear, enjoying the slight bounce as she settled in. They drove to the large, commercial city and as they neared its centre, Contessa could see how badly it had been damaged by what must have been intense bombing. The damage was widespread. Ancient buildings had been reduced to rubble. Piles of bricks and debris sat alongside buildings whose entire facades had collapsed, leaving buildings open and discarded, like skeletons left to rot in the streets. It was sad to look upon. As they continued down a tree-lined street, Contessa assessed that about a third of the buildings were completely destroyed and another third damaged enough to be torn down. Smartly dressed men in suits and ties and jackets, with hats atop their heads, were still trying to make their way down the debris-strewn streets on foot. They were stepping over and around bits of buildings, and merchants were struggling to cart their wares around constant obstacles. Another block in towards the city centre, their car came to a standstill, stuck in traffic that stretched as far as the eye could see. Crowds of people were walking down the street; their voices shrill with excitement, their necks stretched with curiosity.

'What's going on?' Contessa asked of the small party in the car.

'I don't know—it's strange. But we're not going to get very far on this road,' Gina observed.

Contessa did not like strange happenings—they often fore-warned something sinister. She tried to relax and make a joke of it. 'Maybe the Americans have arrived. Maybe a gorgeous American actor came with them, hey?' she quipped.

'You wish,' said Maria, chortling.

'I don't think she is so wrong. I believe the Americans are here. My neighbour said she heard a report on the radio,' Lucas said.

Interested, Contessa craned her neck, but could not see any US soldiers.

Lucas found a side street and pulled in, parking partway on the footpath. 'Better to go on foot from here,' he advised.

Maria and Contessa arranged to separate from the married couple with a view to meeting them back at the car in three hours. They were intent on finding the cinema and doing some shopping, but as they came on to the main street, they got caught up in the wave of people heading in one direction. Without a word between them, the sisters went with the flow and soon they were on the edge of a town square, at the corner bounded by Via A Doria and Buenos Aires streets, near the Unico Prezzo Italiano Milano department store. They were at the back of a crowd, behind hordes of sightseers, buzzing with awe-filled chatter.

'What is it?' Maria asked of the gentlemen in front of her.

'It's Mussolini. They've hung him,' came his curt, shocking reply.

'Oh Mercy!' was Maria's instant response. She crossed herself before turning to her sister to tell her what she'd learned.

They had heard on the radio that very morning of Mussolini's death. He had been shot the day before, April 28th, after failing in his attempt to escape Italy. Found hiding in a German convoy headed toward the Alps, he had been taken prisoner and was later joined by his mistress, Clara Petacci. At that time, it was unclear why the leader had been shot, but they later discovered that a council of partisan leaders, led by the Communists, had secretly decided to execute him.

While horrified, Contessa was also macabrely fascinated. Straining to see the grisly spectacle, a clearing suddenly opened, and through the slightly parted crowd, she could make out six bodies, strung up by their feet from a rafter at an Esso gas station. From that distance, the sisters could not tell which of the bodies belonged to their former dictator, but they did not doubt he was among them. Nearby, lying on the ground, were about six or seven other bodies, seemingly executed not long ago.

Contessa's eyes were drawn to the woman's hanging body and word, spreading around the crowd, named her as Mussolini's mistress, Clara. Her dark skirt had been tied around her knees so it wouldn't fall away, while her coat bunched under her chin, revealing a white blouse that had been tucked into her skirt. She was a slender woman with lovely legs, Contessa thought.

The mood among the crowd was shifting from shock to anger. They were starting to stir, to shout abuse, to spit, to push forward.

'We best get out of here,' Maria said, grabbing hold of her pregnant sister who could not afford to be elbowed or knocked, but they were already penned in, with a sea of spectators all around them.

'This way,' Maria suggested, trying to guide them through, holding Contessa's hand.

People blamed Mussolini for all the hardships suffered throughout the long war. Many hated him for it and it was starting to show. They hurled abuse and edged closer, wanting to take out their hatred on his hanging corpse.

The authorities rushed forth to hold them back and Contessa and Maria were caught in the mad jostling of a crowd out of control.

'Contessa, turn to me,' Maria shouted over the noisy din.

Contessa faced her sister, who held her close, protecting her stomach from sharp knocks. It meant, however, that Maria took several knocks to the back, as she was pushed from side to side by those eager to press forward.

All of a sudden, a large torrent of water blasted to their right.

Fire hoses! The authorities were pushing them back with jets of water. The unrest turned into bedlam and the sisters screamed as they were tossed to the left by a wave of people desperate to avoid the brutal force of the water. Maria kept her footing and held on to her sister. The hose swung to the other side of the crowd, allowing Maria and Contessa a chance to run clear. There was a gap between the blast areas and they ran for it. Contessa was thankful she had not worn her heels. Hand in hand they raced over wet pavement and continued on their way until they were at least a block back. There they stopped to catch their breath, their hearts racing.

'Are you all right?' Maria asked.

'I think so,' Contessa breathed. 'The country's gone mad.'

'So much anger.'

'It was ugly to see.' Contessa straightened her dress. 'Let's keep walking.'

They walked briskly, Maria guiding their way towards the cinema. It would be good to get off the streets and sit down after such a fright. However, while feeling safer inside the darkened cinema, the newsreel did not reveal anything new about the battle for Fiume. Not a word of the city was mentioned. They returned home—downcast by the upsetting and unproductive outing that could have cost them dearly.

But not knowing about the battle turned out to be far less painful than the truth. It came to them by way of the radio only a few days later.

Contessa sat in her sister's kitchen, the radio blaring at full volume. Nonna sat next to it, tears streaming down her cheeks.

The man announced in excitable Italian:

Yugoslav troops have charged down the hills into Fiume and taken the city. The Germans were surrounded and forced to sur-render. Reports put their losses as high as ten thousand, with six-teen thousand believed taken prisoner. The Germans are retreat-ing and burning the harbour as they go. The port is on fire ...

Italy's Fiume was gone.

Where was Ettore?

Contessa rolled out the slip of paper that she carried with her always. *See you in Bergamo*, it read.

With the battle lost and Fiume swarming with Yugoslavs, she did not like his chances. *If he's not out by now*, she thought wor-riedly. *But he could be. He could be out and making his way on foot right now.* Each day she told herself the same thing and each day there was no knock on the door. No message, no note, no news.

She also worried for her friends, for all the Italians trapped in the city. What would become of them?

'It is terrible,' Nonna cried, her face pale, her eyes glistening with unshed tears. 'So many people I know ... What will become of them, of us?'

They stayed by the radio, hoping for any other snippet of news, wondering what was unfolding. It seemed certain that they would not be able to return home.

Maria had served her hot grainy brew, but the brown liquid now sat cold in untouched mugs.

'I am sorry,' she said, moving to sit by her sister.

'Where will we go?' Contessa moaned on her shoulder and Maria, feeling the magnitude of her sister's sorrow, wept with her.

Chapter six

May 1945
Fiume

Ettore awoke groggily, an unknown surface hard and cold beneath him.

The air was foul and stuffy. A throbbing pain in his side made him afraid to open his eyes. When he did, it took a few moments for his surroundings to come into focus.

'He's awake,' he heard someone say.

Ettore was helped to a sitting position. A metal cup of water was proffered. He sipped from it, though the water tasted oily and stale. 'Where?' he asked.

'Can't answer that exactly,' said the man by his side. Ettore lifted his heavy lids and peered at him.

Edrico, the banker.

He looked around and saw four other men, one he recognised—Roberto—the painter, still alive, though his head was wrapped in a bloodied cloth.

'We're in a hold somewhere,' Edrico said, sweeping his grubby hand across his balding head. 'They blindfolded us. It was about a half hour's drive.'

Ettore glanced around. They were in a small square room with stone walls and floor—a solid iron door barred the entrance. High above it was a thick iron grate, which at least permitted some light and air. The cell was bare except for a stinking bucket in one corner. Opposite was a similar bucket but it only held water.

'This here is Gabino, this is Pio and Fausto. You know Roberto.'

Ettore looked where Edrico pointed.

Gabino was young—too young, no older than eighteen—a handsome boy with slender nose, soft lips and slick hair; Pio was about ten years older, pasty and plain to look at, but he was fit, with a solid chest and toned, strong arms. Fausto was large and sullen with heavy lidded eyes that held no warmth beneath bushy brows. Grief rested in his bones—it could be seen in his rounded, defeated shoulders, his down-turned mouth and his absent gaze. Ettore did not like to look upon him for too long.

Instead, he returned his gaze to Edrico.

'How were we taken?'

'I can only guess that the guards who ambushed us had radioed for help before their vehicle veered off the road. At least three patrol vehicles responded.'

'One of them found me,' Roberto piped up, before breaking into a harsh round of coughing. When the hacking died down, he went on, 'I didn't tell them anything.'

'You couldn't. You were unconscious,' Edrico pointed out.

'It only grazed me—just a scratch. Maybe it was shrapnel,' Roberto said, lifting his hand to point to the side of his head that had a small dark bloody patch caked within the bandage. 'I hit the ground and blacked out.'

'They found Roberto and then they probably followed the tyre tracks to our abandoned truck. They spread out to search with torches.'

'They would have picked up your scent. They're like dogs,' Pio spat.

Ettore took another sip of the horrid water.

'We're the lucky ones. You and Roberto were unconscious and thrown into their truck. I was bleeding and slow and surrendered without a fight. The others ... they tried to outrun them ...' Edrico paused and lowered his eyes.

'What? What happened to them? They made it ...'

'No,' Edrico shook his head.

Ettore sucked in his breath sharply. No. He couldn't believe it. 'All dead—shot—one by one.'

Ettore shook his head, not wanting to hear the words, but Edrico kept talking.

'For us, it was too dark to move fast. They had torches. I was taken first, then they found you. A guard stayed with us while five other guards went on. I heard many rounds of gunfire and ... screams. Another guard came back—he was smiling. I was told to carry you, but I couldn't with a bullet in my left arm, so I dragged you with my right hand to their truck. I don't know how ... you're heavy!'

'Thanks.' Ettore knew it would not have been easy. Edrico had been weak and in pain. He could only shudder at the thought of his fate had Edrico not been able to drag him. There were cuts and bruises all over his body, but it was a small price to pay and nothing compared to the fate of the other Italians.

'It was dark ... all they had to do was hide,' Ettore said. He still couldn't accept what had happened.

Pio smiled sardonically. 'You think that would have saved them?' he chuckled sadly. 'They knew you were there. They had you. They would have brought in more men and patrolled the area until morning, when it was light, and waited and watched for days if needed, to make sure they had you all.'

The devastation was clear on Ettore's face. 'They were fathers, husbands ... decent men just trying to live normal lives. We're not soldiers. We were unarmed!'

'They are criminals,' Pio said, seething. 'The men that took you, took me—they are guerrilla forces; nothing fair about them. They will just shoot us too.'

'Shoot us?' the young Gabino squeaked.

'We don't know what will happen to us,' Ettore cut in, noting the fear in Gabino's face. 'We're alive. Our goal should be to remain so.'

'A hard goal. I still have a bullet in my arm,' Edrico stated flatly.

Ettore looked at Edrico's arm, where an undershirt had been wrapped around it twice. It was dark with dried blood. Risk of infection was high.

'I can't move it.'

'They won't let you see a doctor?'

At this, Pio started to laugh crazily. 'A doctor? Them? Those bloody bastards don't have a merciful bone in them. This is no hotel! We get no favours here. Don't expect any. We're dead men to them. Dead! Who knows what they're waiting for.'

'Names,' said the sullen man, Fausto. 'They'll want to learn who we are and what we know. Then they'll kill us. That's it.'

He said it with such morbid conviction that Ettore felt a shudder rip through him. He had only just learned that he was lucky to be alive, and it seemed there was little hope of remaining so.

Roberto spoke—he liked to talk when he got anxious. 'They're right there. We haven't been given any medical attention and only one pot of soup last night—if you can call it soup. I don't think keeping us alive is a high priority.'

'How long have I … ?'

'Two days—not long. We didn't think you were going to come round,' Edrico said.

Roberto coughed again; a deep, nasty bark that once started was hard to stop.

'Your cough is worse,' Ettore commented.

He nodded and coughed again.

There was a clanking sound outside the iron door. The men looked at each other and braced for whatever was coming next.

A guard, with full, ashen beard and black eyes, shuffled in while another waited in the doorway. He placed on the ground, near the door, a pot of brown liquid with a few carrots floating on the top. He backed out without a word and the door was shut. They heard it being bolted on the other side.

'Dinner is served,' Edrico said, twisting his lips into a grin. 'Eat while it's hot.'

* * *

A broth of far superior fare was set down on the table in Maria's tiny kitchen. It contained pieces of chicken in a delightful creamy soup. The eleven children in the house had already had a scoop each with a crust of bread and were now in the bedroom playing cards.

Contessa, Nonna, Maria, and her husband Antonio sat around the wooden table dipping bread into the broth. The meal was warm and satisfying and they washed it down with watered apple cider.

It was the sixth week of their stay and they still had not received any word from Ettore. Contessa fiercely clung to her faith that he would turn up and found her eyes frequently and longingly straying to the front door; her ears listening for the front gate—if she heard it swing open, she was quick to run to the front window to peer out. For her, the door only opened to more disappointment. She prayed often, before bed and during the day, making all sorts of promises to God if He would be so kind to return Ettore to her. 'Please,' she found herself saying, and no other thought would present. She was begging fate almost constantly. 'Please, please, please.'

As she downed the tasty meal, she wished Ettore were beside her. He would have liked that broth. He liked cream.

A voice interrupted her thoughts.

'I was talking to a woman in the park yesterday. Her husband works for the Italian consulate,' Nonna said, in between sips of soup. 'It seems many families are getting out of Fiume and they are amassing in refugee camps. She said many are arriving in Trieste.'

Trieste was part of the same region as Fiume, known as the Julian Region, comprising all of Istria and including the other urban centres of Pola and Gorizia. Like Fiume, it was a cosmopolitan city with its industry based around its port. Also like Fiume, it was subjected to Yugoslavian occupation, with the troops arriving in the city on May 1st. However, with the fear of Communism beginning to surface and an Italian push to retain the Julian Region, Allied forces had descended on Trieste and applied enough political pressure to see Tito withdraw his troops. The Yugoslavs had only held the city for forty days.

'Trieste is unstable,' Antonio stated, finishing his soup and wiping his mouth with the back of his hand.

'There is a safe zone. The Americans and British are there. That's why the refugees are pouring in,' Nonna replied.

'Aren't they dividing the region between the Allies and the Yugoslavs?' Maria asked.

'Yes,' said Nonna. 'Trieste has been divided into two zones. We shouldn't be giving the Yugoslavs anything. Italy should fight for its territory. Should fight for us,' she finished stubbornly

'Fight? Italy has no fight left. The war has crippled her,' Antonio pointed out.

'Then they should get the Allies to fight for us,' Nonna argued.

'The war has ended. The time for fighting is over.'

'Not for the Yugoslavs.'

There was silence. The situation seemed hopeless.

'I was thinking ...' Nonna went on. 'We have already overstayed our welcome. We should make our way to Trieste—be among our city folk. Learn more news.'

'But it is dangerous there. The Yugoslavs can't be trusted to stay quiet in their zone!' Maria squealed, alarmed.

'The Allies will keep them there. Tito has agreed,' Nonna went on.

'Go to Trieste?' Contessa had finally joined the conversation.

She was thinking—if Ettore had got out, he would have gone to Trieste first. Perhaps he was there, injured and unable to get a message to her. 'We would learn more,' she said slowly, carefully.

'But it will be terrible—so little food, and disease.'

'Bless you, Maria, for your kind heart, but we can't stay here forever,' Nonna said, smiling. 'Governments will have to help resettle these people. I feel we need to be with them. We need to be helped. Staying here has been wonderful, but you are a big family and we can't impose on you any longer.'

Weary with prolonged sadness, Contessa put down her spoon and inhaled deeply. It had been their plan to stay in Bergamo until Ettore had joined them. They had thought he would follow only days later. It had been weeks. Sadly, his continued absence meant the plan had to change.

Maria placed a hand on her sister's shoulder. 'I wish things were different,' she sympathised. She felt terribly sorry for Contessa and wished she could pressure them to stay in her home longer, but it was true that it had been difficult managing so many under one roof. They did not really have enough bedding, space or food. Their resources and supplies were being stretched to the limit. She had many children to care for and it was not easy adding her sister's needs to her responsibilities. She could never turn them away; she loved and cared for her sister dearly, would do anything for her ... but if there was another option ...

'We have loved having you here, but ...' Maria said hesitantly.

'But we can't stay forever. Yes. We should at least go look and see,' Contessa said. 'And if we decide to stay there and Ettore should turn up here looking for us ...'

'Of course we would tell him where you are,' Maria said. 'We would send you a telegram immediately.'

'I'd appreciate that,' Contessa nodded gratefully. 'Well, Nonna. Seems we have a new plan. Do you think it will be safe?'

'Safe or not, we need to be with our city's people.'

'Yes,' Contessa said, but she was concerned for her children.

'You must come back here if it is too terrible. I will send you food whenever I can,' Maria said, suddenly tearful. 'I wish …'

'There now, you have done so much for us already. You are a good woman,' Nonna said comfortingly. 'We know you are here for us.'

Contessa held her sister's hand tightly. 'Thank you, Maria. For everything.'

'You must come back here to have the baby,' Maria insisted. 'A refugee camp is no place to give birth. Come here two weeks before your due time.'

Contessa smiled and touched her belly. 'I will. It sounds good. Then it is decided. We go to Trieste and I will come back here to have the baby.'

'I will help arrange transport,' Antonio said. He was a quiet man, but practical and generous. Family meant a lot to him. 'And my wife is right. The baby must be born here.'

Nonna and Contessa decided they would go alone to Trieste to inspect the camp and the city's stability while the children remained in Bergamo. They travelled with a truck, carrying medical supplies to a hospital in Trieste, and were delivered close to the city centre, not far from the port.

They walked around the heart of the city for about twenty minutes, stopping Italian police to ask for directions and eventually found a displaced person's camp in a large, brick building, about the size of a warehouse. Inside, across the extensive ground floor, they saw hundreds of people set up with mattresses, camping out on the floorboards. Grey blankets had been strung up to make tents for family groups. Through the cracks in blankets and in the narrow passages between tents, they could see many people sitting, talking, playing cards and smoking. They were doing nothing in particular but they appeared healthy enough.

A thin, weak man, seemingly aged in his thirties, was sitting on his mattress in a tent left wide open to let in air. He asked them who they were looking for.

'We have just arrived,' Nonna told him. 'Whom can we speak to about staying?'

'The officer is in a room at the back,' he wheezed.

'Thank you.'

They made their way to the back of the building, passing many people, dull-eyed and lethargic. A man, dressed in a grey blue suit and blue cap, stepped out from behind a desk piled high with paperwork. 'Good morning,' he greeted them kindly, but without enthusiasm.

Contessa and Nonna nodded nervously and muttered a polite greeting.

'I'm the liaison officer. How can I help? Are you seeking refuge?'

Contessa explained their situation.

He listened—not unsympathetically, but it was a story he had heard too many times before. When she finished, he rubbed his chin and went back to his desk to retrieve a clipboard. He returned to them, mumbling.

'Ettore Saforo,' he said as he wrote down the name. 'I will check our records and if he is not registered here, I will give his name to the woman from the Red Cross. She is trying to keep track of people coming and going, to help families find each other. She can check other camps.'

'Thank you,' Contessa said. 'That would be most helpful.'

'Two women, four children and one on the way, hey? Let's see. We have space, well, we can make space. We'll give you blankets to string up for privacy, and we'll provide basic meals in a common dining area and water to wash in. We could give you, say … two mattresses. Sound like what you are after?'

'Yes. I think so,' Contessa said. She looked to Nonna, who shrugged.

'How many people are here?' Nonna inquired.

'We have registered nearly four hundred displaced persons,' he replied. 'They are all like yourselves—from areas in the occupied Julian Region.'

'Will this agreement in Trieste, you know, the zones ... what will happen?'

'No one knows the answer to that,' he said, shaking his head. 'They have come up with a line from just south of here in Trieste to Gorizia and then to Ratece, near the Italian-Austrian border. West of the line, known as Zone A, is under Allied military administration and Zone B to the east is under the Yugoslav army. So many Italians are crossing over the line and coming here ... more arrive every day and I expect they will keep coming. I can't tell you what will happen. In the short term, here is safe. We offer food and shelter ... if you want to stay, you will need to fill out paperwork, have a medical assessment and so on.'

'I see,' Nonna said. She had listened intently and made up her mind. 'Then we will stay. We will send for our children.'

'Okay. I'll get someone to take you to your section and give you some blankets. Once you are set up, we will start the registration.'

Trieste, a beautiful town, with house-dotted hills surrounding the port, was very much a border town influenced by Latin traditions and heritage as well as German and Slavic cultures, making it a complex, diverse city with a large working class. As in Fiume, the Germans had taken the city during the war and the Allies had dropped bombs upon it. But unlike Fiume, when the Yugoslavs had come for it, the Allies had pressured them into pulling out— at least part of the way, and a line had been drawn.

'It's uncomfortable,' Contessa said. She was sitting on the scratchy straw mattress, with blankets hanging around her. It was mid-June and hot. She didn't want to stay inside the building, which was smoky, airless and stuffy from too many people crammed inside, and particularly from men sucking on cigarettes. One of the blanketed walls was a shared wall with another family group. That blanket suddenly lifted at the bottom corner and a brown, wizened old face stared at them in greeting.

'Newly arrived?' she squawked and gave an open-mouthed smile, which revealed yellowish stained teeth, but at least she had a full set.

'Yes,' Contessa said. 'Have you been here long?'

'One month. There are six in my family. My daughter and her four children.'

'Children? We have four children too.'

'And soon you will have five,' the woman said.

Her Italian dialect was familiar to them and Nonna was sure the old woman must be from their home city.

'Are you from Fiume?' Nonna put to her.

'Yes.' She stopped smiling. 'Fiume. Poor Fiume. What of your husbands?'

'I believe my husband is still in Fiume. He's trying to get out,' Contessa answered. Nonna, who had lost her husband to an accident before the war, did not reply.

'Worked for the Germans, did he? My son-in-law was the same. They …' She paused. 'I'm not sure whether to say … I don't want to worry you but you need to know. Yes, you will hear it from others. I'll tell you. They put him against a wall and shot him. That's when we left.'

Contessa felt her blood run cold. She put her hands to her mouth to stifle a cry. 'They just shot him?' she gasped. 'No questioning, no trial?'

The old woman shook her head. 'They are rounding them up. Those who worked for the Germans … those seen as a threat— even some civil servants. Shooting them. That's the kindest thing that's happening though. We've heard stories from further out. You don't need to know of them. Your husband is still in Fiume. He might get out. You pray for him. Pray hard because I know what he's up against. Worse than animals, they are. You'll hear the stories soon enough but for now, just pray.'

'He'll get out,' Nonna said and squeezed her daughter's arm.

'Yes,' Contessa sounded unconvinced. 'What's it like here—for children?'

The old woman thought for a moment.

'There's a park across from here where the kids can play. They are going to arrange for the kids to go to school. Some kids are unwell, but they are separated. There's an army hospital set up behind here. They go there. Most are healthy. There's talk of getting them vaccinated.' The woman did not want to say too much more. 'We are making the best of it. It's no holiday camp,' she joked and then limply the blanket fell back across her face, hiding her from view.

'What do you think?' Contessa asked Nonna.

'I think she is right. We will make the best of it.'

'Ettore could be here.'

'Checking out that hospital would be a place to start.'

'Yes. We should go ask there. Let's.'

They visited the hospital and another medical facility nearby but their search proved fruitless. They had no record of a man of his name or description.

'The Red Cross might have more luck,' Nonna sighed as they returned to the camp. 'Well, we best send word for Maria to send the children.'

'Yes,' Contessa replied automatically. Her thoughts were far away. The hospitals had been depressing, and the injuries they had seen consisted mostly of amputations and bullet wounds. The stench of rotting limbs and festering wounds had been too much for her and she had been somewhat relieved to learn that Ettore was not lying among them. Still, if not injured, what then? She thought of how the old woman's son-in-law had been put up against a wall and shot, without trial or question. Hopefully that had not been Ettore's fate. *Let him be alive and well. Please.*

Chapter seven

June 1945
Fiume

A large, iron fist slammed into Ettore's jaw. It was not the first, nor, he thought, would it be the last.

'Your name?' the interrogator asked, his voice dripping with boredom. The man could only speak basic Italian, but he didn't need much more for the crude communications being drawn out in this small, windowless room.

Ettore tasted blood and tried to spit it out, only to find his jaw would not cooperate. *It must be broken,* he thought. The pain in the left side of his jaw and lower right ribs was excruciating. Blood trickled out of his mouth and dripped on the stone floor. His insolent silence was punctured by another blow to the stomach. Chained to a chair, he could not even buckle over. His bonds dug across his bare chest, deepening wounds that had already been pounded by fists and boots. Severely winded, he struggled to breathe, and it was a long time before he was able to gasp more than a short burst of air.

'A name! Say it.' His interrogator held no love for Italians. That was apparent in the glare of his coal black eyes—a cold, cruel stare that held a deep loathing. Clean-shaven and washed, he was clearly a superior officer, able to control his men without raising his dead, empty voice.

'Your name?' he hissed. It was clear his frustration was rising, and rapidly.

Ettore swallowed; the metallic taste of blood lingered on his swollen tongue. He wanted to scream that they would never get his name, he imagined himself doing it, but of course, he couldn't—he could barely whimper. They had beaten him into silence, leaving him to slump against his chains in quiet agony. Ettore knew once they had his name they would recognise his German ties and put him to death instantly. Then he would become just another name scratched off their list. He might be beaten and sore and broken in half a dozen places, but he was alive, though perhaps not for long. Soon they would become tired of this game and kill him—with or without a name. It seemed senseless to fight, but he had a family to live for.

The final slam was a pain-filled blessing. The brute of a guard, over-eager in his assignment, delivered a heavy blow to the side of his head and knocked him out cold.

* * *

He awoke in his cell. Once his eyes focused, he saw that another four men had been crammed into their tiny prison. Two were older—one with silver hair and stubble, whose deeply creased eyes suggested that at one stage of his life he had smiled a lot. The other was bald with a white scar marring his lip. He averted his gaze out of fear and mistrust. The other two, younger and stronger, had recently been tortured and were lying on the floor semi-conscious. They looked how Ettore felt—bruised and battered.

Edrico approached with some water, but he could not open his mouth to receive it. A few drops were sprinkled on his lips instead, just enough to moisten them.

'You okay?' the former banker asked.

Ettore simply looked at him. He did not speak.

'Been better, hey?' Edrico said. He dribbled more water into Ettore's mouth, this time wetting his bloodied tongue.

There was a clanging at the door as someone unbolted it from the outside. Edrico put down the water ladle and faced the door, which jerked open with an ear-splitting squeal.

'You,' the guard said, pointing at Roberto.

'No. You can't … please,' the large man begged as they seized him by his coat and dragged him away. They heard his harsh, racking coughs grow quieter as the door slammed shut.

Bastards, Ettore thought, wishing he could spare his friend the beating that was ahead. Knowing Roberto and his weak constitution, he wondered if he would even return. They might just kill him.

For five weeks now they had been locked in this tiny cell, yet the interrogations had only just begun. It was their understanding that the superior officer must have recently arrived and started the process of questioning. They believed that if he had been on site from the start, they would have been tortured to death by now. He enjoyed his job too much and seemed very impatient to scratch names from his damned list.

'You're going to keep that nurse in Trieste very busy if you keep collecting injuries like these,' Edrico told him.

Ettore smiled internally. His lips were too busted up to show his newfound friend any mirth.

'We are prisoners of war. They will have to let us go eventually. A deal will be done. We'll be exchanged,' Edrico mused, trying to lift Ettore's spirits. However, it was an optimism that was not shared by any of those who had already been interrogated.

'You live in a fantasy world,' Pio said. His pale skin had bruises so dark that he looked like he had been stamped on all over with grease-covered boots. 'They told me many times that they can't wait to kill us.'

The cell was silent bar the moaning of one of the semi-conscious men. The groan of their fellow cellmate seemed endless. Some closed their eyes while wishing they could close their ears instead. It was a discomforting sound, one that reminded them how close they were to pain and death.

Ettore found he could listen without hearing, for the pain had his full attention. There was nothing else for him except throbbing, stinging, aching, stabbing …

Time passed … the bald man got up and took a pee at the bucket. It overflowed and dribbled down on to the stones, spreading out in fast running rivulets. It stank. No one sat near the bucket, forcing the men to cram together on the other side of the cell. Such crowded conditions meant that their captors would need to start clearing space.

The door flung open and Roberto was tossed inside.

He was awake. His eyes showed a rainbow of bruises and his bottom lip was puffy and split. He sat up, shakily, and refused to meet anyone's gaze.

Edrico brought water to him and he winced as he sipped. Another cough erupted, shaking blood from his cracked lip, and tears streamed down his face with the pain of it. When at last his cough settled, he lifted eyes dark with remorse.

'I'm sorry, Ettore. I'm sorry, Edrico,' he rasped. 'I told them. I told them our names.'

He dropped his head in shame. 'I'm sorry,' he murmured over and over.

'Don't worry,' Ettore wheezed through his pain. 'Doesn't matter.'

Perhaps it was for the best. He was marked for death—with or without a name. At least if his name was crossed off a list and published somewhere, there was a chance that one day Contessa could learn what had become of him. He wanted her to know that he had been killed. Better for her, so that she could move on with her life, for he knew she would wait for him for as long as it took. Better she knew.

And now the beatings would stop. The pain would stop and the wait for death would begin.

* * *

At the refugee camp, Contessa was also waiting. Waiting for Ettore, waiting for word from her sister in the hope she had heard from Ettore, waiting for the birth of her fifth child, waiting for water for bathing, for food, for use of the laundry room … life had become one long queue, one long prayer.

More displaced people arrived at the camp every day. Disoriented, sad and hungry, they all had stories to tell. Contessa walked away if they started to mention the executions. She knew it was happening—the tales they told were disturbingly similar—yet it didn't help her to hear them; she had to believe that Ettore would be lucky. He had run into the hills. She had seen him go. He would be hiding and waiting, waiting for the right moment to flee.

At night, as Martino and Marietta shared her lice-ridden mattress, she would indulge in a few secret tears of despair. A part of her had lost hope. It had been three months since she had seen Ettore—every day felt longer than the last.

The old woman they had met on their first inspection of the camp had been a great source of help. She had explained to them about meal times and how to find such things as the laundry, toilet and washroom—not that there was any soap to be had. They learned her name was Gilda. She shared her space with her widowed daughter, the fair-haired Bianca and her four grandchildren—two boys, Elmo and Gian, and two girls, Daniela and Francesca, all under the age of ten. It gave Contessa's children ready-made companions, and every day they raced down to the park, which was really a large courtyard outside the army administration building.

Contessa's older boys both warmed to six-year-old Elmo—a year younger than Taddeo and a year older than Nardo. They became a tight-knit group, going everywhere together but mostly playing soccer, kicking whatever they could, usually a tin can, up and down the courtyard. The game always drew other children and involved much shrieking and shouting.

Elmo's younger brother Gian was the same age as Martino and the two toddlers, of similar height, size and colouring, liked to roll around wrestling on top of each other. Often together, they were frequently mistaken for twins. They were too young to join the games of soccer—though they often tried. However, they soon got the message that they were not wanted on the teams and it was not safe to try.

Marietta and Francesca were a year apart, Francesca being almost four. She was a plain, mousy girl but was quite sporty and liked to do cartwheels, something Marietta struggled to master. They both liked to follow eight-year-old Daniela around as the older girl liked to mother them, making up imaginary games for them to play. Daniela was also the prettiest of the three with blonde hair, cat-like eyes, a pert nose and full lips. To the younger girls, she looked like a princess and they wanted to be just like her.

The two mothers, Bianca and Contessa, became fast friends, which was just as well, as their youngest children had quickly become inseparable. Keeping an eye on them was no easy task as the overly active duo loved to run up and down the street and climb up and down the stairs of a nearby railway station—something Contessa found hard to monitor in her pregnant state. It often fell to Bianca to catch her little Martino if he tried to run inside the station.

As well as helping her with Martino, Bianca was always willing to give practical advice and liked to talk about the past before the war. She had come from a well-off family. Her father was a lawyer and her mother, before marriage, had been an actress on the stage. She had gone to a good school and was quite well educated in music and the arts. Contessa learned that Bianca had once played the violin masterfully, and naturally missed it terribly. Every time Bianca spoke of concerts she had performed, tears would still her words. On one occasion, Contessa had seen vivid memories stirring behind her watery eyes.

'You are hearing the music right now,' Contessa prompted.

'Yes. I hear it all the time. I see myself playing it. My husband loved to … never mind.'

'You don't have your violin any more?'

'No,' she said and did not elaborate. 'Oh look. Martino …'

Martino had climbed the stairs and disappeared inside the door of the railway station.

'I'll get him,' Bianca volunteered. She hurried up the stairs and went inside. It was only a short time until she reappeared with the boy in her arms. He wriggled as she carried him down the long flight. As she was about to set him down on the ground, he grabbed a handful of her hair, pulling some of it loose from its neatly coiled roll.

'Martino, let go. Look what you have done!' Contessa cried, trying to pin Bianca's hair back into place.

Bianca laughed. 'Don't worry. It's always messy,' she said.

Contessa shook her head. 'Your hair is never messy,' she stated emphatically, her admiration clear. 'If only I had your skill. My hair is impossible. Without proper shampoo, it is out of control. Look at it, it is everywhere!'

'Not impossible surely,' Bianca smiled, reaching out and running her fingers through her friend's tangled locks. 'Would you let me try a new style?'

'My hair is not clean,' Contessa said, embarrassment flushing her cheeks red. She still had her pride.

'None of us have that luxury in the silos,' Bianca laughed. 'Let me try to make the best of it.'

'If you don't mind?'

'Not at all.'

They returned to their makeshift tent, their boys tired from the run around. The toddlers fetched their one and only, highly-prized toy—a plastic aeroplane they had been given by a visiting charity group. They had one each and were happily making the toy zoom and fly around the tent.

'Sit here. I'll fetch my brush,' Bianca instructed.

Bianca, although slightly plump, and with a rosy-cheeked face, took great care with her hair, wearing it up in the latest styles. Her bedtime routine involved curling strands of her hair around rags so that in the morning she would have curls or waves to pin up or to leave partly down. Bobby pins were scarce, as metal had been in constant demand for weapon production, and so she had resorted to using pipe cleaners to fasten her hair in place. Contessa envied her such thick blonde waves, and yet, she was aware of another bedtime routine that Bianca partook of—one she did not envy. When they retired to bed of a night, Contessa would hear Bianca crying into her pillow, weeping at the loss of her husband. The unmistakable sound of her muffled sobs reached Contessa's ears every night and every night she felt immense pity for the woman, forced to mourn alone in the dark when she thought her family asleep. In the morning, there would be no evidence of tears, just lovely hair and a smile. She was a strong woman—though she tended to over-protect her children, who meant everything to her.

'See, it is not impossible, though your hair has a few habits that you need to work with,' Bianca said as she twisted handfuls of hair. She inserted a few pipe cleaners here and there, rolling and tucking until all of Contessa's hair had been swept up atop her head.

'Wait. I have a mirror,' Bianca said, scrabbling about amongst her hairnets and make-up. 'Here.' She held up a small handheld mirror with a beautiful ivory handle.

'What a lovely mirror,' Contessa commented, gazing at her reflection. 'Oh my. Would you look at that!'

'Your hair's pretty, Mama,' Martino piped up, having turned to look at his mother on hearing her surprised words.

'Thank you, my sweet. It is lovely,' Contessa agreed. She handed back the mirror to Bianca. 'You must teach me how you did it.'

'Of course. It is not so difficult, just takes a little practice.'

Bianca turned the mirror over in her hands. 'I brought this with me. One of the few things I couldn't leave behind,' she said musingly, putting it away with a fond pat.

'We lost everything in the bombing,' Contessa said, recalling the mirror she had once owned, and remembering her dresses, make-up and jewellery. They seemed a world away. 'Not everything,' Bianca pointed out gently. 'Any news of your husband?'

'No.'

'At least there is hope,' the blonde woman said sadly. She put away her brush and sat down heavily on the mattress.

'What was your husband like? Why did they ... ?' Contessa began hesitantly.

'Execute him?'

Contessa gave a small nod.

'He was not the kind of man to have enemies. He had a kind nature. I can't understand why he had to be killed. He was not a fighter, he wouldn't have caused anyone harm. He certainly was not a troublemaker.'

'Are you sure that they ... ?'

'Sure he was killed?' Bianca considered the question. 'I was told he was arrested with a group of men. When I went to the prison to ask about him, I was told the group arrested that morning had already been executed. They did not even make it to prison. Just put against the wall and shot. I did not hear from him again or hear or see anyone in that group again. I stayed with friends and searched for a few weeks then decided to get out of Fiume and come here.' She shuddered, recalling her visit to the stinking prison and the despair she had carried away from it.

'I'm sorry.'

'Ettore … that is your husband's name. Mine was Roberto. I have one picture—see.' She opened the locket she wore around her neck, revealing a tiny picture of the couple on their wedding day. Roberto had thick, black hair. He was only a little taller than his buxom wife and somewhat wider too. His expression was soft and timid and he looked every bit a nervous groom. Bianca was a radiant bride in a silky, long white gown with stunning pearls at her throat.

Contessa didn't know what to say. Sympathy overwhelmed her. 'It is a nice photo,' she murmured.

'I'll never take it off,' she said, snapping the locket shut. 'Come now. Let's find our children and take them to the dining hall for some lunch.'

'Yes. Hard bread with jam.'

'We mustn't miss such a feast!'

On their third week at the camp, Taddeo was booked in to attend a local school. On arrival each day, he was given a glass of milk and a spoonful of cod liver oil.

'Yuck,' Taddeo told his Nonna and brother Nardo when he returned from his second day at the school. 'They gave us that brown liquid again. It tastes awful,' he said.

'It will keep you healthy,' Nonna assured him. 'And next year, Nardo can go to school too.'

'I don't want to drink the brown stuff,' he said fearfully. 'School sounds bad.'

'It is not all bad. We are learning maths, history, classic writings, geography.'

'Good, good,' Nonna said, very pleased to hear it. 'Learning is good. You must listen to everything they tell you. You will need an education more than ever in the future.'

'You get to meet lots more kids and we get to play soccer too.'

Nardo was impressed at that. 'Do they have school teams?'

'Class teams.'

'I want to go to school.'

'We can start teaching you. Tomorrow I'll teach you numbers,' Nonna said.

Nardo considered his grandmother for a long moment. 'All right,' he agreed. 'Teach me now.'

Nonna laughed and found herself forced to give him a lesson straight away.

Nardo, almost age five, picked up number recognition quickly, and soon developed a love for counting. He began driving everyone to distraction, calling out a number whenever he spotted one. This progressed to a passion for counting backwards from twenty, very loudly. Impressed, Nonna continued to teach him, proud of his enthusiasm and ability. Before long, she was teaching him how to add numbers and soon he was constantly requesting sums to work out.

* * *

It was Sunday. Outside the rain was pelting down, its heavy drops splashing on the road. Nardo and Taddeo stood by the tent opening, their expressions long and dismal at being forced to stay inside.

'It is just a shower, it will clear,' Nonna told them.

The morning shower had not cooled the air and Nonna shook her blouse, wanting to shift the heat. With so many bored children, Bianca and Contessa pegged back the blanket that acted as their common wall, making one large room between them and organising a card game.

'... three, four, five,' Nardo said, counting the cards that were being dealt to him.

'Must you count everything?' Taddeo sighed.

'Yes!' Nardo shouted assertively.

'Come on. Look at your cards. It's Francesca's turn first,' Contessa said.

They were sitting on the mattress in a circle, Contessa leaning back on her hands, as she was heavily pregnant and uncomfortable. The baby's due date was nearing, and the day after next she would travel to her sister's house. She was looking forward to seeing Maria and tasting her cooking again!

Martino and Gian were too young to play cards and were crash landing their planes into a pair of shoes.

Contessa studied her hand of cards, not liking those she had been dealt. The numbers swam in front of her for a moment.

'Your turn, Contessa,' Gilda called.

'Yes. It's just …' A stab of pain in Contessa's side cut off her thoughts and she turned to her side with a loud groan. 'What is it?' she heard Bianca ask. 'The baby?'

'Mama!' shouted Martino, worried by his mother's obvious distress.

Nonna reached Contessa within seconds and made her lie down.

Contessa felt an agonising grip tighten and clench across her belly. She had felt that intense pain before and knew exactly what was happening. It seemed the baby wasn't going to wait for her return to Bergamo.

Old Gilda gathered up the cards. 'Come children. We can play in the dining area.' She then turned to the two older children. 'Taddeo and Daniela, go together and fetch the officer—the man in the room at the back. Taddeo, tell him your mother needs a nurse or a midwife straight away. Tell him she's having a baby. That will get some attention.'

'She is?' Taddeo looked dumbstruck.

'Go now!'

The other children, too young to comprehend, complained over the abrupt ending of their game. Martino and Gian cried as they were wrenched away from their mothers and bustled away with the other children.

Only Nonna and Bianca remained to assist the mother in labour.

'It is my fifth time. I know what to do,' Contessa assured them in between quickening contractions.

'We all know what to do,' Bianca said, smiling. 'As long as the baby knows what to do and we don't have any complications.'

Contessa had a short labour. The baby arrived well before a nurse or midwife—though when she did finally arrive, the very competent senior midwife was helpful with the post-birth proceedings.

There, on a mattress in a displaced persons camp in Trieste, on July 14th, 1945, a baby girl was born. Contessa knew what to name her. Ettore had wanted her to be named after his late mother. She would be called Isabella.

She's here, Ettore. Our Isabella is here, she thought. Tears rolled down her cheeks unchecked. *Will he ever meet her?* she wondered, feeling desolate as she was starting to believe he never would.

Nonna squeezed her hand. 'She's beautiful—beautiful Isabella. She'll make her Papa proud.'

Contessa had no response. She turned and kissed her baby's cheeks in an effort to hide another rush of tears. Where was he?

Chapter eight

July 1945
Fiume

Ettore was in the back of a truck.

Four guards had come suddenly to their overcrowded, cramped cell, which for the past couple of weeks had housed twelve men in all. Their hands were bound in front of them and a cloth tied across their eyes. Their filthy, bearded faces held the same expression of grim apprehension. Once bound and blindfolded, they were led single file out the stone enclosure and down a narrow hall. As they tripped down the steps onto a gravelly road, they inhaled their first breath of fresh air in months. In this new light, it was easy to see they were malnourished and scrawny. Many had tied knots in their trousers to keep them from falling down. Like unruly cattle they were prodded with the butts of rifles and pushed up into a truck. As they sat and waited, it seemed that another ten or so prisoners were rounded up from somewhere and pushed in with them. They heard them grunt as they were thrust inside the army-style vehicle, many forced to sit on the floor.

Ettore felt men at his feet and to either side of him. His heart was pounding so hard he felt someone must hear it. Where were they being taken? To a firing squad? Would their cloths be removed so they could see their fate or would they remain blinded to the row of guns directed at them? Would this dark world end only in a darker grave? He had much time to consider it, for the drive went on and on, a long series of rough roads and sharp turns. Then the truck started to climb—the engine roaring during the steep ascent, heating the already hot interior. After a while, as they levelled out, he could hear the chirping of birds and smell the distinct, rich scent of the forest. It felt dank, as though rain was coming. The road might have levelled out, but it was still winding.

Roberto, as always, was coughing. Ettore could hear him on the opposite side of the truck. The stench of the men's infected wounds was almost overpowering. Ettore's hip wound had healed, but in his current situation, he found there was not much comfort in dying wound-free.

They came to a halt. Ettore felt the sweat gush down his face from beneath his blindfold. His thin, filthy clothes were clinging to him. Doors opened and guards shouted to each other.

'Oh Christ, be done with it,' he heard an Italian mutter angrily.

No one else spoke. Ettore heard a whimper—not quite a cry, but a mewling sound of deep despair. Be brave, he wanted to tell the man—or perhaps it was a boy. But who was he to speak of bravery, he with his heart pounding to a deafening beat?

They were wrenched out of the truck and left to drop like sacks of potatoes on the damp ground, at times landing sprawled over each other. Roughly pulled to their feet as their shirts were yanked by rough fists, they were made to stand and wait. The trickle and stink of a man urinating filled their senses—the guards laughed.

There was some terse discussion, and then their blindfolds were pulled down, the outside light causing them to squint painfully. Ettore saw it was mid morning, though the sun was not easy to detect in a sky dark with dense clouds. He could see it had rained not long ago; droplets still dripped from trees and clung to the grass. They were gathered on the edge of a seemingly remote forest, an arrangement that could only bode ill.

The Italians did not meet each other's eyes. They hung their heads, afraid if they glanced up they would look upon fear or reveal it on their own faces. It was a fear they knew if shared would quickly intensify. Ettore stared at his scruffy boots without seeing them. In this gathering he knew there were only two types of men: those preparing to die and those preparing to kill. The tension quickly uncoiled into action; all too soon they were being shoved towards the forest's dark centre, ushered along a damp dirt trail.

Ettore heard coughing at the back of the group—Roberto was somewhere behind him. He could not spot Edrico, but he could see the youthful Gabino ahead of him. After no more than ten minutes, they came to another clearing. There, the trees thinned out and the ground became rocky and slippery. They approached a narrow opening, a hole in the ground's limestone surface. Ettore knew such sinkholes existed in the Karst regions and the hinterlands of Trieste. They were cavernous pits that had eroded from the limestone, plunging hundreds of metres into darkness. Thin grasses, moss-covered rocks and overhanging branches surrounded this one—it looked peaceful and innocent enough. Here they were brought to a halt.

The Italians, for the first time since their blindfolds had been removed, exchanged looks. What was the horror that awaited them? Were they to be shot and thrown down this natural chasm? Down there their bodies would lie broken and mangled, perhaps never to be found or exhumed.

The guards—eight in total—trained their rifles on them, expecting them to run. They wouldn't get far if they tried.

A burly soldier walked around the other side of the hole to face the group. He had a broad, deep-lined forehead, a lump in his nose that suggested it had once been broken, and a square block for a chin. His expression was stern—he had a job to do and he wanted to get on with it. He spoke at them in Yugoslav, his glinting eyes barely blinking, his words short and brisk. Then in Italian, he called lazily: 'You!' His pointed finger rested on Fausto.

All eyes fell upon the big, round-shouldered man. He was a head taller than all else present.

'Fuck you,' the miserable Italian exclaimed.

Ettore was impressed at his bravado but his admiration quickly turned to horror as two guards grabbed hold of the giant man and started dragging him towards the hole. Fausto fought them; he struggled and spat and cursed them, but his hands were bound and the end result was the same. Eventually there was no ground left beneath him and he was falling ... they heard his scream, followed by a sharp, permanent silence. Perhaps his head had hit the side of the chasm on the way down. All they knew for certain was that a man had been thrown alive to his death. He had been with them a moment ago and now he was gone, consumed by the hole that stared back at them expectantly. He had been the biggest and strongest of the group; they now had little hope of saving themselves from a similar and imminent fate.

The shock took a moment to register, but then there was pandemonium. The Italian prisoners threw themselves back away from the pit, shouting hysterically, but the guards had expected this and blocked their retreat. A rifle blasted and one of the Italians screamed like an animal. They all stared at the squealing man and saw his kneecap had shifted sideways, a gunshot wound gushing blood. The men froze, glaring warily at the Yugoslav guard.

Ettore glanced to his right and saw Gabino had come to stand beside him. He was wide-eyed with abject terror.'

You,' the guard said, pointing at the sobbing prisoner who was clutching at his blood-soaked leg. The injured Italian had a bushy beard covering a round face, at the centre of which was a red, stubby nose. His wide nostrils were flaring with pain. The same two guards grabbed hold of him. He squirmed in their grasp, but his wound had weakened him. A final push and he slipped over the edge—a longer scream haunted their ears. It trailed off, another life swallowed by the hungry chasm.

'This is barbaric,' a young, feisty Italian shouted, and his reward was to be thrown in next, forever silenced within seconds.

Hell, thought Ettore. He could still hear the man's screams—or was that just his mind playing a trick on him? What horror! Who could have thought that this would be how it ended? All those months of crawling around on that urine-soaked stone floor, sipping at stale water and foul soup—fighting to stay alive, trying to cling to some false hope that they might be released, that he might somehow make it to Bergamo. He had never stopped believing even though the situation had always appeared hopeless. But this? This was beyond anything he could have imagined. He hoped Contessa would not learn of his tragic end. Don't let her know of this!

He looked around, desperately searching for a path he could run for—better to run and, at worst, be shot in the back. However, he quickly realised he had no hope of cutting his way through the fierce-looking, heavily armed guards that were barricading them in. As he surveyed the area, movement caught his eye. Someone was coming up the trail they had followed from the roadside. It was a slender, bearded man dressed all in black. He had a rifle slung over his shoulder. Ettore knew that figure—it was familiar to him.

The man stepped into the clearing and the shadows dropped away from his face.

Cappi!

Cappi—Dino and Lisa's boy—the one who had come to the house to warn him. Why was he here?

The young man did not break his stride, walking up to the commanding guard on the other side of the yawning pit. He greeted him formally. His superior eyed the intruder warily, his square chin jutting out. Heated words were exchanged and

Cappi presented a piece of paper. The guard snatched it from him, read it, and examined its official seal.

'Ettore Saforo,' the guard read out the name.

Ettore was too stunned to respond. What was happening?

'Saforo?' the guard shouted irritably.

Ettore took a small step forward, unable to find his voice.

Cappi turned to him to explain in Italian. 'You have been spared execution by our Military Commander. You are skilled in repairing naval ships and submarines. The Germans destroyed the harbour when they retreated and your skills are urgently required. You must immediately present your skills to assist the new Communist regime.'

The burly guard studied Ettore's face, mostly concealed beneath a dark, sweaty beard, and awaited a response. Ettore nodded, too fragile to take any joy from this life-saving reprieve. There was relief, but the shock of what was happening here meant he did not feel any lighter—he was only numb. The other Italians stared at him in awe.

Cappi spoke again.

The guard shook his head and snapped a command, which Cappi then translated. 'You are to stay. After the executions, he will have my paper checked by his superior, only then will he release you to me.'

Ettore was brought to stand to the right of the pit, next to Cappi, where they would have a good view of the killings.

At that point, Roberto started coughing. He was at the back of the group, but his dry hacking drew the guard's attention. His mouth twitched with distaste, and then he smiled and pointed, demanding Roberto be brought forward.

Concerned that his friend had been singled out, Ettore failed to notice that his hands were being freed from their binds. He felt them break apart and looked down. Cappi had slipped a sharp knife between his wrists, cutting effortlessly through the rope. He had enough sense to put his hands back together and not to look at Cappi even though he longed to thank him.

'You,' the guard said cruelly, pointing at Roberto.

Roberto was seized. Terror spread across his face and he tried helplessly to shake off the men gripping him. For once he was not coughing. Fear had smothered his ability to breathe, let alone cough. They had to drag him, his feet lifting off the ground, over to the edge of the hole.

Something inside Ettore snapped. He couldn't watch this man die—not again. Ettore had learned in the cell that Roberto had two sons and two daughters under the age of ten and a wife with long, fair hair—Bianca. He adored talking about her. A lifetime ago, before the war, Roberto painted houses for a living and loved to tend to his rose garden. He liked music and enjoyed taking his beloved Bianca once a year to the opera. He used to be healthy and happy and did not deserve such an end. None of them did.

It took only a couple of seconds for him to snatch the rifle from Cappi, lift it and fire—once, then twice. Both guards on either side of Roberto fell dead; their hands dangling down into the hole. Ettore had taken a risk—he could easily have shot Roberto—but it was a risk worth taking, and if he had shot his friend, it would have been a mercy.

The shots raised bedlam. Pio, his bruised face twisted in rage, let out a war cry and slammed his elbow into the nose of the guard beside him, spraying blood everywhere. The other Italians responded to the cry and, despite being bound, swung their fists around to hit whichever guard was closest, stopping them from firing their rifles.

Cappi had not expected a fight but had been prepared for anything. He slid out a pistol tucked in behind his waist belt. Whenever a guard stepped clear of the throng, he fired. His careful aim took out two guards, leaving only three to be kicked and beaten by more than a dozen half-crazed Italians.

Ettore looked to the commander on his left and saw that he was aiming his gun at Gabino's back.

He didn't hesitate to react; swinging Cappi's rifle around he took aim and fired. The bold-faced guard took the bullet in the shoulder, was jolted backwards and dropped swiftly to his knees. His teeth clenched in pain, but the bullet was not enough to stop him. Again, the guard lifted his gun. Ettore leapt towards him, wrenching the rifle from his clenched hands. Outraged at being disarmed, the guard kicked hard at Ettore's chest. Ettore responded with a firm punch to the man's jaw, a hit that made a cracking sound on impact. He was about to hit him again, when three prisoners, now free of their ropes, sidled up to the guard and grabbed him. They hoisted him up above their shoulders.

In unison, they took a step towards the hole.

'No, no, no,' the guard cried, his courage instantly evaporating. Another step and his screams, so piteous, grew hysterical in their bid for mercy.

But his assailants were deaf to his pleas. They had watched this man send their fellow Italians to their deaths—now it was his turn.

Without a word, they tossed him down into the sinkhole. His shrill cries were suddenly cut off. It grew unnaturally quiet. All the prisoners stared at the hole. They were pleased to see justice done, but repulsed by the method.

The other guards lay unconscious on the edge of the woods.

They were free. Yet there were no cheers, no smiles—their spirits were too low to be so easily lifted. For a long moment, they simply tried to catch their breath and recover from their sudden attack. They were weak; many nursing new or old injuries and others were shivering with long burning fevers.

Roberto stumbled around the hole and embraced Ettore. 'Thank you,' he wheezed.

Then everyone was shaking Ettore's hand and slapping Cappi on the back.

'We must hurry,' Cappi told them. 'You take the truck and I'll show you the direction of the border. I can tell you how to get out.' The men did not need to be told twice. They turned and retraced their steps, shuffling up the trail through the forest, a path they never thought they would live to see again. Only Edrico and Roberto stayed back, waiting to walk with Ettore.

'You won't come with us?' Ettore asked Cappi.

'I can't leave without my family. I've got to get my parents. My sister will be fine—she's married to an engineer. She is safe. But I can't keep fighting with the Communists. It is not my fight and yet, if I pull out, I'll be seen as a deserter and my parents will be killed.'

'I'll come with you,' Ettore said solemnly.

Roberto stared at him as though he were mad. He put an arm around him. 'Ettore, come away with us now. You have a wife and children,' he said, not wanting to part from his friend.

But Ettore would not be swayed. 'His family has done so much for me. I have to help them.'

Cappi shook his head. 'Your friend is right. You should go,' he urged. 'I can do this alone.'

'Alone is harder. I want to help you—I must.'

'You are a good man,' Roberto said, tears welling in his eyes. He coughed into his hands. 'No, you are a great man.'

Edrico too was filled with admiration. 'You are crazy but … don't take any risks. Think about your wife.'

'I will.'

Cappi and Ettore saw the men to the truck. As Cappi advised the driver of the best route, it started to drizzle with rain. 'Take it slow,' Cappi said. At least they were not far from safe territory and, with just a bit of luck, they were assured of an easy passage and quick escape.

'Good luck,' Ettore called after his friends as they climbed into the back of the truck.

'You too,' Roberto rasped.

'And get that cough seen to!'

The truck rumbled to life. At last, some smiles could be found in the eyes of the prisoners. They were going home—to Italy, to families who had fled, or to families who lived in other Italian cities. While they were relieved, sadness lingered as their thoughts strayed to those so recently lost. They wouldn't get to make the journey home but would remain in there, in that cavity hidden in the forest. They looked at the opening to the trail, trying to store the place in their memories, in case they ever returned and could request the bodies be recovered and buried appropriately. It was the least they could do—for the families.

Ettore waved goodbye, sad to be farewelling Edrico and Roberto. They had been his cellmates and had shared the worst of times. Chances were, he would never see them again. He hoped this time the escape would go smoothly.

'Sure you don't want to go with them?' Cappi asked.

'Of course I do. But your mother and father are good people. I'll leave with them.'

They hurried to Cappi's Jeep and climbed in. They took the winding road back down the mountainous terrain. The light rain ceased. They slowed at an intersection for Cappi to decide on the safest path to take. Ettore turned to the younger man; there was something he wanted to know.

'Was that paper real? Was I to be pardoned for my skills?'

'No,' said Cappi. 'It was a forgery. I knew you were being held, but I didn't dare try to get you out until you were away from the prison. Here the numbers were better. Though my plan was just to get you out—once that guard said he wanted to check the orders, I knew my plan had to change.'

Ettore let out a long whistle. 'You took a huge risk.'

'You once took a risk yourself.'

Ettore looked at him questioningly. 'How so?'

'You saved my sister one night from an attack. They would have killed her—those two men. They had raped and killed before. She told me what you did. Now I have repaid you.'

Lena! Yes, he had helped her that night. 'You didn't need to, but … thank you.'

'No problem.' Cappi smiled. 'Now let's get my parents and get the hell out of here.'

Chapter nine

They waited in the forest until nightfall. As they waited, they nibbled on dry army biscuits and sipped on water that Cappi had stored in the Jeep. They talked little. At one point, Ettore dozed for a few precious minutes.

When the dark day grew into an even darker night, they began making their way down to the outer suburbs of Fiume. Ettore had a little trouble keeping up with Cappi, who was as familiar with the forested hills as a rabbit would be, and moved almost as deftly. He darted in and around trees, moving down the slopes, never slipping. They bounded down a grassy hillside for a long time, past houses and streets until the back of his parents' farmhouse appeared. The farm held many memories for Cappi. He had grown up there, helped his father, Dino, with the chickens and goats and learned how to extract honey from the beehive. He had chopped wood and packed the storehouse with supplies. His mother, Lisa, had seen him well fed and schooled. He had also played there with his brother Marco and sister Lena.

But the farmhouse was now in darkness—not a candle lit anywhere. They did a brief search and found it deserted. Strange!

'What should we do? Wait?' asked Ettore, not liking the quiet. He remembered the place filled with the noise and laughter of family. The fire had roared through winter, keeping them warm, making them feel safe. They looked around. The chook pen was empty, and the goats were disturbingly missing.

'This is not good,' Cappi said, trying not to be alarmed. 'There is a friend's house—not far. They might know something.'

Ettore kept up with the fast lad as he raced along the back of properties, finally spying the one he sought. They approached warily and watched for a long time. At last, Cappi was rewarded with a glimpse of a person within the small cottage—Lisa.

'Mama—she's there. Why?' He did not like it. It wasn't right. His mother never went there after dark. 'Let's go in.'

Ettore followed his lead.

The back door was unlocked, and they slipped inside. When their eyes adjusted to the dark, they were just able to make out that they were in a small bedroom, with a single bed against the left wall. On the far side of the room was a door, which Cappi opened a crack. From there, he could see straight through to the living room where his mother sat, hunched over, staring into a fireplace of a few glowing embers.

'Mama,' he whispered. His soft voice reached her ears and she turned around. Her face, heavy and drawn, was a picture of heartache. On spying Cappi, tears flowed anew down her cheeks in well-worn paths.

'My Cappi,' she croaked. She rose, Cappi bundling her in his arms within seconds.

The owners of the house, a couple with serious, worn faces, were also in the living room. Respectfully, they slid out to the kitchen to give mother and son some privacy. Ettore remained in the dark of the bedroom, waiting for Cappi to call for him.

They embraced for a long time. She was afraid to talk; he was afraid to ask, to hear what he had already guessed. At last they separated.

'Papa?' The question was barely audible.

She shook her head and rested her face on Cappi's shoulder, hiding her misery. 'I must tell you …' she said, but she couldn't continue—only more tears fell.

Cappi brushed her hair with his hand, patiently waiting for her to calm.

The woman who had left the room re-entered, carrying a cup of boiled grain, its steam carrying a scent of herbs.

'Sit down, Lisa,' she urged. 'Here ...'

Lisa slumped in her spot by the fire and the beverage rested next to her on a side table. She nodded her thanks. 'Can you tell him?' she pleaded to her friend.

'Ettore,' Cappi called at that point.

Ettore emerged. 'Good evening. Sorry to come unexpectedly,' he mumbled, uncertain what to say in the circumstances.

Lisa lifted her hand in acknowledgment of his presence.

'Please sit,' said the woman. 'My name's Ciana. I can tell you ... I can tell you only terrible news. Sit first.'

Unwashed and filthy, Ettore sat on the floor against the back wall.

Cappi knelt by his mother and took her hand. She cupped her own hands around his and looked to Ciana. 'Go on.'

Ciana had long hair that trailed over her shoulders and fell almost to her lap. She had a kind, older face and was wearing a black dress with lace trimmings. Around her neck hung a grey scarf. She pulled the scarf nervously across her throat, and then began.

'Your brother, Marco, returned from the war. He had fought for the Germans among the Italian forces. He was one of the lucky few to survive and, with the war over and news of the Yugoslav occupation of Fiume, he made his way home.'

'He shouldn't have come,' whimpered Lisa. 'He shouldn't have ...'

Cappi felt his skin grow cold and clammy. No, not Marco, not his big brother ...

'The Yugoslav soldiers came for him. They had heard he was home and your father tried to hide him in the cellar.'

'He shouldn't have …' Lisa shook her head; her tears in constant flow.

'The soldiers searched the cellar and dragged your brother out.'

'He was brave,' Lisa added, a faraway look deepening the emotion in her eyes. She wiped at her tears angrily. 'Marco told his father to let them take him.'

Lisa paused, took a deep breath and Ciana continued.

'Your father knew that if they took Marco, he would be shot. They are killing many Italians known to serve the Germans.'

'I know this,' Cappi said. 'Marco and Papa … ?'

'Your father tried to stop them. He pulled out a rifle and shot one of the soldiers. There were three of them. The other two shot your father and when Marco tried to stop them, they shot him too.'

'I saw it happen,' Lisa said quietly. 'It happened in the backyard. They were shot several times and they fell, near the chopping block, among the chooks. They were both lying there, dead. The soldiers took everything worth taking. They looked at me, but didn't … when they left, we buried them straight away.'

'When? When did this happen?' Cappi asked, his face white, his fists clenched.

'They were killed this morning. We buried them in the afternoon. Father Giovanni came to say the prayers. We did it quickly. Lena came.'

Ettore felt a pang of guilt so strong it hurt. Cappi had been rescuing him that morning when he could have been saving his brother and father. He should have been at home, watching over them, not him.

'I'm sorry,' Cappi said and buried his face against his mother's side. She held him tightly.

'I'm sorry too,' she cried, sobs convulsing her body. Their grief was raw and tangible and Ettore was embarrassed to intrude on it. He looked away but he could hear it and feel it and absorbed it until he too had to wipe at hot tears. Damn war. Dino was a good man, a good husband and father.

Leaving mother and son consumed with sorrow, Ettore rose on aching muscles and shuffled out the front door on to the porch, remembering how he had once shared a cigarette with Dino on a similar porch. It seemed so long ago. There, he took a deep breath and as he exhaled, he tried to breathe out his compassion and guilt. He took breath after breath until he was dizzy with it. Damn it. If only they had come a day earlier … they could have got Dino, Marco and Lisa out safely. If only …

Ettore spent the night on the porch, gazing at a sky that had forbidden the stars and the moon from shining.

In the morning, Ciana ordered him inside. He was told to bathe and shave with some warm water in a china tub. He dabbed water on his wound, washing the caked blood from it for the first time. A dark scab on his hip remained. With a small mirror to guide him, he shaved off his short, grotty beard, glad to feel the smoothness of his skin again. Fresh clothes were brought to him. He didn't ask to whom they belonged. He dressed, grateful to be out of the clothes he'd been wearing for months. They fit him well in length, but a belt was needed to keep up the trousers as he had lost a lot of weight. For breakfast, he was given honeyed bread and a hot drink of boiled grain.

Cappi joined him at the kitchen table and they ate and drank together. He too had washed and dressed in fresh clothes, though he had just trimmed his beard, which was as dark as his eyes.

'Today, we leave for Trieste. Mama will come with us.'

Ettore nodded.

'I've arranged a ride. Lots of trucks headed west.'

'Thank you.'

'Mama is packing.'

'Whatever she wants to take, I will carry,' Ettore said.

'What she wants to take can't come.'

'No.'

'We will leave soon. We'll be picked up. I have papers for the three of us. I had papers prepared many months ago ... you'll have to pretend to be my papa.'

'Yes. Cappi, I'm sorry.'

'Don't apologise for something you had nothing to do with. I'll go see if Mama is ready.' Cappi left the table abruptly.

Ettore finished his beverage. It was a sunny day outside and soon he would be in Trieste and after that, heading for Bergamo. He couldn't wait to see Contessa and the children. How worried she must be for him! In Trieste, he would be able to send word to her sister and let them know he was coming. He couldn't believe it was actually happening. In prison, he had lost hope of returning and, many times in his mind he had prepared to die. Now he had to relearn to live—if only he didn't feel so damned guilty about it.

Chapter ten

July 1945
Inner-city Fiume

Lena learned of the death of her father and brother by way of a letter, delivered by courier—a young, shabbily clad boy no older than twelve. He had arrived by bicycle and climbed the stairs to the third-floor, inner-city apartment and knocked on the door. Nursing her six-month-old baby, Lena had answered and simply stared at the boy without comprehension. She was surprised when he placed a letter in her hand and became alarmed when she saw her mother's scrawled handwriting on the single sheet of paper. She was so overcome with dread that she had to sit down before her eyes could focus on the words.

Her eldest brother Marco and her Papa were dead—shot by Communist soldiers at the farmhouse. It didn't hold much detail. It was short and shocking and she received it like a punch from nowhere.

The letter had fallen from her hands as the colour drained from her face. Sensing her distress, her baby daughter, Vittoria, had started to cry, and she felt the infant scraping her little nails at her neck, trying to gain her attention. Dazed, she hugged the wriggling baby tightly, seeking comfort in the soft touch of her milky skin. She felt like life—glorious life—she wanted more of it, more for her father and brother. The war was over! *It wasn't fair*, she thought, increasingly despondent.

'Are you all right?' the courier had inquired. He had delivered much bad news in his short career as a messenger and had seen that blank, vacant stare before. When she didn't answer, he fetched a blanket from the bedroom, returned and wrapped it around her shoulders. She didn't even seem to notice.

'Do you want to send a reply?' he asked gently. 'I won't charge you.'

Lena took a while to register his kind offer and formulate a response. 'No, no. I will go myself. I'll take the tram,' she whispered.

She had left the apartment as soon as possible and arrived in time to help her mother bury her father and brother in a swift and quiet service. This was to attract few mourners, out of fear the soldiers would come and use the ceremony as a means to question and detain more Italians—many of their friends were being sought for arrest.

The next day Lena received another letter. This time her hands shook as she held it and scanned the scrawled words.

Cappi had visited. He was no longer safe in Fiume and was taking their mother with him to Trieste. 'Mama! Leaving Fiume!' It was hard to take in. She had lost her father and brother and now her mother was fleeing … when would she see her again?

While happy her mother and Cappi would be in a safer place, she knew she was going to miss them dreadfully. A part of her longed to leave too, and she had asked her husband about it, but he was not ready to let go of his job, his friends, his apartment. They were not in any danger—Rico was an engineer and his skills were in high demand, so they stayed and her brother and her mother, whom she loved and relied on heavily, left the city.

Over the following year and a half, they became aware of more and more Italian families leaving. Whenever she heard of other Italians exiting the city, she was sure to let her husband know of it.

'I heard that the Scipione family have left and the Ottore family,' Lena told Rico when he came to the small kitchen table for breakfast one morning.

'I know. They don't trust the Communists.' Rico dipped his bread in his coffee, only to find Vittoria dipping her biscuit in it too.

'What are you doing?' he smiled at the cheeky girl with round, red cheeks and glassy eyes.

She giggled and sucked on the biscuit only to find coffee not to her liking. She spat it out.

Lena and Rico laughed. They handed her a cup of water and she drank thirstily.

'I don't trust them either,' Lena continued after a long while. 'The schools are not teaching Italian,' Lena said. That worried her. She looked to her daughter and wondered how she would be raised among so much anti-Italian sentiment. 'They are even changing the street names from Italian to Yugoslav.'

'I've heard a couple of schools are still Italian—we'll just have to find them.'

Lena didn't like it. She didn't want to be struggling to find Italian teachers and books.

'Maybe we should leave too?' she put to her husband, holding her breath. She had asked him before but he had been reluctant to leave.

'Tito is promising everyone will have a pay rise, everyone will soon own a car and be wealthy,' he said. 'Maybe it will get better.'

'I don't believe him. Look at this city. The Germans destroyed everything on their way out. It will take years to rebuild.'

'Shh, my sweet. Keep your voice down. I know, I know. You are right. But it is not easy to get out now. They are forcing skilled workers to stay. Too many have left already. The Yugoslavs are coming here to work but they don't have trades. They are farmers, peasants ... They will never let me leave."

'We could find a way out,' she pressed. Yugoslavs had moved into their apartment building and she could feel subtle shifts away from the Italian ways of doing things. She was constantly nervous. She had heard stories, terrible stories. It was said that Italians had been thrown alive down old mineshafts and sink-holes … it was too horrible to think about.

'We could leave … but where would we go? Refugees are overrunning Italy. Let's give it time. At least here I have work and we have a roof over our heads.'

'All right,' she said in a depressed tone, not meeting his steel blue eyes. She didn't want to give it any more time. She missed her mother and brother. The last time she had received word from them, which came by way of a short letter some six months ago, they were residing in a displaced person's camp in Trieste. Then she had not heard anything from them since. Were they still at the camp? Surely that was a temporary arrangement. Soon Cappi would find work and they would rent somewhere. She was concerned that they hadn't written again. Surely they had but the letters weren't getting through to her. How she wanted to go to Trieste to join them. They should all be living together in Italy. She knew her mother would love to be a nonna to her child. How could she make Rico understand such things?

'I know you don't like the changes. I don't like them either. And I don't like working Sundays,' Rico said. He was working six days a week on low pay and then had to give up Sunday, his only day off, to work for free to help clean and repair the city, which had been reduced to ruins by bombs and the retreating Germans. It was the government's forced voluntary work that he resented most. He had pride. He was a mechanical engineer and yet on Sunday he was sent to clean streets of rubble, shovelling rocks for hours on end. It was mindless, hard labour and he had to do it without pay.

'I'm tired. I never see you. I never see Vittoria,' he complained, pulling on his old boots. It was Sunday, and he didn't want to leave them.

Vittoria started chewing on the other end of her biscuit,

crumbs flying everywhere. The sight made her parents smile. Rico stroked the girl's hair—it was dark, soft and fluffy. She smelled sweet, like condensed milk.

'I don't want to go,' Rico sighed, rubbing his thumb against the nape of Vittoria's tender neck. 'What a mess she makes,' he said, laughing.

'Such a mess.' Lena smiled.

They sat quietly as a family, watching their daughter drop the biscuit and run on chubby legs to a wooden toy. She put that in her mouth and bit down on it. Rico stood, kissed his wife and little girl, and headed towards the stand by the door to fetch his cap. Before he reached it, a knock was heard.

Lena and Rico looked at each other.

'It is early,' Lena said, surprised.

'And a Sunday,' Rico added.

'I'm not expecting anyone.'

The knock came again, sharper this time and Rico hurried to answer it. There on their threshold was a high-ranking Yugoslav army official.

'Good morning, sir. Come in,' Rico said, battling to steady his nerves.

Italians were still being arrested and executed throughout the city for supporting the Germans during the war. He had worked as a fireman for a time, though that was before his engineering studies had finished. The palms of his hands were sweaty as he pointed to an armchair. 'Please take a seat—be comfortable,' he said, clearing his throat.

The official sat. His face was stern.

Vittoria stared at the man; a scowl equally severe was stamped on her young face.

'Excuse me. I'll leave you to talk without interruption.' Lena said. She rushed over and picked up her toddler and took her to the bedroom, where she closed the door behind them. She grabbed some crayons and paper and told her daughter to draw, while she raced to the door and pressed her ear to it, hoping to overhear what the official had come about.

'Would you like something to drink or eat?' Rico offered.

The thin-lipped, straight-backed man shook his head and waved his hand.

'Then, how can I be of assistance?' Rico asked and sat opposite. He wished his heart would cease its pounding, for it was making him feel light-headed.

'Let me come straight to the point. You are an engineer—of which there are too few. We urgently need your skills in Belgrade,' he stated. 'You must know there is a severe shortage of engineers and much construction work to be done. If you move, we will give you a nice apartment. Of course, your family can come with you. You will be looked after, I promise.'

'I see.' Rico felt sweat break out above his upper lip. Belgrade! He could not imagine Lena ever agreeing to such a move. She was finding it hard in Fiume! 'I see,' he repeated, forcing a polite smile. 'It is a good offer.'

'It is an excellent offer. You will receive a pay rise, of course.'

'That is kind.'

'You will be in charge of a big project. We will explain the details at a meeting next week on Thursday. Can we expect you there?'

'Thursday? Yes. No problem! I'd like to hear more about it. See if my expertise is up to the job.'

'We need any expertise. I know you will want to do your part for the state.'

'Yes. It is good work. A good offer.'

The man stood. 'Here is my card. It has the address of the headquarters on the back. The meeting will be held there. You can ask for me. My name is on the card. Be there—Thursday, ten o'clock sharp.'

'Yes. Ten o'clock. Understood. I will see you then.'

The official, having delivered his message and believing it well received, nodded his head curtly and took his leave. As soon as he had left, Lena opened the door and swept into the living room, her face pale.

'I don't want to go,' she whispered, horrified at the notion.

'No, me neither,' Rico said sadly. 'It can't happen.' He looked at his worried wife and gave her a weak smile. 'I believe the time has finally come, Lena. We must leave, find a way out. We have to go quickly.'

They embraced, frightened by the idea. Would they be allowed to leave? Would Rico be punished for refusing to take work in Belgrade? Would they be regarded as disloyal? Where would they go? When? So many questions and fears flickered through their minds.

'We must go,' Rico said so softly that Lena had to strain to hear him. 'Belgrade is not for us.'

'I will start packing.'

Chapter eleven

July 1945
Trieste

Ettore, Cappi and Lisa sat in the back of a truck, their weary, sleep-deprived bodies rocking with the motion. They had reached Trieste, but they were yet to travel across the Morgan Line, a demarcation that had been established in Trieste to separate two military administrations. The Yugoslavs administered Zone B in the east and the Allied Military Government, comprising of British and American peacekeepers and law enforcers, governed Zone A in the west.

The papers that Cappi had prepared would hopefully see them safely admitted into Trieste's Zone A. The truck pulled up at a well-guarded checkpoint, where their papers were scrutinised over a fifteen-minute period. Lisa could hardly hold her anxiety in check; she was terrified of the heavily armed guards. The papers were eventually accepted and the truck was permitted to cross the line.

Zone A was teeming with American and British servicemen and, from the badges on their uniforms, Ettore saw infantry, signals, engineers and military police. An American in a well-cut uniform and cap directed them to a displaced persons camp. This one was set high on a hill, allowing its occupants a view over Trieste. It was crowded and only about two kilometres from the Yugoslav border, which made Ettore nervous.

It is too close, he thought, wishing to put a thousand kilometres between him and the border. Ettore was carrying two bulging suitcases and Cappi had a large bag that might as well have been a sack slung over his shoulder. As well as clothes and toiletries, Lisa had packed sentimental items, among them precious plates, gold-rimmed cups and silver cutlery. She brought a lighter, which had belonged to Dino, and playing cards and recipe books and an embroidered tablecloth. They were things she didn't necessarily need but could not bear to part from. It made the cases an effort to lift, though Ettore did not complain. He bore the weight gladly.

Quietly, they set their luggage down in their cell-like room. There were four other people in the room; two couples, one aged in their fifties, the other aged in their seventies, though they were not related. With seven people in the tiny space, there was only room when they were lying on their bunks. Had they all stood together, they would have been shoulder to shoulder, with hardly room to move. At least the beds were reasonably comfortable. *Better than sleeping on a stinking cement floor*, Ettore thought.

Lisa took a bottom bunk, allowing her luggage to slide underneath, freeing up some precious space. They slumped wearily on their bunks and one of the men offered Ettore and Cappi a cigarette.

'They give us a little pocket money to buy a few extras,' the man with silver hair explained gruffly. 'You travel far?'

'Not far enough,' Ettore replied, accepting the cigarette.

'From Fiume,' Cappi told the man, also taking a cigarette. They lit up and breathed in deeply.

'We're from Zara.'

Cappi nodded but, not in the mood for conversation, lowered his eyes while Lisa lay down on her bed and turned to face the wall.

'I want to see the officer about contacting my wife,' Ettore said. 'She has not heard from me in months. Probably thinks I'm dead.'

The silver-haired man nodded, not at all surprised, and his wife piped up with a suggestion.

'Go to the office of the Red Cross. They are helping families find each other,' she said. 'It's down the hill to the right. You can't miss the big red cross.'

'The Red Cross? Thank you. I'll do that. I'll go straight away.'

Eager to get out of the hot, cramped room, Ettore slipped down from the top bunk. 'Thanks for the cigarette.'

'No problem. You looked like you needed it.'

He shuffled around Cappi and the two couples and pressed his way into the crowded hall. He weaved around people until he found the door leading outside. His yearning to see Contessa and the children again was so strong and raw here; it was all he could think about. Outside on the top of the ridge he had a sweeping view of Trieste. A cloud-streaked sky stretched over the red roofs and jutting chimneys of the houses set into the hillsides surrounding the port. He could see Miramare Castle facing the sea from its perch on a rocky spur, its white walls reflecting the sun. There were uniformed troops around the castle and on the long pier that stretched out from the port's quays. He descended the hill as instructed and, looking to the right, easily spied the Red Cross tent. He called out on approach and was urged to enter. Three Italians, an older man and two women, welcomed him. Could they send a telegram to his family for him? It was not a problem. They set about drafting his message and arranging for it to be delivered to Bergamo, with the promise they would alert him immediately should they receive a reply.

'I also need help travelling to Bergamo. Can you assist?'

'Of course,' said the older man. 'We can arrange it for you. Come here tomorrow morning and we will give you the details.'

Buoyed by their kindness, Ettore was thrilled at the possibility of beginning his journey the next day. Hoping the arrangements would work in his favour, he hurried back up the hill to the camp. He couldn't wait to travel west—the further he was from Yugoslav territory, the safer he would feel.

On his return, Ettore was met by the camp's liaison officer, who demanded he fill out some paperwork and have a medical assessment. The assessment turned out to be fairly invasive, but at least they examined his hip and reported that it had healed well, despite the unhygienic conditions he had been forced to endure. He also learned that his jaw and sore ribs had not been broken during the prison interrogations, only badly bruised and were on the mend. He was told that overall, he had satisfactory health, though the doctor said he was malnourished and anaemic.

Dinner was a cup of brown soup and hard bread. They collected their food from the soup trucks and took it back inside to eat. As breadcrumbs spilled on the floor, Ettore thought about rats and disease. They would need to create a dining area soon, he mused, or they would certainly have health problems. The camp had an early curfew and once it grew dark, little light was available to them. It was easier to just lie down and sleep. At first, Ettore found sleep elusive. If he was not remembering the horror that had unfolded at the sink hole, he was thinking of his family. If he blocked out those intrusive thoughts, he was all too aware of the hunger in his stomach. However, weakness eventually ushered sleep in, although when it came, it was spasmodic and troubled. The others sleeping in the room rustled and twitched, snored or coughed. Occasionally the silence was broken by a quiet sob. It came from below him; no doubt it was Lisa, struggling to contain her searing grief. His heart ached with pity. She had lost a good man, a man he had considered a true friend.

The next morning, after the weak cup of boiled barley that constituted breakfast, he wandered down the hill to the as yet unopened Red Cross building. When the two women and older gentleman arrived, they greeted him by name. They were holding a shopping bag that smelled like heaven.

'Come inside. We can give you a real breakfast,' they told him. Sure enough, the shopping bag held several paper packets. They unwrapped the packets to reveal sweetbread rolls with jam. 'Here, have one.'

He took it, his mouth watering at the sight of the pretty rolls. In an attempt to remain civilised, he took a small bite, immediately followed by a bigger bite. It was delicious. He could not wolf it down fast enough.

'Thank you. It is very good,' he told them and they laughed knowingly.

'They are made by a local baker. We help him get what he needs and he repays us with these.'

'Better than money,' Ettore smiled.

'Now, you have come about your travel. You are in luck. We have talked to a priest at a nearby church,' said the elderly man. 'He is organising a group of nuns to be driven to Milano for a special service tomorrow. When we explained your situation, he agreed to let you join them. You can ride at the front of the truck—the nuns will be in the back. From Milano, you should be easily able to make your way to Bergamo.'

'Tomorrow?' Ettore repeated hopefully.

'Yes. They will leave at dawn. You have to be at the church by then.'

'I'll be there.'

'I'm sure you will.'

'Thank you for organising this. It is wonderful news.'

'We're happy to help. If you like, I can walk with you to the church now, so you can see where it is. It's not far.' The man, aged in his seventies, was tall with thin, white hair and a prominent, pointy chin. He looked strong and fit for his age.

'That would be very helpful, yes, thank you. I have no other plans for the day.'

The man took a moment to finish his roll and then got to his feet. He picked up a distinguished looking hat and placed it on his head. 'Come this way then.'

They walked side by side, without talking. Ettore noticed the town was only now beginning to awake. Well-dressed workers and merchants were starting to make their way to the city; their faces were grim, the mood on the streets was heavy.

'How are things in Trieste?' Ettore asked the man at his side.

'You can see for yourself.'

'Explain it to me. I am out of touch.'

'Well,' the man said, deep in thought. 'The Allied Military Government is both welcome and unwelcome. They bring hope and stability to the economy. But many see them as intruders. Some are talking of an independent Trieste—that we should break away from Italy and have our own free territory. Some look favourably on Communism and wonder if life will be better under Tito. Most remain loyal to Italy and want to be returned to Italian rule. What is clear is that the Allies have formed only a temporary government, so what comes next? We are in limbo. It is a city divided, literally and ideologically. There will be political conflict for years to come, I fear.'

'You follow politics,' Ettore observed.

'Politics is about people. I know people and society and that is why I serve the Red Cross.'

'You serve it well.'

The man bowed his head in recognition of the compliment and glanced sideways at Ettore. 'And what will you do once you find your family?'

Ettore considered the question. 'I don't know. What do we do? We are displaced with nowhere to live.'

'There is a housing shortage here and jobs are hard to get, though there are some low paid ones if you are willing to work hard.'

'I've always worked hard and I have nothing to show for it.'

'Keep working. You are young—you can't be more than thirty. Plenty of time to rebuild.'

'I have time, but do I have opportunity?'

'Men like you find opportunity.'

'What kind of man is that?' Ettore asked.

'Men who know how to get what they want.'

'And how do you know I am that kind of man?'

The man stopped walking and turned to him. 'What do you want?'

'To find my family,' he replied instantly.

'And there is the church. Tomorrow you will have your family.'

Ettore felt his mouth slide into a wry smile. 'Yes. I believe so.'

'You should go in and meet the priest. He can confirm the arrangements with you.'

'I'll do that.'

'Stay safe.' The man held out his hand to him and Ettore shook it warmly. Stay safe—once, a long time ago, his wife had given him the same advice. It had rung in his ears until the bombs had fallen, but he and his family had stayed safe. He took the words as a good omen.

'Goodbye and good luck to you,' Ettore said in reply.

The church was made of roughly cut, old bricks of various sizes and a doorway flanked by stone pillars embedded with sculptured faces, eroded and ghost-like. He walked up the three stone steps and knocked on the large wooden door, which was open, hesitating before taking a tentative step inside. The priest came out of the darkness to meet him. He was short and stocky with prominent shadows beneath heavy, bloodshot eyes. His hair was black and scruffy, as though it was rarely washed and combed. He looked in dire need of a good night's sleep. He offered Ettore a blessing, which he accepted.

'I've come about the ride to Milano,' he started and the priest nodded.

'Yes, yes. The Red Cross asked me about it. It is all organised. You come here tomorrow before sunrise. The truck leaves at dawn. All right?'

'It is perfect. I will come early tomorrow.'

'Good, good. You look thin and pale. Come, I'll give you breakfast.'

The priest gave him no chance to reply but ushered him out of the dimly lit church into a small cottage at the back. The door opened directly into a tiny kitchen where a woman was cooking up some eggs. 'Any chance of cracking another egg for our friend?'

'Of course, Father,' the woman said obligingly and reached into a basket full of eggs to add two more to the pan.

'Sit down, have a glass of apple juice. Sorry I don't have anything stronger.'

'I don't have a stomach for anything stronger,' Ettore confessed.

'Then drink this up.' The priest had fetched a bottle of juice from the icebox and poured him a glass of cloudy, cool liquid. 'How's that?'

'Cold.' Ettore was delighted and it showed in his sparkling eyes. 'Very nice.'

'You look like you needed it. I can't help everyone—wish that I could, but every now and then, one like you wanders in and I want to do something more.'

'Thank you. Trieste is overrun with people like me.'

'People like you are swarming all over Europe. We have to help. You are too many to ignore.'

'Can they help so many?'

'Not overnight, but give it time. The world is a big place.'

'I'm not interested in the world. I just want to find my family, get a job, start over.'

The priest listened and the shadows beneath his eyes appeared to darken. 'Start over … yes. I hope you can. God willing. After so much death, must come beginnings, must come life.'

Ettore studied the priest's face and saw pain and turmoil and stress. 'You take on too much, Father,' he said.

'There has been a lot to take on. If only you knew the half of it, the half of what I've seen and what I've heard. Spirits were not made for breaking but ...'

'You have done your best.'

The priest glanced up at Ettore. 'My best hasn't been enough. Sometimes I've wondered ... questioned ...'

'Everyone's faith has been tested. You'll be stronger for it.'

'What is happening here? I ask you in to give you food and hope and you are counselling me!' The priest's face lightened and he leaned back in his chair. 'Stronger? Perhaps so! The world is stronger, more united.'

'There you are, going on about the world again,' Ettore pointed out.

'These Americans are fascinating creatures. They are young, innocent in many ways. They come in friendship. They've come to help.'

'Just in time too,' Ettore commented.

'Yes, but they can't stay. We have to step up.'

'As a free Trieste or as Italians?'

'Whatever the majority wants,' the priest said. 'But for me, I am Italian born and Italian proud. I'm a traditionalist, a Roman Catholic. And after that, I serve Trieste.'

The eggs were served. 'Tuck in, my friend.'

Ettore did not have to be told twice. He ate well that morning.

On his departure from the church, the priest kissed him on each cheek and gave him a second blessing.

'Find your family.'

'And when I do, what then? What can I give them? I have no job, no roof, nothing!'

'When your wife looks upon your face ... after believing you dead for so long, tell me then you have nothing to give her.'

Ettore nodded, understanding.

'Go now. And may God go with you.'

* * *

Ettore had spent half the morning at the church and he walked slowly back to the camp, meandering through the streets, in no hurry to return. He wished he could take some of those sweet rolls to give to Lisa and Cappi. Hell, he wished he could give them more than that! How Dino's death haunted him. Here he was walking around Trieste, very much alive. His life had to mean something; he had to be more than just a displaced person living on handouts. Surely, he could offer his family more than that. As he walked, with the sun beating down on his back, he resolved to one day put a roof over his family's head, put decent food on the table and give his kids a good education. He wanted those things and he would make them happen or die trying.

The hearty breakfast had given him a burst of energy and his feet took him to the port, where people of all ages were milling around the piazza. It was a vast square with grand buildings and a gold-trimmed palace facing the ever-changing Adriatic Sea. On this day, the Adriatic was uncharacteristically sullen. He strolled the square, his eyes transfixed by the grey water, all the while thinking of Fiume. American soldiers watched him curiously but saw he was harmless and left him alone to wander with his thoughts and memories.

By tomorrow afternoon he'd be in Bergamo. It was a thought both heartening and disturbing. His future was as murky as the wild sea before him. He turned away and began his trek back to camp. His energy from breakfast vanished and he began to realise how weak his muscles were after spending weeks sitting listlessly in the prison cell. His pace was very slow and he stopped frequently and sat where he could to rest. Eventually, he climbed the hill and the camp came into view. Thirsty and out of breath, he crossed the road, only to hear a familiar voice calling his name. He turned to see two men hurrying towards him—one had his arm in a sling and they were both wearing hats. It took a few seconds to recognise their faces.

'I didn't know you, not without the beards and—look at you, in clean shirts!'

Ettore embraced and kissed the cheeks of Edrico and Roberto, who were both very happy and relieved to see him.

'You made it,' Edrico said, his eyes glistening.

'Yes.'

'I did not believe …' Roberto started, shaking his head.

'First thing! You should go see the nurse, she's very pretty. I promised you that, didn't I?' Edrico chuckled.

'He's lying—you can't trust a banker! She was old and looked like a man and was twice the size of one,' Roberto reported and coughed. 'She gave me awful tasting cough medicine too.'

'That was your nurse. Mine was blonde with big boobs.'

'You saw the same woman that I did!'

That made Ettore smile. 'I have seen the nurse—not pretty,' he chortled.

'You are a hard man to please,' Edrico laughed. 'And so how are things? The young man's parents … did you help them out?'

The smile, so brief and wondrous, was gone. He shook his head and shuffled his feet. 'We got his mother out. His father … and his brother—we were too late. Both shot.'

Edrico's eyes glazed over sadly. 'That is too bad,' he said. 'You talk to anyone here—terrible stories everywhere.'

'Have you found your own families?' Ettore asked the men.

'I have. My wife and son are making their way to Trieste,' Edrico said.

'I'm still searching,' Roberto replied downcast. 'We have seen the Red Cross. They will help find them but it may take time.'

'People are leaving Fiume every day,' Edrico explained. 'There is no place to go. Camps like this one are everywhere.'

Their conversation was interrupted by the arrival of trucks, turning into a driveway at the far end of the camp.

'The food trucks. Lunch. We were on our way to join the queue. Come with us,' Edrico beckoned.

The men joined the snaking line of people waiting for handouts. Each person, in turn, would be given a chunk of hard bread, a cup of soup containing some small pieces of meat and vegetables, and a cup of water. The soup was delicious compared to their prison swill and Ettore, having worked up an appetite again after his long walk, eagerly poured the contents into his mouth, burning his tongue and scalding his throat in the process.

'Slow down. You look like you just got out of prison,' Edrico remarked dryly.

The men had taken their hot meal over to the shade of a tree, where they found a rocky wall to sit upon. They sat there, preferring the outdoors after their lengthy confinement.

'Here we are,' said Edrico, tilting back his newly acquired felt fedora hat, which a charity group had given him. 'Outside.'

'I never thought we'd do this. Sit under a tree,' Roberto agreed. He wiped at his nose with a hanky. His hat was concealing the large scab on the side of his head.

As they sat relishing the fresh air, they watched other people, including families and a few children, spill out of the camp to wait for soup. As they watched, more and more people poured outside, until there were hundreds of them, in ill-fitting clothes, waiting to be served.

'What happens now—to all of us?' Ettore wondered out loud.

'The country will rebuild,' Edrico said. 'Growth will follow impoverishment.'

'But first the poverty and for how long?'

No one had an answer to that.

'We have families,' Roberto pointed out.

'And where are they?' Ettore wanted to know.

'Yours are in Bergamo.'

'Are they? My wife's sister has only a small house. It has now been three months; they could not have stayed there that long. And how do I know for certain they made it out?'

The two men fell silent, draining the last squelching bits at the bottom of the soup cups and longing for more.

'You'll find them soon enough, you and Roberto,' Edrico promised firmly.

'I miss my wife. I don't know if I will find her or my children. It may take years,' Roberto conceded. 'They won't be waiting for me or searching for me. They think I'm dead—shot. I was taken with a group of men who were put against a wall and executed. On our way to the wall, the group fought back. They were quickly overcome but I was at the back and was actually knocked down a slope, I took that as my chance to run. I ran and ran. For some reason they didn't give chase. I think they had to tend to the group and couldn't afford to lose a guard in search of just one man. I didn't look back until I was down in a gully … I tried to get word to my wife, but she fled quickly. I had told her if anything happened to me to leave Fiume and she did.'

'You will find her,' Edrico affirmed, without substance.

At that moment, Ettore saw Cappi walking away from the queue with his bread and soup in hand. 'Cappi,' he called to him. The young man heard his name and turned in their direction. They waved him over and moved along the wall to make room for him.

'Where's your mother?' Ettore inquired.

'She was in the queue before me. She has her soup and is sitting inside. She wants to be alone,' he said. 'I wish my sister Lena was here. She would be better for my mother in this situation.'

The men did not know what to say. They chewed on the bread.

'Don't know how long we can stay here,' Cappi continued, looking around at the dozens of families sprawled about. Children were running amok, babies were crying and exhausted mothers looked close to collapse. 'It's crowded. We are packed like sardines.'

'Better here than back in Fiume under Tito,' Ettore grumbled. The men agreed, but they were aware their futures were now very uncertain. It was not going to be easy resettling in a war-ravaged country, its economy crippled.

'Take each day as it comes, son,' Edrico told Cappi. 'Look after that mother of yours and try to find a less crowded place— get work if you can. You're young. You will make your way.'

Cappi nodded. He was trying hard not to think of his father and brother, but their faces were imprinted on his troubled mind. He wished they were there with him, drinking soup, talking of the future and its challenges. Everything wouldn't seem so bleak if he had them to share it with. Feeling alone despite the company, Cappi abruptly stood.

'I best check on Mama,' he murmured quickly and left them.

'He's suffering,' Roberto commented.

'He lost his old man—a good man,' Ettore said.

'The war took many good men.' Roberto lifted his hat to wipe his brow.

'Not us. We are here. We made it,' Edrico announced. 'Your wives will be happy for it. When do you leave for Bergamo, my friend?'

'Tomorrow I have organised a ride with the nuns to Milano.'

'Nuns? You're assured of a blessed trip then,' Edrico quipped.

'Don't suppose there's room for one more on the truck?' Roberto asked. 'Bianca has a close cousin in Milano. It's possible she went there or the cousin may have heard something.'

'I'll find out, but I'd welcome you along.'

'Good. Thank you. I must start my search somewhere.'

'So I could lose two good friends on the morrow,' Edrico said, holding his hands up with exaggerated woe.

'You have a wife on the way. When she gets here, you'll forget us soon enough,' Ettore put to him with a sly smile.

'Forget? No. Never forget,' he said seriously, and for the first time Ettore thought the banker sounded sincere.

'Rise before the sun tomorrow and come with me to the church, Roberto. If they have room, they will take you.'

'How about I meet you here—under this tree—before dawn?'

'Perfect.'

The plan was set. The next morning, despite the early hour, Edrico, Cappi and Lisa waved off both Ettore and Roberto as they set off down the slope. Ettore was not one for showing emotion, yet he felt a sense of loss as he farewelled the sleepy trio beneath the branches of the tree. For a moment his mind played tricks and he thought he imagined Dino standing behind his son and wife, but he blinked and the image vanished. He waved without joy. Tension clenched his jaw, leaving him with no parting words. If only he could express what he felt, but even if he could, what difference would it make?

When they reached the church, a large group of nuns was already secured in the truck's canvas-covered back. Roberto was readily accepted along for the ride and the two men joined the driver in the front cabin. They left in the dark and the sun rose behind them as they travelled west. Along the way there were plenty of roadblocks and detours and they passed dozens of American soldiers on tanks and jeeps. The driver, wearing a flat cap with a small brim, kept his thoughts to himself, mumbling only when he became stressed navigating the detours, frequently glancing at his watch. He was overly conscious of time. They had a funeral to make. It was a long five-hour drive but they had left early, so it was only mid-morning when they drove into Milano.

Ettore was shocked at the extent of the city's war damage. He shuddered at the sight of ghostly buildings, left open and exposed and partly crumbled. This was one of Italy's commercial hearts and much of it lay in ruins. It was disturbing to see.

The church they arrived at was significantly more impressive than the one they had departed from. Gothic in style, its high arched windows and detailed facade was incredibly still intact, though neighbouring buildings were not. The nuns alighted hurriedly and were met by a priest at the arched doorway who ushered them inside in great haste.

Ettore and Roberto thanked the driver and, carrying a small roll of spare clothes and some food, hopped out. They shut the truck door and glanced about at the well-dressed men and women picking their way around debris to walk through the streets. The young women wore short-sleeve blouses and straight skirts to the knees with their hair rolled up. The businessmen were in suits and ties and hats.

'Where is this cousin?' Ettore asked Roberto as they wandered up the block.

'It's a fair walk from the city centre but I know the way. I best get started if I want to make it there by night,' he said, turning to his friend. He coughed but only briefly and his chest sounded much clearer. He was on the mend.

'Well, good luck,' Ettore said and held out his hand.

Roberto shook it and smiled. 'Best of luck to you too.'

'Find that wife of yours.'

'And yours.'

They met each other's eyes and embraced for a long time. They had shared a lot and were both emotional at the thought of moving on.

Their hands fell apart, and then they were walking in opposite directions, but with a common purpose—to find their families among a backdrop of ruin. Ettore's hopes were high but that only made him nervous. It was not good to hope, not when so much was being taken away. Yet there was a spring in his step. He was only an hour from Bergamo … one more hour and he would have word of Contessa. His letter should have arrived by now. They should know he was safe and alive and on his way to them. He wondered if he had another child awaiting him and the thought put more energy into his steps and lifted his spirits higher. Not long now!

* * *

In a dingy laundry area behind the camp building in Trieste, it was Contessa and Bianca's rostered wash time. Nonna and Gilda were helping them. The two nonnas fed clothes into the boiler, a huge metal tank into which they added some yellow soap shavings. Soap was scarce but they had traded their pocket money for a small bar.

Contessa and Bianca were at the mangle, where their dripping sheets were being squeezed through two rollers. Contessa was turning the handle, while Bianca pulled the sheet clear for hanging on nylon string that had been strung up between two posts. It was tiresome work, but made easier with the four of them sharing the duties.

Bianca peered around the washing to fetch more wooden pegs, and let out a sudden shriek of amazement. She fell back into the wet sheet, which slowed her fall long enough for her husband to grab her by the arms and pull her to him.

'Sweet Jesus, am I dreaming?' she gasped, then she was hitting him and kissing him and hitting him, while he laughed and kissed her back.

'You're alive. How?' she was sobbing too hard to say anything more, and he was burying his head in her glorious hair, his breath coming too hard and fast to give a response.

Gilda watched the two, a huge grin on her face. 'It is a miracle,' she said, shaking her head. 'A miracle.'

'Roberto. This is my Roberto,' Bianca said, turning to face Contessa and Nonna.

'Yes. It must be! It is incredible,' Contessa said, smiling broadly.

'You have given your wife a shock,' Nonna said.

'The children?' he asked, apprehensive.

'All well and fine. They are in the courtyard playing. A friend is watching over Gian.'

'That's good. Good that they are playing,' he stammered, finding it hard to believe the conversation was truly happening.

'How did you find me?' Her teary eyes were fixed on him. She was afraid to look away lest she might discover she was dreaming, that she was not really here in his arms.

'I was in Trieste but I didn't know you were here. So I went to your cousin's apartment in Milano.' He paused to cough and then continued: 'She told me you were here. I stayed the night with them and in the morning they arranged someone to drive me back. I couldn't believe it was going to be that easy, but they dropped me off out front and the officer at the desk knew exactly where you were.'

'In the laundry room!'

Roberto laughed. 'I don't give a damn where, as long as I found you!'

'And you have,' she sighed, feeling so much love, wonder and relief, all at once, that she became lightheaded.

'You have had a shock. Come. Let's find somewhere you can sit,' Roberto suggested.

'Take him to the garden,' Gilda suggested. There was a small park with a pretty garden down the street.

'Yes. Come.' And the couple, locked together, arm in arm, wandered down the path.

Contessa's smile was so broad it hurt, but as she returned

her gaze to the washing and started rotating the handle again, her heart ached wistfully. How she longed for such a reunion. She imagined what it would be like to have Ettore's strong arms around her again, to lean against him, feel his breath on her skin. He had been gone without a word for so long. And yet, miracles were happening. Families were being reunited. Men, believed dead, were turning up. Surely her day would come. The washing was eventually all hung out.

'I must hurry. Isabella is due for her next feed,' Contessa told Nonna.

'I'll come with you.' They walked back to their sleeping area. The baby had been left fast asleep with one of the older nonnas while they attended to their washing.

'She has just woken up,' the old woman reported as they walked in. The baby was in her arms and starting to whimper.

Contessa took the baby, whose cry intensified, letting her mother know she was hungry. Unlike Martino, Isabella took the breast well and suckled greedily. Once fed, Nonna took the baby and put her against her shoulder, tapping her back in attempt to bring up wind.

'Here.' Contessa put a small hand towel on her mother's shoulder, in case the baby should have a sick up.

'Go rest,' Nonna urged, knowing Contessa had been up most the night with the baby.

'Thanks. But first, I'll go check on the children in the courtyard.'

Contessa left the camp and walked across to the military administration building, where there was a large courtyard complete with lawn, paths, fountains and statues. She sat on a rock in a side garden next to a terracotta statue. There, she watched the children playing—Taddeo and Nardo were rolling marbles and Martino was busy filling a bucket with stones. Marietta was skipping rope with Daniela and Francesca.

'Don't put the stone in your mouth,' she called to Martino, who was about to do so. He looked up and saw his mother and smiled. He dropped the stone into the bucket and kept picking up more.

She straightened out her skirt. It was a nice morning, warm but with a cool breeze that aired the back of her neck. Under Bianca's tutelage, her hair had been swept into a roll and encased in a knotted net close to the back of her head. Everyone in camp had been treated for lice the day before and their mattresses sprayed, so her head, which still itched, at least didn't feel as assaulted. She stretched her legs out in front of her and for a moment closed her eyes, wishing she could have an afternoon siesta.

All of a sudden, she felt strong hands rest on her shoulders. Her eyes flew open and she twisted at the waist. A man was standing behind her. The sun was to the back of him, blinding her and casting him in shadow. Trying to block the sun with her hand, she squinted and peered up.

No. It couldn't be. She was just seeing it because she envied Bianca her reunion. Her mind was surely playing tricks. She blinked hard and looked again. He was thinner and his clothes different ... but there could be no mistaking it, could there? She didn't want to hope.

'Ettore?'

He smiled. 'Contessa.'

They were in each other's arms instantly, hugging so tightly she could barely breathe, but she didn't care. It was him. She clung to his shirt, revelling in the kisses he planted on her cheeks, her eyes, her lips ... He was back, alive and well. Her prayers had been answered. It was too wonderful. Suddenly, their children were around them, screaming and shouting with joy.

'It's Papa. Papa, Papa—you came back!'

'I did!' He bent down and hugged all his children at the same time. When he stood, his hand flew to Contessa's flattened stomach. 'The baby?'

She smiled and was about to reply when a similar commotion erupted at the other end of the courtyard. Contessa glanced over to see Bianca and Roberto with their children also screaming and shouting.

'It is a day for reunions. My friend also had her husband arrive today. Look how happy they are.'

Ettore gazed across the courtyard and saw a blonde woman in the arms of his friend Roberto. He couldn't believe what he was seeing. What were the chances?

'That is Roberto—we came together. We survived prison together,' he said in a rush, his tone astonished.

'Prison?'

'I will tell you later. Come.'

Holding his wife's hand, Ettore crossed the courtyard in three strides, his children following.

Roberto saw him approach and was equally as stunned and confused. 'How can it be? What are you doing here? I thought you'd be in Bergamo?'

'I went to Bergamo and discovered that my wife is here.'

'As is mine!'

The men laughed.

'How is it you know each other?' Bianca asked. 'Contessa and I met in this camp.'

'Hear that, Ettore? Our wives have been keeping each other company, while we sat together in prison! It is crazy!'

'It is strange. It seems we both have good taste in friends,' Ettore said, grinning.

'This is a great day,' Roberto declared. 'A great day.' He looked at Contessa.

'You failed to say how pretty your wife is,' Roberto boomed. 'Such a sweet face.'

'And your wife is as you described, lovely in every way.'

They kept their arms tightly around their wives' waists while a sea of young faces hovered around them, eyes shining. Ettore noticed how much his children had changed and grown in such a short time.

'Where were you, Papa?' Taddeo asked.

'Questions later,' Contessa cut in. 'For now, there is still one more child yet to meet her papa.'

'Her?'

'That's right. Our Isabella.'

'Isabella,' he smiled. 'Where is she? Take me to her.'

Contessa led Ettore to the large brick building that was housing hundreds of displaced people. Taddeo, Nardo, Marietta and Martino hurried along behind them.

Nonna was inside, nursing the newborn, whose eyes were wide and searching. They lit up on seeing her mama, but when she was placed into the arms of her papa, her lips curled up in the shape of a smile.

'Look! She smiles for me. Smiles for her papa,' Ettore beamed.

'She brings up wind more like,' Nonna said. 'Ettore, you are a sight for sore eyes. We had almost given up on you.' She grabbed hold of her son-in-law's head in two hands and turned him left then right to plant a wet kiss on both cheeks. 'Welcome back. Thank goodness you're here with us.'

'I almost gave up on me too,' he said.

'I can't believe you're here,' Contessa said dropping to the mattress and starting to weep. It was too much for her, seeing Isabella in her husband's arms. The relief was overwhelming, revealing just how little she had believed Ettore would actually return to them. She put her face in her hands and cried uncontrollably.

'Don't cry. This is a happy day,' he told her, bending down to kiss her cheek.

Yes, it is, she thought. She looked at Isabella, content in her husband's arms. All was well. They were back together and the future would be better for it. She dried her tears with the back of her hand and, gazing at Ettore and all her children, allowed a smile to emerge.

Chapter twelve

January 1947
Fiume, Italy

Lena packed hurriedly. Vittoria watched on curiously, confused at the commotion.

'We're going on a trip,' she told her two-year-old daughter. 'So we must pack your clothes and your doll, yes?'

'Yes,' the girl agreed.

Rico entered the bedroom. 'I have submitted the paperwork at city hall. We are to go back tomorrow to pick up the pass-outs.'

'Okay, I'll wear my best dress for that,' she said, thinking aloud.

'You don't have to. You always look a picture.'

'Thank you.' Her laughter rang high and thin. They were both terribly nervous about leaving Fiume, but didn't feel they had a choice. They couldn't move to Belgrade.

The next day, the couple visited city hall as required, to see if their application had been processed.

'What name?' the sleepy-eyed officer asked for the third time.

'Corona,' Rico replied, trying not to show his anxiety. He knew he had to stay calm and agreeable if they were to provide him with the necessary documents.

The officer went through his files, searched down a list and even made a phone call. Eventually, after all his searching, he shook his head. 'Nothing here. Seems I can't find your application.'

'Should I come back in a few days. It might turn up then?'

'We'll call you if we find it,' he said. His dark eyes held no hint of promise.

'I see. Come on, Lena.'

Lena stood and picked up Vittoria, who had been playing with a doll at her feet. They left together.

As soon as they were a long distance from the government offices, Rico said solemnly, 'I don't think we're going to get permission.'

'No.'

'Don't worry. I can get it.'

'We don't have much time. You are meant to meet at headquarters in two days. Best to leave tomorrow so they can't come after us!'

'I know, I know. I can get a pass.'

Rico had friends who owed him favours, for he often did mechanical repairs for free. With so few tradespeople available and no money for maintenance, they were extremely grateful for his services. One such happy customer happened to work at the city hall and Rico decided it was time to call in a return favour.

'Yes, yes,' the short and stocky man promised, as they sat over a coffee in his office. 'Come back tomorrow morning and I will have a pass for you and your wife. Happy to help after all you have done for me ...' He gave a knowing wink and grinned broadly.

Rico smiled back, but harboured doubts. Could he trust this man? He had been too quick, too agreeable about carrying out what was a highly risky task. What if he changed his mind, decided to report him? Would he return to get the pass, only to be arrested?

The following day, Rico and Lena were the first ones at city hall, arriving just as the doors were opened. Apprehensive, Rico told Lena to wait outside.

'Lena, if I'm not out in half an hour ...' he began.

'What do you mean?' she asked, alarmed. 'This man is your friend, isn't he? He will get the pass for us?'

'I think so, but I can't be sure. Just wait and if I don't come out ...'

'You will. I will not discuss another plan. You will come out.'

She watched her husband enter the building and waited across the road with her sleepy toddler. Vittoria complained of being cold and leaned heavily against her mother's legs, trying to block out the wind and find warmth. Lena was shivering too, with both cold and fear. What if he didn't come out? What if a trap had been laid?

Half an hour went by and Rico was nowhere to be seen. Lena's teeth bit into her lip repeatedly and she tasted the metallic taste of blood. He should be out by now. She took a deep breath, and was suddenly overwhelmed by the tears she had been fighting to keep back. She was afraid. He was taking too long.

'Where's Papa?' Vittoria whined.

'Coming soon,' she choked, hiding her face from her child.

Then she saw him running hard down the side of the building, not the front as she had expected. He was waving to her, papers in his hand, but he was not smiling. He was sprinting towards her at high speed. As soon as he reached them, he scooped up Vittoria.

'Run,' he cried, and raced frantically down the nearest alley.

Lena followed, hating that the heels on her shoes slowed her down, but she kept pushing her legs as fast as she dared to keep up with her husband and child.

Two blocks down, Rico stopped in the shadows of a low awning and explained what had happened between deep ragged breaths.

'My friend had the papers. But he was not careful. Someone saw him preparing them and reported it. Security was waiting for me to collect them. But, fortunately for us, my friend became aware of the guards and I was given some warning. As soon as I arrived, he rushed up to me and shoved the papers in my pocket. He whispered: 'Back up slowly and run'. He turned around, blocking the guards' view and made a huge production of opening his drawer with his key, pretending to get the papers out and sort through them, but by then, I was by the exit and had a good head start. I ran in the opposite direction for a few blocks to lead them away from you, and then doubled back. Did you see anyone running behind me?'

'No, I don't think so,' Lena panted, but she could not be sure what she had seen. Rico had come upon her all of a sudden, out of nowhere.

'Are we in trouble?' Vittoria asked, her eyes resting on her father's anxious face.

'No, my beautiful girl. We are going to be fine.'

Lena looked at Rico and bit her lip.

'We must get to the roadside and find a truck,' he went on.

'Yes,' Lena said. She took Vittoria in her arms. 'We'll follow you.'

'Okay. Let's go.'

Husband and wife kissed for luck and walked briskly up towards the main road. They hailed the first truck they saw travelling west and were very surprised when it stopped. Rico hurriedly showed the driver their papers and he squinted long and hard at them from beneath his black cap, trying to make up his mind whether to give the family a ride. He was young and sunburnt and obviously in need of a wash. He stared at Lena and the rosy-cheeked infant on her hip. Feeling his gaze, she glanced up, looked at him with her large, shining hazel eyes and smiled as casually as she could. She was wearing a blue and white scarf around her head and it was tied in a pretty knot beneath her chin. Her coat was her best one—made of soft, navy wool with large black buttons. It hung well on her tall, slender form.

'Okay. Climb in.'

As fast as he dared, knowing the security guards and by now

probably the police too were looking for them, Rico helped his wife and child into the back of the truck. They sat low and Lena buried her face against her daughter's shoulder. *A ride! They had a ride to Italy*, she thought. *Such relief!*

'We're in,' Rico called and thumped the side of the truck to indicate they were ready to the driver.

The truck took off, destined for the nearby harbour city of Trieste. They huddled tightly for warmth, feeling better the further they travelled from the town centre. Soon Fiume was behind them ...

Vittoria was asleep on Lena's lap when they drove into Trieste. But they were not safe yet. They needed to get across the Morgan Line and into the city's Zone A. The truck slowed as it approached the checkpoint separating the city's Yugoslav-ruled zone from the Allied Military Government zone.

The fierce looking Yugoslav guards, guns held for the world to see, demanded their permit papers in curt, hostile tones. Rico did as instructed. The guards stared from the papers to them. Rico and Lena struggled to appear relaxed under such intense scrutiny. Vittoria awoke and began to cry on seeing the harsh-faced men.

'There, there my beautiful girl. They are just making sure everything is in order,' Lena cooed to her daughter, kissing her cheeks. The girl quietened but buried her head against her mother's shoulder.

'Occupation?' they asked Rico.

'Fireman, Fiume's city division,' he answered quickly, having prepared the answer in advance. He had worked as a fireman during the war and so could provide more details if requested. If he had told them that he was an engineer, they would have become suspicious and detained him.

'Why Trieste?'

'Family reasons.'

'What reasons?'

'My wife's sister is having a baby.'

The guard shifted his gaze to Lena. 'Is it true?'

'Yes. My sister is almost at full term. I want to help with the birth.'

The guard turned to the others manning the checkpoint and there was a long discussion.

At that moment, Vittoria turned her face from her mother to peer at the guards. She saw one of them, a huge man with a grizzly beard and blank eyes, staring at her. Desperately wanting to make the man smile and be nice to her parents … she did the only thing she could think to do and winked at him.

The guard's eyes flashed warily for a second, but when he saw how innocent it was, his lips went slack with mild amusement. He erupted into a string of Yugoslav, all the while pointing at the child.

Rico and Lena grew alarmed. Why was the guard talking fast and pointing at Vittoria?

Lena looked to her daughter, wondering what had caused such a stir. 'What did you do?' she asked. 'Why is he pointing at you?'

'I just winked,' the girl replied and did it again to show her mother.

The guard actually laughed this time, only to earn a punch in the arm from his comrades. They wanted him to concentrate and be serious. Don't let a little girl distract you, they told him. Still, it seemed to have worked.

'All right. Your papers check out. You can go,' they were informed soon after.

Lena and Rico could not show the true depth of their relief, but they grasped each other's hands tightly in celebration. They had done it. They were out and just in time. By now, the military would have been searching for them.

In Trieste's Zone A, Rico sought out Italian police to ask for help and they were directed to a refugee camp—a brick building with arched windows. At that time, there were about four hundred people camping out on the floor. They were hoping to find Lena's mother Lisa, and brother Cappi, somewhere within the camp, but gazing across the tent-like city, it seemed an impossible task.

'Just grab a mattress from over there and find a spot,' a gruff man told them. 'Come see me later to register.' He was busy and flustered and didn't even have time to explain the house rules or help them with any of their queries.

Rico fetched one of the uncomfortable straw mattresses from a pile and managed to find somewhere to lay it down.

'It is awful here. So noisy,' Lena complained. Vittoria was unsettled by the raucous environment and was starting to contribute with shrill demands and protests.

'I want to go home,' the toddler wailed. 'I don't like it here. Take me home.'

'It's all right. We won't stay long. We want to find your nonna. You do want to meet her? You were only a baby when she left. Come, help me search.'

Vittoria and Lena held hands and wandered around the silos, asking families if they knew of Lisa or Cappi Coletta. The people they asked shook their heads but then wished them well with their search. Finally, it was suggested that they should check in with the Red Cross.

That afternoon, Rico, Lena and Vittoria walked to the Red Cross office and were met by a tall woman wearing a straight skirt and matching jacket. She made them a hot drink while she searched through the files, seeking anything related to the Coletta family. After an hour, by which time Vittoria had fallen asleep on her father's lap, the woman emerged with news.

'I have it. Your mother and brother have been transferred to

Germany. They have been registered as displaced persons under the care of the International Refugee Organisation and are being processed for offshore emigration. I have a note here explaining that they did send a letter to you in Fiume, advising you of their change in residence. Obviously, you did not receive this notification?'

Lena shook her head. She was shocked. Her mother and brother in Germany!

'Well, this is why we keep a record of such transfers, so families can keep track of one another. We can apply for you to join them in Germany or you are free to stay in a camp in Trieste or another Italian camp. I can notify your family of your whereabouts. As long as you keep a Red Cross office informed of your movements, communications and tracking can be arranged.'

'I see,' Lena said hesitantly.

'The camp where we are now is very crowded. We wouldn't want to stay there too long. But I don't think we want to leave Italy for Germany,' Rico said, looking to his wife for confirmation. She nodded.

'That's fine. Of course, you must think about what you'd like to do.'

'Are there less crowded camps?' Rico inquired, hopeful.

'Try going south—some of them are better. When you find a camp that you like, go to the Red Cross and have them get in contact with your mother and brother in Germany. They can advise them of your whereabouts. I'll write down the details of the German camp for you.'

'Go south, you say?' Rico was considering it.

'How long will my mother and brother have to stay in Germany? You mentioned they were going to emigrate. To where?'

'Processing for emigration can take a long time. They will be asked for their preference, if they have family who live overseas who can sponsor them, their work skills … that kind of thing.

A lot of matters will be taken into account to help decide where they are sent.'

'I see. Can we emigrate with them?'

'They are trying to keep family groups together. Yes. If I were you, I'd find a camp, get in touch with the authorities and start the process.'

Lena looked at Rico, who was staring down at his sleeping daughter, deep in thought.

'Give it some time. These are big decisions,' the woman went on. 'There is no hurry. As I said, the processing is quite an ordeal. There are hundreds of thousands of displaced people throughout Europe. Some are being helped back to their home countries, but your family is not in a position to go back, are they?'

Lena shook her head. 'There's no going back,' she stated emphatically.

The woman from the Red Cross looked at Lena and, with sympathy, softened her voice. 'Then explore your options. You are lucky. You have a husband, a beautiful daughter. You decide what's best for you all.'

Lena and Rico thanked the woman and took their leave. They returned to the camp, Rico carrying Vittoria all the way. They supped on bread and cheese and tried to lie down to sleep, but it was impossible. The room was noisy, smoky and stuffy, the foul air rich with the smell of grime and sweat.

Lena stayed awake all night, listening to people moving about, coughing and talking. In the morning, at first light, she begged Rico to find them somewhere else to go.

'I can't stay another night,' she complained. 'It is too crowded. I can't breathe in here.'

'Then let's go south and see what else we can find,' he said.

Seeking a means of travel, they walked to the nearby railway station and found a train that was running. Bombing during the war had disrupted many rail lines, but it was now operational and taking passengers south. They caught the train and at each main station along the line, they stopped to check out the closest refugee camps. They stayed overnight at four camps before they finally agreed to stay for a length of time at one in Napoli. It was in a building that had once served as a mental institution. It had security grills across all the windows, giving it a prison feel. What made it attractive to them was that it wasn't overcrowded and they could sleep on steel and wire beds with a decent mattress.

'We could stay here for a while,' Lena said, liking the view of the shops from the window.

'Sure. We'll give this a try. We have to settle somewhere.'

'At least it's not Belgrade,' Lena felt the need to point out.

'Yes. At least it's not that.'

The next day, Lena visited the office of the Red Cross and advised them of where they were. She asked that her brother and mother be notified. She then visited the liaison officer at the camp and asked about the paperwork for emigration. The process had begun.

Chapter thirteen

July 1945
Trieste, Italy

The wind was gusty, threatening to trip them up as they climbed the hill to the displaced person's camp. Ettore and Roberto did not talk as they trekked up the steep road, putting one tired, sure foot in front of the other. They were thirsty and hungry and had plenty of time to think about it.

When they finally arrived, they sought out Edrico and Cappi, whom they quickly found lying on their bunks, doing nothing. The foursome strolled outside and sat in the sun: they all had a tin cup of water in one hand, a cigarette in the other.

'So you found your wives in Trieste! I knew it would work out for the two of you,' Edrico drawled, smiling. 'My wife found me. She's taking our son to the local parish to see about some shoes. The ones he has are falling apart.'

Roberto nodded. 'We got lucky.'

Ettore cleared his throat, preparing to broach what he had come to say.

'The camp down town has more space. We're going to stay there with our wives for a while. You should come with us— transfer across. Cappi … your mother would do well to have the company of my wife. They're close friends.'

Cappi's dull, lifeless eyes lifted. Within his despair there was a flickering of hope.

'Your wife? Yes. That's true. It's a very good idea. My mother needs another woman right now. We'll definitely come with you. I'll go tell her.' He got to his feet, almost automatically.

'Stay. Finish your cigarette and then tell her,' Ettore advised, and the lad sat down and put the cigarette back to his lips.

'What happened in Fiume ...' Ettore began, wondering how to finish what he wanted to say. It was a subject too distressing for words. Screaming men tossed down gaping holes in the ground plagued his dreams. It was something he didn't want to share with Contessa. He didn't want to share it, to give it life, to make it real. He wanted it never to have happened. 'Some things aren't for talking about,' he stressed.

'About the ...' Roberto too was suddenly lost for words.

'I haven't told Tazia,' Edrico agreed.

'It's not easy to talk about,' Roberto put in.

'Then we never mention it again,' Ettore asserted. 'Except ... Cappi ... thank you. We owe you.'

'Don't owe me. You're right. We never talk of it again,' Cappi agreed vehemently. He stood. 'I want to tell my mother to have her suitcases ready.' Then added, 'We hate it here.'

He tossed the remnants of his water onto the dry ground in one angry movement and, stern-faced, purposefully strode away from them in search of his mother.

The men fell silent. Cappi's pain was clear, and in that silence, as they considered their good fortune in having families who they would lie with that night and many nights beyond that, they felt the depth of what they owed the boy.

'We'll transfer too. It can't be worse than this place,' Edrico said at last. 'Besides, I'm getting used to the two of you. A few months in prison and it's like I've known you my entire life.'

Ettore and Roberto grinned.

'Come meet my wife,' Roberto sang, obviously proud of his Bianca, keen to show her off.

'I've heard so much about her, I feel I've known her my whole life too,' Edrico laughed.

Ettore chuckled. 'It's good you're coming. We'll show you the way. Good thing your wife is getting your boy some shoes. It's a hell of a walk.'

'At least it's downhill on the way back,' Roberto pointed out.

'My boy will be fine. He'll run it. My wife ... Let's hope I don't have to carry her the last mile.'

'You might be carrying me the last mile if I'm carrying Lisa's suitcases,' Ettore put in.

'We'll help with the load. Come. I best go advise the camp officer,' Edrico said. 'We'll want to go soon to make it by dark.'

* * *

When Ettore joined Contessa at the camp, they were permitted one more mattress and could extend their living area by another metre. Bianca and Roberto did the same. It required some manoeuvring on the part of other families, but they were used to needing patience and having to accommodate others.

Edrico and his wife Tazia found an unused space further down and Lisa and Cappi were assigned a single mattress each and strung up sheets around their bedding, allowing for their own private tent.

As soon as Lisa had stumbled into the camp on the cusp of nightfall, Contessa had rushed to meet her. The women embraced in a tearful greeting.

'I'm so sorry,' Contessa cried, still shocked by her friend's losses. Dino would be missed by all of them and Marco had been a handsome, reserved young man who had excelled at his schooling and was hoping to become an engineer. Contessa could still remember visiting Lisa after she had given birth to the squalling boy. How Dino had celebrated the arrival of his first child—a healthy son! She recalled many bottles of red wine being uncorked ... that was such a long time ago.

'I can't believe it,' she cried tearfully.

'I still can't,' Lisa breathed. Her body went limp with grief and Contessa took her weight and helped guide her to a seat near the doorway.

'You have us and Cappi,' Contessa told her, trying to offer her friend some comfort. 'I will help you set up here and show you all you need to know. You're not alone.'

Lisa's tears choked her words, but she eventually blurted out, 'I can't think straight.'

'You don't need to. Cappi is setting up your sleeping area. You will be very close to us. Just rest and if you need anything, anything at all, come and see me.'

'Thank you,' Lisa sighed. Her dark, knotted hair was limp around her face, dropping to her waist. It was unlike her. She always rolled her hair up and kept it back from her eyes. Her dishevelled state alarmed Contessa, but she could well understand it. She curled an arm around her friend and sat and wished that life were not so cruel, even though they knew it was, and worse, that there was nothing they could do about it. They sat, without speaking, grappling with the loss. They were beyond denial and so, with acceptance, came a slow torturous sorrow. And their hot tears kept falling ...

* * *

The families stayed at the camp for a year, always believing it was just a temporary measure. However, that would not be the case. While the four men did gain lowly paid jobs - Ettore and Cappi worked in security and Roberto and Edrico found menial cleaning jobs - they could not afford the high rents brought on by the city's severe housing shortage.

The camp's conditions were only just bearable. They had enough food to survive, but they were often weak from hunger and, consequently, slept a lot. The men's pay ensured they could buy some extra meat, but it was still hard to come by and made for intense negotiating on the black market.

As Isabella grew and her demand for breast milk increased, Contessa struggled to produce enough to satisfy her. She sought help at the hospital and they gave her some powdered milk with which to supplement her baby's diet.

'I'm sorry I don't have my jars of tomatoes to offer you,' Lisa joked, recalling how she had helped Martino to thrive when they had presented at the farmhouse, only a single baby bottle in hand.

'At least this baby will take milk,' Contessa exclaimed, remembering all too well the trouble she had encountered trying to nourish her third son.

The women smiled and Lisa took the baby girl in her arms for a cuddle. As she did so she thought about her only grandchild, Lena's daughter, Vittoria, and wondered what kind of girl she was growing into. She would be pretty, if she were anything like Lena, she thought. She had only received one letter from Lena, telling her that Vittoria was walking and talking well ... such precious news. Mail was unreliable between Fiume and the displaced persons camp in Trieste but still she wrote to Lena once a month in the hope that a few of the letters would reach her.

During those long months in the camp, Contessa, Lisa and Bianca became an inseparable trio. Physically, Lisa and Bianca changed the most, losing what little weight had padded their bones. All too quickly they grew thin and gaunt and mildly jaundiced. Contessa had always been slim, but now she became bony; her frizzy hair turned brittle and clumps fell out. Together, they battled to keep themselves groomed and presentable, trying to help and support each other as best they could. As for Edrico's wife, Tazia, the group accepted her, but they were wary and didn't seek out her confidence.

Tazia was a stout, short woman with a head of tight black

curls and beady black eyes. She laughed and gossiped a lot, perhaps too much, Contessa thought. She was inclined to be nosy and pushy, especially when it came to her son, putting his interests above everyone and everything else. Her precious son, Monte, was seven years old and always finding mischief. Tazia was either unaware of his antics or laughed at them. Now her only child, having lost an older boy to the war, she absolutely doted on her cheeky-faced Monte, but her adoration was not generally shared, as he was too fond of initiating trouble.

Life stretched on at the camp—every day similar to the next. After a year, the liaison officer approached the families.

'Do you want help in returning to Fiume?' they were asked.

No. A return was not possible.

'Then how about emigrating abroad?'

Silence.

They gave this idea considerable thought, wondering if they could move to America or Canada. What would it be like? Would they get jobs there, earn big money? The American soldiers in Trieste had been good to the people of Fiume, so the idea of going to America was looked upon very favourably. After all, it was the land of movie stars, the vast land of opportunity.

'Why not?' Ettore put to Roberto and Edrico.

'Why not indeed?' said Edrico, flexing his fingers in excitement.

'I'm not sure,' Roberto said grimly. 'To leave Italy? Leaving Fiume was hard enough.'

'Staying in Italy means staying here,' Ettore pointed out.

They were all sick of the camp; the scratchy mattresses, the woeful food, the lice, the queues, their mundane jobs ... so any other option was something to be thoroughly examined.

'I guess it could be an adventure. We could go to America for a couple of years, make some money then come back. Italy might have recovered from the war by then,' Roberto mused aloud.

'And what an adventure,' Edrico beamed a big smile. 'There is money to be made in America. Come on. Let's apply.'

'Together,' Roberto stressed. 'Bianca won't go anywhere without your wives!'

'Yes, all of us, together,' Ettore agreed. 'Cappi and Lisa too. We must convince them to come with us.'

Husbands talked to wives and Contessa talked to Lisa. Despite some reservations, they decided that anything had to be better than life in the displaced person's camp. As a group, they approached the liaison officer and sat down to the paperwork.

Once they had applied, an Allied Military Government official interviewed them and, a few months later, they were all approached about being transferred to Germany.

'Germany?' Contessa shrieked. 'I thought we're to be resettled in America!'

'It's a long road to America,' Ettore said, smiling. 'We're just going to Germany for processing. We have to wait there for our papers to be looked at. Many emigration officers are interviewing in Germany. It seems we have to go there.'

'But Germany! I don't know.' Contessa did not want to swap one dreadful camp for another. Conditions might be worse in Germany. She was nervous and the other women equally so.

'Germany lost the war. It was heavily bombed. It'll be in ruins, worse than here,' Nonna told the group of women. 'I wonder how long we'll have to stay there … months or years? And I can't imagine there'd be too many other Italians! Mostly Poles and Jews in the camps.'

The other women had come to respect Nonna's counsel. She was wise, listened to the radio daily, and was more politically aware than most. They already harboured many concerns and Nonna raised more issues than they cared to think about. Despite their many reservations, it seemed they were locked into a process, and when they were told to be ready for transfer to

Germany, they packed their few belongings.

'Change can't be bad,' Ettore said to Contessa. 'The thought of staying here another year ... well ... it's not worth thinking about!'

So they packed their few remaining possessions and then, one drizzly afternoon in September 1946, they left.

Lisa and Cappi had sent a letter to Lena in Fiume, informing her of their transfer to Germany, but they did not know if they could trust the postal system across the Morgan Line. So, they made certain to inform the Red Cross, which would help Lena find them should she come looking ...

* * *

The group was officially recognised as displaced persons under the care of the International Refugee Organisation and transported by train to Germany. There they were delivered to a former military barracks in a rural area of Germany's American zone.

Ettore carried one suitcase, containing his entire family's clothing and belongings. On arrival at the camp, they were assessed as being in need of extra clothing. Ettore was issued with a dyed army uniform, which was drab and unappealing. However, when he put it on, he felt the heaviness of the material and knew it would keep him warm through the German winter. Contessa was given a woollen black and white checked skirt and a thick, heavy coat. Their children were also given coats. Nardo was handed an adult-sized jacket. His arms were lost in the sleeves, which had to be rolled up to reveal his hands, while the jacket came down to his ankles. Marietta was given trousers to wear beneath her skirt as the winter would be bitterly cold, and she was warned that her legs would need the extra coverage.

They were escorted to their lodgings. The Italians had a long, grey stone building at the back of the camp. Inside, there were many bedrooms off a long hall. However, there were no doors on any of the bedrooms. In the rooms were several bunk beds, a window without any curtains or coverings and stone floors. The Saforo family had a room near the front of the building.

Ettore walked down the hall and counted twelve rooms. He saw that Bianca and Roberto and their children had the room next to theirs and Edrico, Tazia and their son Monte were in the same room as Lisa and Cappi. At the end of the hall was a small common area where he saw a black, old-fashioned stove and a few chairs.

He stuck his head back into his family's room, where the children were shouting excitedly to each other about whose bed was the best. 'Quieten down,' he called, to no avail.

'It's all new to them. Let them be excited,' Contessa said, smiling. She too was feeling nervous and dazed by the change of scene. The stone floors and walls were drab and cold but the room, mattresses and scratchy army blankets were clean and dry.

'Let's go in search of the toilets,' Nonna suggested to Contessa.

'Good idea.'

They found a shed of communal toilets, with no walls separating them. Nonna was horrified.

'I can't go there,' she blurted out, staring in disbelief. 'People will see.'

'This shed is for the women. Only women will see,' Contessa said, trying to make the situation seem less daunting, but she too was embarrassed by the notion of using the toilet without any privacy.

'I'd rather go behind the shed and dig a hole.'

'You may have to,' Contessa smiled lamely, unable to help her amusement at the image that sprang to mind. Nonna would have a hard time digging into the hard, cold ground.

'It's not funny. What if you have an upset stomach?'

Contessa's mirth ceased, and she was forced to agree that

going to the toilet was certainly going to challenge their pride and dignity.

'Maybe we should go in groups and stand around each other with our backs to them to create a wall,' Contessa suggested.

'I'll try digging first.'

Mid-afternoon, the food, consisting of Red Cross packages, was served. It would be the only food doled out for the day and they would be expected to make it last until the next afternoon. They were given half a loaf of black bread, a dab of butter and marmalade, a small piece of cheese and wurst and a tin container of soup. Often the brown soup would contain small pieces of meat and vegetables. Once a month, the ration would extend to a piece of fruit and the children who attended school would also be given a cup of powdered milk each day.

It was when they all amassed to receive their food rations that Contessa became aware of how many others were at the camp. Looking around, she guessed there would have to be over a thousand people.

'More like two thousand,' Ettore estimated.

'There's not many Italians here,' Contessa observed.

'No. Mostly Poles.'

They soon learned there were also some Latvians, Estonians, Ukrainians and even a few Hungarians at the camp.

In Trieste, the men of their group had jobs and the extra pay had helped to supplement their food supplies, allowing them a few luxuries such as processed meat, fresh bread and sweets. However, in Germany, with the nearby town almost completely destroyed by bombs, there was little work around or money for rebuilding. As such, they had little purchasing power and Ettore, Roberto, Edrico and Cappi found themselves with nothing to do all day. Like many of the other men at the camp, they grew bored and restless.

It was not much different for the women, though at least they had some domestic chores—looking after the young children, helping in the kitchen and washing the clothes—to occupy some of the hours that trickled by drearily.

With so much time to fill, the people in the camp began to dream and talk of what life would be like when they migrated. They had to keep their spirits up.

'It won't be long now,' Edrico said. 'I heard an emigration official was visiting next week to take a ship full of people to America.' He was speaking to a group of Italian men sitting around a table, playing cards. 'They've got the ship ready to set sail,' he went on.

'How did you come by this news?' Ettore asked sceptically.

'I overheard some people talking.'

'In what language?' Roberto quipped.

'German. I know a little German.'

'We'll see,' Ettore said.

A week went by and there was no news of a ship to America. Such rumours circulated regularly. A month went by and another month and another and there was still no sign of ships.

By that time, winter was upon them and the cold made a drastic difference to their comfort in the stone barracks. Freezing drafts of cold air whistled through every crack and, try as they might to block them with blankets, the cold still managed to creep its way inside. They battled to make a fire in their stove for warmth, as they had not been allocated any firewood. After a while they ran out of fuel and the cold, empty stove merely taunted them.

The food packages became inadequate for bodies burning energy to keep warm. They were all but starving and their regular complaints fell on indifferent ears, as the American soldiers trying to run the camp were powerless to help them. Germany was in the grips of a food shortage and they were not the only ones feeling it.

One Sunday, the Italian children who had come from the camp in Trieste decided to walk beyond the camp's boundary, dragging their feet up a dirt road. They headed for what they called 'the hill,' although it was actually a particularly deep bomb crater with slopes they could slide and roll down or test their throwing skills by pegging rocks as far as they could across it. However, this time they weren't in the mood for 'the hill.' It was a cold, gloomy day with thick, grey clouds that hung low and the ground was frozen solid. They wore their coats but still couldn't get warm, even though it was the middle of the day. It had snowed lightly overnight but not enough to give them snow to play with. There was a small dam on a farm further up that had iced over. They thought to check it out and continued past 'the hill', walking up the dirt trail. They would have kept going to the dam; however, they came to an intersection, which Monte declared promised better adventure to the left.

'It goes into town. Let's go exploring,' the dark-haired boy shouted, already scooting down the trail.

'We don't know for sure where it goes,' Nardo called after him, but as he kept going, the others felt a sense of responsibility to stick with him. They followed, though reluctantly.

A few minutes more, they came across an abandoned wooden farm shed, and heard a mewling sound coming from within. They stood still: the three-year-olds crashing into the backs of the other children.

'What was that?' Daniela asked, frightened.

'A ghost?' Francesca offered uncertainly.

'No such things,' Nardo scoffed.

'Then go in and find out what it is,' Monte urged him. He flicked his hair back from his forehead, as was his habit. He had a face that was nice to look at, with bright, dark eyes, a short, curt nose and lovely curved lips. But those eyes always showed more mirth than was warranted, and there was coldness to it, as though he was always laughing at you, not with you.

'No, don't,' cried Martino, grabbing hold of his brother's arm, afraid he would go in. Nardo shook him off.

'Go on, Taddeo. You're the oldest. Go in there.' Monte turned his sights on the serious-faced boy.

'You and Daniela will be the same age as me in a few months,' Taddeo said.

'Age has nothing to do with taking stupid risks,' Daniela snapped.

'What's risky about going into a shed?' Monte asked.

Taddeo hesitated. His father had told him to keep to well-worn paths, as there were still a lot of unexploded bombs, grenades and ammunition lying about from the war. 'I don't know,' he murmured.

'Scared like your little brother?' Monte taunted.

'Leave him alone,' Nardo snapped.

The mewling sound came again, louder.

'It's a cat,' Francesca announced and, taking them all by surprise, her long, fine brown hair whipping behind her, she ran through a door that was dangling open on one hinge.

'Francesca!' Daniela shouted, alarmed for her younger sister. She instinctively followed.

Once the girls had rushed forth, Taddeo felt he had no choice but to enter. With three of them inside and all quiet within, the rest of the children crept towards the door, curiosity overcoming their fear. They stared into the dimly lit shed and saw the two girls sitting on the floor, a skinny kitten in each of their laps: one all black and one white with black paws. There were two other kittens, both black and white, lying against a sleepy white mother cat and, sadly, one unmoving grey ball of fluff nearby.

Monte watched the girls patting the kittens. 'They would make a nice dinner,' he surmised, licking his lips.

'No!' the girls squealed in unison.

Martino puffed up his chest and cried, 'No way. You're not eating them.'

'They're meat. We're all starving,' Monte said, smiling slyly. He picked up one of the other kittens and pinched the skin at its neck. 'Not much meat on it, but it would be tasty. Better than those fatty, smoky sausages we keep getting in the brown soup.'

Marietta frowned. 'Give me that kitten. It's not for eating.'

'They're going to die anyway,' Monte insisted. 'Tell them, Taddeo. Tell them it's silly to keep kittens when people are starving.'

'We're not starving,' Francesca pouted.

'I'm hungry and I bet you all are too.'

'Not hungry enough to eat these cute little kittens,' she spat back at him.

'Fine. Suit your stupid selves,' Monte said, tossing the kitten. The little bundle rolled on the dusty wooden floor and squeaked as it hit the wall.

'Don't!' Francesca shouted. 'Poor thing.'

Marietta raced over to the kitten and gathered it up carefully in her hands, brushing the dust from its fur. 'Are you okay?' she asked, looking into its big, timid eyes.

'By the time you skinned these kittens, there'd be less than a mouthful to eat,' Taddeo said calmly. 'But there is another way we can help the camp.'

'How?' Elmo asked, intrigued. The seven-year-old was the tactful one of the group. He liked to calculate the risks then act swiftly and capably for the betterment of all. If there was a way to help the camp, he wanted to be part of it.

'We need firewood. Look at these wooden boards.'

The children glanced around the unused shed, which was on a slight lean. It was made of enough wood to keep the fire burning in their stove for a month.

'We can take the cat and kittens to the barn at the farmhouse next to the hill. They'd be warmer there.'

'Yes, and they would grow fatter there too,' Monte pointed out.

But no one was listening to Monte. They were examining how easily the old boards would break away. The wood was mostly weather-beaten or gnawed away, probably by rats. Taddeo and Nardo tried to break a few loose. They snapped easily in some sections and needed a little prying in others. Elmo developed a method for loosening the boards and then the girls and even the three-year-olds joined in. Eventually Monte was seen pulling up boards from the floor, though he worked slowly, not wanting to overexert himself.

The others worked hard with a common purpose. The past week had been painfully cold in the barracks and those in bunks of their own had sought the warmth of other bodies and happily shared mattresses to survive the below zero temperatures. The mere thought of having a fire burning to take out the endless chill was enough to make the children work as hard as they could to rip up boards. Their fingers collected splinters and cuts, but they pushed on regardless, intent on what they considered a very important task.

Taddeo carried four boards, the other boys carried three; Martino and Gian carried just one each. Marietta and Francesca carried the kittens, hiding them in the pockets of their coats, and Daniela carried the mother cat.

They walked past the bomb crater, and veered off to the right to the farmhouse, delivering the cat and kittens to the small barn, which was only used to store tools and seeds. They found a bale of straw and pulled some loose to make a bed for their new feline friends. Then the girls helped the boys to carry the boards the rest of the way to camp. When they finally reached the camp, taking care to go the long way around so that they wouldn't be seen, the sun was starting to set and the chill in the air made their splintered fingers icy and sore.

'What have you there?' Contessa asked as she opened the

back door to their insistent pounding. She looked again and saw they were carrying wood—lots of lovely, dry, solid wood, perfect for a fire.

'Where did you find it?'

'An old shed with nothing in it but some chains and old clay pipes,' Taddeo replied. 'It's practically falling over.'

The men had now heard the commotion and saw the boards placed inside the back door.

'Wood!' Roberto announced, staring gleefully. 'We need to break it up.'

'Not a problem,' said Ettore, and he and Cappi grabbed the planks and started snapping them, using their feet and knees to crack them apart. Other men joined in, smiles in their eyes. Armed with wood, they would easily fight off the cold that night.

It wasn't long before a robust fire was roaring in their stove, with everyone cherishing the crackling, dancing flames. The fire heated the small common area that quickly filled with bodies eager for its warmth. The compacted crowd and the fire put colour into the cheeks of the Italians and they stayed up late, talking and telling stories and singing songs to pass the time. No one wanted to return to the cold bunks in dark rooms, but eventually exhaustion forced them to retire and the flames were left to burn low.

The next day, the children proudly showed the Italian men where the shed was located and, after that, many strong hands raided the wood each day until every board had been fed into the hungry stove.

'It was my idea,' Monte told his mother sweetly. 'I told them to go down that path and I noticed that the shack had useful wood.'

'You are the clever one,' Tazia smiled, kissing him on the lips.

Nardo had overheard the exchange and ran to tell Taddeo.

'He thinks it was all his idea,' Nardo complained to his brother. 'All he wanted to do was cook up the kittens. He didn't tell his mother about that!'

'Don't worry. Only his mother believes him.'

The successful escapade had Nardo thinking. In town there was a railway line and where there were trains, there would be cargo. What if they could bring back more than just wood? He talked to Taddeo about it but his older brother was the cautious one, and was unsure about venturing into town.

'Come on, it's worth a look. If Monte is right and that path leads to town, we should explore it.'

'All right. Let's get a group together. We'll be safer as a group. We'll go after school,' Taddeo relented.

Martino and Gian were too young for school but they enjoyed waiting for their siblings to come home. They kept a keen look-out from the branches of a tree that dangled over the camp's gate. Their high perch allowed them to see the dirt path, which led around to a stone building where a middle-aged teacher was giving lessons, mostly involving religious instruction, to all school-aged Italians.

'Here they come,' Gian said excitedly. He was happy to be the first to spy them that day.

Martino swung from his branch to one closer to the gate. He peered down the path and saw twenty children straggling back towards camp. However, his brothers and sister seemed to be heading in a different direction.

'Hey, where are you going?' he called to them.

'Can we come?' Gian added.

The boys' siblings, along with Monte, were taking another path, winding away from them instead of continuing up the road along with the others.

'No. You two go back to the barracks.' Taddeo's voice came loud and firm.

Martino and Gian looked at each other, wondering what was going on. They watched their siblings disappear from view and fell quiet, feeling sad to be left out of the adventure. The pair did not go home but stayed either in the tree or around it, determined to wait for their siblings to return. It was about two hours later when they were finally spotted again; they were running up the road shouting to each other, appearing hot and flustered. Taddeo, Nardo, Elmo and Monte were carrying a crate each, while the girls, huffing and puffing, were sprinting alongside.

Martino and Gian leapt from the lowest branch and joined the group, eager to run with them back to the Italian barracks.

On hearing the mayhem, Contessa came outside, Isabella on her hip.

'What's going on? What have you got now, Taddeo?' she asked, and the children raced over to her, placing the heavy crates at her feet. As they hit the ground with a thud, there was the distinct sound of squawking chickens. Contessa's eyes widened in surprise.

'What is this? Where did you get them?' she asked suspiciously.

'They fell off the back of a truck,' Nardo shouted and they all laughed and nodded.

Contessa found it difficult to stay serious or to condemn their behaviour—they had not savoured chicken in over a year. She bent down and peered through the wood slats, counting how many were inside.

'You found them then?' she asked, though she was not really waiting for an answer. She was wondering about the best way to cook them.

'There's four in each box,' Taddeo informed her.

Other Italians were wandering out, wanting to know what the commotion was about. On learning of the chickens, their eyes widened in amazement. Nonna, Gilda, Lisa and Ettore took in the children's report with a slow smile.

'I think we will have a nice dinner tonight,' Nonna declared. And everyone laughed.

Nonna addressed them all: 'Children, what you did was wrong. The crates were not yours to take. But as they were lost, and no one was claiming them, I suppose you did well to bring them to us.'

The children stood taller, their eyes gleaming with pride.

Martino, struggling to gaze through the legs of the bigger kids, was relieved to see the women's excitement. They had been unhappy and complaining about things for months. *So this is what cheers them*, he thought.

The Italian men and women fell into earnest discussion about how to prepare their chicken dinner, and before long, the men set about killing the chooks, breaking their necks. Afterwards, Tazia, Lisa, Nonna, Gilda and Contessa went to work plucking feathers. Other women gathered food from each person's daily rations to create a tasty stuffing. Another woman set off for the kitchen to see if she could beg, steal or borrow a cooking pan of some description or be granted some extra spices. The men saw to an outdoor bonfire, scoring extra firewood from a couple of soldiers who had been invited to join the feast. The fire was carefully concealed behind their barracks. There was a sense of purpose and elation as they snapped a few of the boards from the old shed that they still had in storage. It would be the first decent meal they would consume in months, certainly since their arrival in Germany.

'What is this? What special occasion has warranted such a feast?' Bianca asked, returning to the camp from the washroom with a small bundle of clean clothes. She looked upon the roasting chickens, breathing in the smoke wafting with the smell of cooking meat. Her mouth watered and she felt dizzy with hunger. She was not the only one. All the Italians had gathered to watch the chickens cook and some Polish people had also found their way around to the bonfire, drawn by the tantalising aromas.

Nonna was already carving one of the chooks and delivering morsels of the white meat to the children.

'The children found crates of chickens,' Contessa explained to Bianca.

'Found them? Not stole them?'

'Does it matter?' Contessa said, lowering her voice and staring at her directly, a brow lifted.

But it did matter. Bianca didn't like the notion of her children scouring neighbouring farms to steal like scavengers. Chickens were quite a prize and much too valuable to be taking. If they had been caught ... The thought had her drawing in breath sharply.

'I don't think it's right,' she blurted out, her voice breathy and anxious.

'Nothing is right about war,' Contessa sighed.

'The war is over and ... these are our children. We must bring them up to respect property.'

'Our children are malnourished and need to eat meat. Respect property? My children have no property—it was all taken away from them. All they have is charity.'

'So you condone stealing? Your children can steal?'

'They can take what is needed.'

'And what if they get caught? What if a farmer comes out with a rifle?'

'What farmer is going to shoot starving children taking food to eat?'

Bianca's eyes widened. 'Why, a hungry farmer whose crops can't grow in the frozen ground!'

'My children can run fast,' Contessa said, shrugging. 'At least it wasn't the little ones. Martino and Gian weren't with them. I agree they are too young for such activities.'

'All children are too young for it.'

Tazia, overhearing the exchange, moved close to the women. 'I have to agree with Bianca,' she chimed in. 'Our children were lucky this time, but it is too dangerous for them to be wandering around stealing food. I will be telling Monte never again.'

'You do that while you enjoy your dinner tonight. I'll be telling my children I'm proud of them but they're not to take risks. You think they are the only children doing it? All the kids from the camp are pinching here and there.'

'They are pinching nuts and berries. Our children took four crates of great value! From where?' Tazia wanted to know.

'Right now, I'm so hungry and that meal smells so good, I don't care!' Contessa said, raising her voice. She strode away from the two women to go help Nonna cut up the other chickens.

'What was that all about?' Lisa asked Contessa.

Lisa had been one of the first adults to be served the roasted meat, for she was considered one of the weakest Italians. Grief had whittled away her fighting spirit and more and more often she was missing meals, wanting only to lie around and stare into space. Contessa was worried about her friend and was glad to see she had eaten a chicken leg.

'They're angry at the children for stealing,' Contessa told her.

'Then they're the only ones. Right now, I want to kiss them.'

Contessa smiled. 'I understand it. They are mothers. They worry.'

'You're a mother. You worry!' Lisa pointed out.

'I worry all the time. But how can I scold them for wanting to eat? I can warn them of the dangers but ...'

Lisa placed a hand on Contessa's. 'Go eat. Be happy. Soon we'll be on a ship and all of this will be behind us.'

Contessa kissed her friend on the cheek. 'I hope so.'

'In America, we'll eat until we're stuffed like chickens.'

'I can't wait for that.' Then Contessa grew serious. 'I'd like to see you eat well again,' she said, holding her friend's hand.

'Thanks to your children, I feel quite full now.'

That made Contessa feel somewhat better about the stealing and she went in search of her own piece of crispy chicken.

Half an hour later, the Italians were sitting around the bon-fire, licking their fingers and the grease of meat from their lips as chicken bones were tossed on to the flames. Contessa, sitting next to her husband, saw Bianca scolding her children, no doubt over their involvement in taking the crates. They stood near the barracks. Elmo and Francesca bowed their heads in shame, but Daniela, being the oldest and feeling the most responsible for the escapade, tilted her chin defiantly.

'Mama, they were just there, really,' Daniela said, her voice rising. 'Everyone loved them. Look around! We didn't do any-thing wrong!'

Bianca saw before her a scene of contentment. In the fire-light, she could see people smiling and laughing and talking with more vigour than normal. She looked back at Daniela, who had pride in her eyes.

'That is the point. You don't see it as wrong and it is. For the next two weeks, you are to come straight home from school and stay in the barracks with me.'

'You've got to be joking! There's nothing to do here. I hate this place,' Daniela cried. She was nine years old, with long fair hair like her mother. She had a pretty face, with her father's dark eyes and brows and full, rosy lips.

'You will do as I say. I will have Nonna give you some chores to do.'

'I hate you. You don't understand!' Daniela screamed at her mother and suddenly took flight, running off into the darkness beyond the light of the fire.

'Daniela, come back here. Come back now!'

But the girl ran hard and fast and her mother had no chance of catching her.

Ettore stood up and spoke to the teary-eyed Bianca. 'I'll get Taddeo to bring her back,' he offered kindly.

'No. I'll tell Roberto to look for her.'

Roberto was nearby, enjoying the fire's warmth, when his wife approached.

'Daniela has run off. You have to go in search of her,' she implored her husband.

'I thought I heard Ettore offering to send his boy after her.'

'Yes, but …'

'But nothing. Taddeo will find her quicker than I could. Ettore …?'

'I've already sent him. He's a good kid. He'll do his best.'

'Thank you,' Roberto said to his friend and then, turning to his wife, he gently bade her sit down.

'Now stop your worrying. The boy will find her. Here.' He handed her a piece of chicken. 'I got you some.'

'I'm not eating it.'

'Eat. You won't get any better for another year!'

Bianca reluctantly took the chicken and bit into it. The tender meat broke away in her mouth. It tasted divine, but that didn't change anything. She had no intention of forgiving her children. She continued to eat, then felt her husband's gaze upon her.

'I just don't want our children growing up into thieves,' she said, wanting to explain her stance.

'Thieves? Daniela? I don't think so,' he chuckled lightly. 'Our children are just hungry and tired of slop like everyone here. Now go on and eat. Your children want you to.'

Bianca took her husband's counsel and ate. Afterwards, she stayed by his side, waiting for Taddeo and Daniela to appear, but an hour slid by and there was no sign of them.

'She's not back! I'm worried,' Bianca fretted. She stood, hands on her hips, and peered as far as the firelight allowed.

'I'm sure they're okay,' Contessa said gently, though she had to admit to herself that she would feel better if the children were to return soon. It was cold out there—she could feel the chill against her back.

'If they're not back in another half hour, we'll gather a few men and go in search of them,' Ettore suggested.

Bianca did not reply, but kept staring into the moonless night that was hiding her little girl. *Come back,* she thought, wanting nothing more than to wrap her arms around her. Her anger had dissipated and all she had for company was unmerciful anxiety.

* * *

Taddeo found Daniela easily. She was around the side of the barn at the nearby farm, a black kitten in her lap. She had been hard to see, but he knew it was a place she liked to visit, ever since they had delivered the cat and kittens there, and so once he had reached the barn, he just had to listen for the sound of her ragged breath.

'I'm not going back,' she asserted tearfully as soon as Taddeo plunked down beside her.

'Why not?'

'Because I hate it there. No one asked if I wanted to come to Germany. It's cold and miserable here. I want to go back to Italy.'

'To Italy, or to Fiume?' Taddeo posed.

'Fiume is not Italy, but I miss it. I had friends there. Here, all I have is this kitten,' she sniffled.

'You have your sister and my sister to play with.'

'They're too young. They don't even remember Fiume.'

'I remember it.'

'What do you remember?'

The two children recalled early memories, their images taking them back to times before the war. They talked about friends they once had and things they used to do. It was such a dark night. No stars could penetrate the cloudy evening and with the dark came the cold. They sat, side by side, their bodies touching in need of warmth. Taddeo held a kitten too, its tiny body heating his hands.

'We should go back,' Taddeo said at long last. He had practically lost feeling in the tip of his nose.

Daniela instantly got to her feet. She walked over and plopped down the kitten next to its mother. 'All right. We best go.'

Bitterly cold, they hurried across the farm to the path, their strides keeping pace with their pounding hearts. Taddeo thrust his icy hands into his pockets, while Daniela's arms were crossed against her chest. As they came up the dirt path and the light of the fire reached them, they heard Bianca's cry of relief.

'Daniela,' she sighed and rushed to her daughter. 'I'm sorry,' she said, holding the shivering girl close.

'I'm sorry too,' Daniela murmured. 'Taddeo walked me back.'

'Thanks,' Bianca said to the boy. 'Where were you?'

'Nowhere.'

'Come inside and let's find a blanket. You're freezing.'

Mother and daughter walked together inside the barracks.

Off to the side, Martino was having fun, finding chicken bones and throwing them into the fire, sending up a spray of sparks, which delighted his younger sister Isabella. Used to tasteless food, he felt he had never tasted anything so delicious as the meal he had demolished that night. He looked upon his older brothers and sister with admiration. They had done this. They had made the camp a better place to be for one night, for the campfire and the slow-cooking chickens had put everyone in a festive mood. It made for a strong and lasting impression.

Chapter fourteen

Hands shoved in pockets as they left school for the day, Taddeo and Nardo walked side by side earnestly discussing the possibility of another visit to town to forage for food. Bolstered by their hero-treatment after their previous venture, as everyone except Bianca had personally thanked them for the meal, they thought it couldn't hurt to try their luck a second time. Their sister Marietta was keen to join them. Their mother had told them to be careful, but she hadn't banned them from such escapades.

Monte wanted to come too, as did Daniela.

'I thought your mothers don't want you taking food,' Taddeo queried Daniela and Monte.

'My mother doesn't have to know,' Monte replied.

'Mine neither. We want to help. It's important. Kids are better at this kind of thing. The Polish kids are raiding farms all the time,' Daniela said, her chin jutting forward in defiance. 'I'm coming.'

Francesca and Elmo also longed to come but were afraid of defying their mother. However, on hearing their sister, they gathered their courage.

'If you're going, I'm going,' Francesca stated.

'Me too,' said Elmo, sounding uncertain.

Martino and Gian were in the tree, watching their siblings standing in the middle of the road, talking. Then they saw them turn away from the camp.

'They're going to steal food again,' Martino concluded.

'Are they? My mother will get mad at them!'

'I'm going too!' Martino jumped down from the low branch and broke into a run.

'No, come back. You'll get in trouble!' Gian wailed behind him.

Martino didn't care. He wanted to be part of the adventure and bring back nice food for the camp. He could help, he was sure he could. He wanted to be a hero too.

Taking care not to be seen, Martino followed the bigger kids all the way into town.

Nardo finally noticed him when they were crouched down behind some bushes on the top of a hill, watching a train pull into a railway station.

'What are you doing here?' Nardo turned to him, alarmed.

'I can do it,' the small boy whimpered, blinking hard. He was on his knees, looking down on the train.

'It's too dangerous. You shouldn't have come.'

'I want to help.'

'You can't help. Taddeo! Look who's here!'

Taddeo turned and was dismayed to see his little brother kneeling between Nardo and Elmo.

'No. We told you not to come,' he scolded, but when his little brother's face crumpled and Taddeo saw he was about to cry, he quickly added, 'But now you're here, do what we say. You stay here. You don't move and when we say run, you run to camp. Got it?'

'Okay.'

Taddeo, Monte, Daniela and Nardo edged closer to the freight train, commando crawling on their bellies down the hill. The train had come to a standstill just outside the station, awaiting clearance. Taddeo climbed up on the side of the train and, with a yank on a handle, slid open a door. He disappeared into the carriage.

'Where's he going?' Martino asked Marietta, Elmo and Francesca, who were watching from the top of the hill. He was terrified for his brother who had disappeared inside the train.

'Quiet,' Marietta said. 'Just watch and when we say run, you better run as fast as you can.' Martino, despite his young age, was light on his feet and could run swiftly when he wanted to. He nodded and waited breathlessly for his next instruction.

One, two, three crates were pushed out the door, off the train and on to the tracks, where the other kids picked them up and hauled them up the hill. Marietta, Elmo and Francesca raced to meet them and helped drag the crates behind the bushes. Taddeo joined them, huffing and puffing for air, his chest rising and falling from speed and exertion.

'Got the crates? Let's go!' Taddeo ordered.

Taddeo grabbed a crate, Elmo and Daniela picked one up together and Monte and Nardo lifted the last one between them. They stood, balanced the heavy crates, and then ran for it.

'Run,' Nardo told his younger brother. And run they did.

However, the sudden motion caught the eye of an old railway guard. He glanced up the hill on the other side of the tracks and saw crates being carted away beyond the row of bushes.

'Hey stop! Thieves,' he shouted. He immediately reached for his gun.On hearing the man cry out, Nardo glanced back and saw Martino trailing the group. Despite his skinny legs pumping as hard as they could, he was not able to keep up with the big kids.

Angrily, Nardo dropped his side of the crate.

'What?' Monte looked around in confusion as their crate slid to the ground.

'Forget it. Just run,' Nardo told him. 'I have to get Martino.'

Monte reluctantly let go of the crate and bolted for camp, while Nardo dropped back and scooped up his little brother. Cradling him close against his body, he began to sprint.

A gunshot rang out.

Nardo fell to his knees and his brother rolled out of his arms.

The shot cracked the air like a thousand whips, giving Daniela and Elmo such a jolt that they dropped their crate. It bounced down the hill and split open.

The other children peered back to see what prize had been lost and saw apples rolling down the hill towards a body lying on the ground. A blood-spattered Martino was leaning over it, tears streaming down his face.

Taddeo froze in his tracks. *Oh my God*, he thought, his heart thudding. *Oh no.* 'Nardo!' he shrieked. He didn't even remember dropping his crate, but he sprinted back towards his brothers, not caring whether more shots would follow the first.

'You all go. Run,' Taddeo told the other shocked, pale-faced children, but they did not move. They watched in horror as Taddeo turned Nardo's body over.

Nardo winced with pain. He was conscious. His arm lay unnaturally limp and was blood-soaked.

Martino gave a small scream. 'I'm sorry,' he cried, sobbing uncontrollably and covered his face with his hands. So much blood had to mean his brother was going to die.

'Are you hurt?' Taddeo asked Martino, for the small boy had blood on his face and hands and it was impossible to know whether the blood had come from Nardo or whether Martino had sustained an injury of his own.

'Nardo got shot,' was all he managed to blurt out between shrieking wails.

Their sister Marietta flew to Martino's side and wrapped her arms around him, trying to calm him. 'We'll get him to a doctor,' she said earnestly.

'Nardo ...' Taddeo examined the body quickly. The only wound seemed to be in the arm. 'I need to wrap it.'

'Here.' He glanced sideways. Francesca was stripping off her thick, white woollen stockings from beneath her long skirt. She handed the bundle to Taddeo.

'Thanks. It's perfect.'

He was able to loop it tightly around the arm several times and tie it off in a secure knot.

'We have to get you on your feet,' Taddeo spoke gently to Nardo.

Daniela was suddenly on Nardo's other side. 'I'll help,' she said, tucking a hand beneath Nardo's shoulder, where she felt him shivering. 'He's cold. Give him another coat.'

Taddeo threw off his own coat in an instant and draped it around Nardo. 'Lift him now,' he commanded urgently.

Daniela and Taddeo tried to get him to his feet, but it was difficult. The wounded boy was weak, losing blood, and in shock.

Elmo stepped forth and added his strength by pushing on Nardo's back from behind. At last, he was on his feet, leaning heavily on Taddeo with his uninjured arm.

'Elmo, run ahead and get help. We'll be too slow like this,' Taddeo said.

'I can get help,' offered Monte, standing away from the group, staring at Nardo's bloodied arm with fascination.

'Elmo is faster,' Taddeo said bluntly.

'I'm a year older. I'm faster,' Monte disputed.

'I'll go.' Elmo broke into a run.

'Me too,' Monte shouted and took off, though he was hard pressed to keep up with Elmo's long strides.

'Francesca and Marietta, take Martino back as quickly as possible. Run.'

They each took one of the hysterical boy's hands and started to run. Forced to go with them, he began to sprint, his skinny legs once again pumping hard.

Taddeo and Daniela tried to help Nardo walk, but he could only take small steps. His eyes shut frequently, and it seemed he was drifting in and out of consciousness. Often Nardo's weight would become twice as heavy and Taddeo would stumble and almost fall. However, Nardo would wake just in time to take another step. They pushed on, knowing they had to get him back to camp and raise the alarm.

But help soon came to them.

A man appeared on the dirt track, seemingly rising out of nowhere: a young, slender man with black eyes and a capable swag. *Cappi!* They knew him to be Lisa's son.

He didn't say a word or ask any questions, for he had surmised the emergency at a glance. He picked up the injured six-year-old like he was a bag of grain and moved towards camp at a gentle trot to keep the boy's arm as still as possible.

'Let's catch up to the others,' Taddeo told Daniela, and they ran as hard as they could.

This time when Contessa came to the back door to answer the loud knocking, she had to clutch at the doorway for support. Her eyes were unable to take in what she was seeing and she felt drained of all strength.

Taddeo, Marietta and Martino were standing there, panting for breath, covered to varying degrees in blood. In a similar state behind them, were Francesca, Elmo and Daniela. The blank looks of horror on their faces confirmed that something terrible had happened.

'What?' she stammered, her voice barely audible. She had noticed that Nardo was the only child missing. Gian was safe inside with his mother.

'Nardo ...' Taddeo said hoarsely.

'He was shot. He was shot,' cried Martino.

Lisa appeared at the doorway in time to hear Martino's words. 'Who's been shot?' she asked alarmed.

'They say Nardo,' Contessa answered. 'Where is he? Is he ... ?'

'He's at the camp's hospital—not dead ...' But Taddeo did not want to add what he was thinking. Nardo had lost a lot of blood. The stockings around the arm had been soaked through when he had handed over his brother to Cappi.

'Let's go to the hospital. Tell Ettore and get to the hospital,' Lisa said.

Contessa nodded frantically.

At that moment, Ettore came around the side of the barracks; Edrico and Roberto were with him.

'What is it?' He stopped and stared in bewilderment at his three children, whose faces, hands and clothes were smeared in blood. Roberto also looked at his children, who were trembling in shock.

'It's not our blood,' Taddeo stammered.

'Whose … ?'

But no one could find the courage to answer.

'It's Nardo's,' Martino exploded. 'It's all my fault! I shouldn't have followed. I should've just stayed at camp and not cared about stupid apples …'

'Apples … ?' Contessa gasped.

Martino was screaming. 'I was running too slow. I should've got shot. It's all my fault.' He was hysterical again.

'Nardo's at the hospital. His arm was shot,' Taddeo said, his senses coming back to him.

'It's my fault,' Martino kept yelling.

Ettore closed the distance between himself and the out-of-control three-year-old and held him firmly against his chest.

'No, Martino. Never say that. It's the war's fault. You are an innocent boy. Just a little boy! You would never, ever harm your brother and you should never have to see him get harmed. It's not your fault, you hear me, not your fault.' Ettore was on his knees, tears pouring down his own cheeks, while clutching the screaming youngster against him.

'Papa …' Taddeo had never seen his father cry.

'Ettore, Contessa … you are needed at the hospital. If your boy were to wake …' It was Cappi. 'I can take you there. Come.'

Lisa helped Contessa find the strength to walk. Roberto and Edrico helped Ettore up.

As a united group, they walked around to the camp's medical wing. Behind them were all the stricken children who had been a part of the misadventure; all of them except Monte.

A German doctor came out of a room to meet them in a crowded hall. A translator stood beside him, ready to assist.

'You are the parents of the boy who came in shot?' the doctor inquired, looking to Ettore and Contessa standing at the front of the group. Ettore had his arms around his wife to keep her steady on her feet.

'Yes,' Ettore croaked. His throat was dry.

'He is alive but not conscious. He has lost a lot of blood. We will do our best but our medical supplies are limited. There is a hospital in town. We might be able to move him there, but not just yet. We need to stabilise him.'

Ettore and Contessa nodded as the information was translated. They were relieved to hear he was alive, but knew his life was still in danger.

'Do what you can,' Ettore whispered. 'Please doctor ...' He wanted to say more but words failed him. His boy, brave, serious, and quick on his feet, who put loyalty before all else, who knew to fight for what mattered; his boy, impulsive and hot headed, but generous and loving ... he couldn't just get shot over some apples! How could he share such thoughts with the doctor, thoughts that flashed so rapidly through his mind?

'We will do what we can,' the doctor promised, but there was not much hope in his grim expression. 'I can't let you see him yet. If there's any change ... I'll come and get you.'

The translator explained the situation. When he had finished speaking, the doctor bowed his head at the parents, turned on his heels and walked back into the room. The translator told them they could wait in the hall, and then disappeared into another room. It was narrow, stuffy and full of people, waiting for treatment or in recovery from a range of illnesses and diseases.

'Take Contessa and the children outside. I'll wait here,' Ettore instructed Lisa.

Outside in the cold, fresh air, Contessa and Lisa sat on the steps while the children wandered further away. The sun was low in the sky, casting long shadows. Martino and Taddeo sat on a stone wall together, both silent and downcast.

'Bianca and Tazia were right. I should've banned the kids from looking for food,' Contessa said to Lisa in a desperate tone.

'Banning doesn't stop them,' Lisa whispered. 'Bianca's children were there too. They were right behind them.'

'Still … if I had banned them, maybe none of them would've attempted it.'

'You can't think like that.'

As guilt churned in Contessa's stomach, two shadows loomed before her. She glanced up to see Bianca and Tazia approaching, their faces solemn. Surely they were going to be upset with her. After all, it was her weak rules that had resulted in their children being shot at! If she had taken a harder stance, they wouldn't have gone into town … The women stopped at her feet.

Contessa lifted her head, ready for their attack. She knew she utterly deserved it. 'Say what you have to say,' she put to them, breaking the torturous silence.

'Contessa …' Bianca breathed. 'How is he?' Her lips quivered in forming the question. Tears welled. Nardo was a well-loved playmate of her son Elmo.

'We're sorry,' Tazia said.

'He is alive but …' She couldn't think beyond that.

'We've been told to wait. He's not out of danger just yet,' Lisa said softly.

'We'll wait with you and pray with you,' Bianca assured her.

Contessa nodded. She was uncomfortable accepting their kindness. 'I'm sorry …' she found herself saying. 'I should've …'

'No. I won't hear of it. When these things happen we can't

look for reasons. If you want reasons, maybe we shouldn't have come to Germany. How far back do we go to find reasons? Let's just pray there are enough reasons for him to live. Yes?' Bianca lectured, wanting her friend to relinquish her guilt.

A few minutes later, Nonna arrived, white-faced and frenzied. Isabella was on her hip, thumb firmly planted in her mouth.

'Where is our precious Nardo?' she cried, rushing to Contessa and embracing her daughter. Until now Contessa had remained strong, keeping her overwhelming emotions in check, but on seeing the depth of Nonna's love and concern, she felt the floodgates open and tears gushed down her cheeks.

'Oh Mama ... don't let him be taken,' she sobbed. 'I couldn't bear it.'

Nonna shook her head. 'How can this be happening? Where is the doctor?'

'They are doing all they can,' Lisa told her. 'Come sit on the step.'

But Nonna couldn't just sit. Agitated, she plunked Isabella on Lisa's lap then began to pace, her hands fretting with her hair, pulling strands loose from its net. How could Nardo be shot? He was only six. Then she saw Taddeo and Martino sitting on the wall. Taddeo's eyes were wide, his jaw tense. Martino was pale with shadowed eyes. She saw the blood stains on their clothes and skin.

'You poor dears,' she muttered, hurrying over to them. 'Don't you two be fretting. Your brother is strong and will be fine. Like a lion he is. Don't worry your young minds. Perhaps it's best if you come back with me and we'll find you something to eat.'

'No,' Martino interjected. 'I want to stay here.' He met his Nonna's eyes, challenging her to force him away.

'We're not hungry,' Taddeo said tightly.

Nonna nodded, understanding. 'All right you stay. But if you stay, you start talking to God and making your peace with Him. You understand?'

The two boys closed their eyes, immediately intent on prayer.

Nonna wanted to hug them but dared not interrupt their loving thoughts. She finally sat on the embankment next to the wall and began to wait in earnest.

Inside, Ettore was also trying to come to terms with what had occurred.

'Who would shoot a child?' he grumbled, slamming a fist into the palm of his hand. 'I mean really! A six-year-old!' He was outraged.

'We'll find out soon enough,' said Cappi, his voice low.

'Whoever they were, they were firing on a bunch of kids all under the age of ten,' Roberto said, shaking his head in disbelief.

'It could've happened to any of our children,' Edrico said.

For all the Italians at the camp, it was a long night. No one could rest knowing that one of them was hovering between life and death, especially one so young. As the moon rose high in the sky, Lisa took the exhausted and shivering children back to their beds. Taddeo and Nardo didn't want to go, but their father commanded it, and reluctantly they were led away. The rest of the group stayed and waited, wanting to support Ettore and Contessa for as long as it would take.

Hours passed but there was no reported change in Nardo's condition.

Lisa returned from putting the children in their bunks and sat beside Contessa, holding her hand.

'Are the boys and Marietta all right?' Contessa asked.

Lisa shook her head. 'The boys aren't sleeping. Marietta cried herself to sleep. Before putting them to bed, I found a basin of water and washed their hands and faces. The water turned red. It upset them.'

Contessa nodded and gulped down a sob. She felt Lisa's grip tighten on her hand. 'There's still hope. No news is good news.'

At last, just before dawn, the doctor reappeared with a different man by his side.

'In some ways, the boy is lucky. The bullet grazed his upper arm.' The man translated the doctor's words into Italian. 'The bone is not broken. The wound is clean with no sign of infection, but the blood loss has been extensive—it was quite a tear—and his body is already weak from a lack of minerals and vitamins in his diet. He has not as yet regained consciousness.'

The words floated through Ettore's mind as though they were not real. They couldn't really be talking about Nardo.

'We don't want to move him. We'll see how he is in another couple of hours ...'

The doctor was gone again.

The new day brought a visit from the master of the railway station. He had come to apologise to the boy's family, though Ettore and Contessa did not want to see him. However, a message was passed on and they learned that an old railway guard had fired his gun before realising he was aiming at children. He had acted recklessly on seeing crates being stolen but would never have intentionally shot a young child. The guard next to him was quick to see he was firing at children and had ordered him to lower his gun, but it was too late. A few at the station had seen the small form flop to the ground after the gunshot. It had shocked the onlookers and rail workers and they had moved to assist, but the train had already started to depart and they had to wait before crossing the tracks. The children had scampered off before anyone could reach them.

The guard offered to pay for any costs involved in having the boy treated at the larger hospital in town, an offer Ettore accepted.

By noon, Nardo was transferred to the hospital in town and on the second day there, he opened his eyes to a hugely relieved mother and Nonna.

'Contessa, he wakes. Look,' Nonna cried, clutching Contessa's hand. 'His eyes open!'

Contessa leaned forward, stroking her boy's face gently with her fingers. 'I'm here, my sweet. I'm here,' she said repeatedly.

'Give him some water,' Nonna urged.

'Nurse! My boy is awake,' Contessa called. Her hair was loosely tied back, but much of it was falling across her pale and strained face. Her bloodshot eyes followed the nurse rushing over to them.

'Can we give him some water?'

'Try a sip,' the young woman advised.

Nardo took in some water, then looked into his mother's tearful eyes for a long time. He saw that she was happy.

'Where am I? Are we in America?'

'No,' Contessa said, shaking her head, laughing and crying at the same time. 'It is better than America. You are here with us. You're back.'

'Where did I go?'

'Asleep. You've been asleep and unwell for a long time, but now you are okay. You feel okay?' Nonna asked.

'I can't move.'

Contessa looked nervously to the nurse, who was quick to reassure her. 'He will be sore and weak but he will be able to move in time. The bullet only wounded the arm.'

'Bullet? Was I shot?'

Contessa looked to her son and exhaled steadily. 'We will make you better. I promise. You will get stronger.'

'What happened?'

She hesitated then thought it best to tell him. 'You were getting apples. Martino was slow. So you bravely decided to go back and carry him. If Martino had been shot, he would've been killed.'

Nardo's face screwed up, trying hard to think, to remember.

'I'll go tell the others you're awake. You will have many visitors ...' Nonna said, '... but just family first.'

Moments later, Martino, Taddeo and Marietta bolted in—they had not quite believed that Nardo was awake and were eager to see if it was true.

'He is! He's awake,' Martino squealed excitedly.

Ettore, with Isabella riding on his back, came up behind the children; his smile was euphoric.

'How are you? What a fighter you are!' Ettore praised his son while swinging Isabella down and seating her on the edge of Nardo's bed. She smiled at her brother, having missed him.

'I'm not a fighter. I can't even move,' Nardo confessed to his father, feeling sorry to have to disappoint him.

'Your body may be weak but that spirit is strong,' Nonna explained to the boy, cheering him.

'I'm sorry I didn't run fast enough,' Martino cut in. His serious eyes were fixed on his big brother's arm, wrapped in bandages and secured in a sling.

'You were fast,' Nardo replied. 'We didn't know we would be shot at.'

'And no one can outrun a bullet!' Contessa said.

'No. You're not Superman!' Nonna exploded, looking pointedly at Nardo.

'But my spirit is strong like Superman,' he replied. 'Papa said I'm a fighter.'

'And you did save me,' Martino added. 'I'll never forget it.'

Nardo smiled weakly. 'What are brothers for?'

'That does make you a superhero,' Ettore asserted. 'I'm proud of you.'

They all smiled, but Nardo was already starting to drift off. His eyes were half closed. They could see he was still very frail; so small and pasty, leaning back on a pillow too big for him. They could see death's haunting in the dark shadows beneath his eyes; shadows too ominous for comfort.

'I think it best we give him more time to rest. The doctor will be here soon and will want to check him over. Best not to tire him out,' the nurse said.

'Goodbye Nardo,' his brothers and sisters called.

Contessa and Nonna kissed him on the cheek.

'Get well now,' his Papa told him and picked up Isabella.

The family moved away. They were happy he was out of imminent danger, but they could see that full recovery was a long way off. At least in hospital, he should receive better quality food. Relief made their steps lighter than they had been in days.

Thank you, God, Martino thought. *I won't ask for anything else ever again.*

Chapter fifteen

February 1947
German Displaced Persons Camp

Ettore had called Cappi's bluff and lost again. He folded the cards and slammed them down on the table.

'I think I should stop playing. My mind is not on it,' he confessed to the men.

'It makes a nice change to have you losing,' Edrico mocked, smiling.

'We should not just be sitting here,' he continued irritably.

'We're not. We're sitting and playing cards—well, some of us are,' Edrico pointed out smugly.

'What should we be doing instead?' Cappi asked, wondering what was on Ettore's mind.

'I can't stop thinking … it should never have been left to the children to scavenge for extra food. We should be doing it,' he said, springing to his feet and pacing around the small common room. He wanted a cigarette but had finished his last one that morning.

As though reading his mind, Roberto held out his packet in which two cigarettes were remaining. 'Take one,' he urged.

'I can't. No. Thank you.' Ettore sat back down. 'We should scout around. See what we can bring back.'

Roberto put away the cigarettes. He shook his head, a frown etching lines into his forehead. 'I don't think so—still a lot of guns around and nervous fingers. I'd rather go hungry than get shot again.' He tipped his hat to reveal the scar on the side of his head.

'We all got shot,' Edrico said flatly. 'Not that I'm keen for it to happen again, mind you.'

'I'm not keen about getting shot either but I'm prepared to risk it,' Cappi declared.

Ettore gave a half smile. 'That's the spirit. But I don't think we'll be going near the rail lines and those bloody stupid guards. There are plenty of farms around. If we go at dusk, keep low and go alone, we should be right.'

'I don't know …' Roberto sighed, rubbing his cheek with the back of his hand. 'It's a lot of ground to cover.'

'I'm in,' Cappi said.

Ettore looked at Edrico, who was hesitating. 'I'll go once, maybe twice,' he caved.

They all turned to Roberto, who was trying not to meet their eyes. 'I'm not much of a thief. I'll be seen a mile away. I don't get down low. I kind of bumble around.'

The men laughed and Ettore slapped him on the back. 'I knew we could count on you.'

From then on, the men met just before dusk, decided which farms they would raid, and set out with cloth sacks they intended to fill. Roberto was always allocated the nearest farms. Their efforts meant they were digging into frozen ground to pull up potatoes or turnips, or returning with nuts or grains or berries. Every Italian at camp appreciated their booty, which they generously shared around. A few other men joined their efforts, reaping even more productive yields, and helping the Italians to thrive throughout the remainder of winter.

Warmer weather brought higher food rations for the displaced persons and fewer raids were needed. It also saw Nardo return to his family with a hero's welcome. He had stayed at the hospital in town for a few weeks and then in the hospital at camp, with the doctors reluctant to release him for fear of infection. On his return many Italian families brought the boy gifts of whatever they could find, make or steal—even if it was a bunch of flowers taken from the cemetery in town. They did what they could to make his homecoming as memorable as possible.

The children were thrilled to have Nardo back in their fold.

'Come to the hill,' Taddeo invited his younger brother on his second week back at camp. He couldn't wait to show Nardo what had happened to the bomb crater.

'No, he's not to leave the camp until he builds up his strength,' Contessa told the boys and girls who were surrounding him.

'I'm strong enough. I can make it to the hill. It's not far,' Nardo argued, thrilled to have all the children's attention. His arm was still in a sling but he felt much better.

'Please let him come,' begged Martino. More than anything, he wanted Nardo to come and have fun at the hill.

Contessa was touched by Martino's show of affection. 'All right, he can go. But I'm coming too to make sure he is all right. I'll get Nonna to mind Isabella and I'll go get my hat. Tell me where this hill is and I'll follow shortly.'

'You just take the dirt road past the farm and poppy fields and keep going straight for about ten minutes,' Taddeo explained.

'All right. That sounds simple enough. I'll see if Bianca and Lisa want to come too and we'll meet you there soon.'

The children wanted to run to the hill, but Nardo could only manage a slow walk, so they resisted the urge to speed ahead, instead strolling alongside their friend. They couldn't wait to see the joy their surprise would bring, and they were not disappointed. Nardo yelped in pleasure as they neared the site.

'It's a swimming pool,' he shouted gleefully.

The crater had filled with water after a week of rain and it was warm enough to take a dip. The older children slipped out of their clothes, keeping their underwear on to protect their modesty, and leapt in.

'It's cold,' Daniela cried, but she didn't hop out.

Nardo stripped off his clothes and waded in. The water quickly came up to his waist and he had to hold his bandaged arm up high to keep it clear of the water.

Martino and Gian kept to the edge where it was most shallow.

'I don't think this a good idea,' called Monte from the far side of the crater. He was addressing Taddeo. 'I mean, what if Nardo slips? You couldn't protect him from being shot. How are you going to save him from drowning?'

Taddeo turned, shocked at Monte's words. 'What did you just say?' he asked, dumbfounded.

'He's trying to start a fight. Ignore him,' Daniela advised wisely.

'Say sorry,' Martino shouted at Monte.

'Listen short stuff. This is no place for babies,' he responded sharply. Monte looked back at Taddeo and added, 'Take your little brothers away or they'll both fall in and drown. Nardo can't swim with one arm and Martino could fall in the deep end. If they drown, we'll all get in trouble again. You know I'm right,' Monte went on.

'I'm not a baby,' Martino cried angrily.

'No you're not and I can carry you,' Taddeo argued and put his back to Martino. 'Come on.'

Martino climbed on Taddeo's back and he walked in, allowing the small boy to be partly submerged in the cool, muddy water.

'It's freezing,' Martino laughed.

'I want to go in,' Gian cried and his brother Elmo came over to give him a piggyback into the water too.

'Don't say I didn't warn you,' Monte said, jumping into the pool.

The next voice they heard was their mother's.

'Nardo! Taddeo! What are you doing? You know Martino can't swim! Nardo you just got out of hospital!'

Contessa had come running to the crater's edge, shocked to see 'the hill' was a large body of water. Lisa and Bianca followed close behind.

'Get out now,' Contessa demanded.

'I won't let go of him,' Taddeo assured his mother. 'Besides, you're here and you're watching.'

'I'm all right. I won't get my arm wet,' Nardo told her.

Bianca was also concerned. 'Elmo! Take Gian out now!'

Elmo and Taddeo walked over and allowed the small boys to climb off their backs and out of the waterhole. Nardo was so thin he looked hardly capable of walking, let alone swimming. He too climbed out and sat long-faced on the edge and dangled his feet in the water.

'Let us stay, Mama,' Taddeo pleaded. 'Look how fun it is! Nardo has been bored in hospital for so long. Let him have some fun. Why don't you put your feet in too?'

Contessa's expression softened at her son's urgings. Nardo did need to get some sun and time to play and be a child again.

Bianca, Lisa and Contessa exchanged looks.

'I guess we can stay for a while and dip our feet.'

The next hour proved a wonderful time for the children as they jumped and splashed and played chase, climbing in and out of the pool. Nardo was only allowed to go in knee-deep, but it was enough for him to enjoy the games. Contessa sat on the grassy side of the crater and put Martino on her legs, lifting him up and down in the water, while she held his hands and he squealed in delight. Water sprinkled over her spotted dress but she didn't mind. It was a warm day.

'I want to do that too,' shouted Gian to his mother.

'Look what you've started,' said Bianca, struggling to give Gian a similar ride, as it required some strength in the legs.

'Elmo, why don't you give your brother another swim,' she conceded, unable to help her youngest enjoy a dip.

At the end of the hour, the women, tired of being out in the sun and watching all the activity, stood and called to Nardo, Martino and Gian.

'Time to go,' they said, and the boys did not resist. Nardo and the youngsters were exhausted and ready to return. They needed a drink and a rest.

Once the women and boys were out of view, Monte returned to his sniping.

'Daniela, you always stand up for Taddeo. Is that because you like him?' he started to tease, flicking his wet hair back from his fine-featured face and smiling at her with knowing eyes. He was handsome and he knew it.

'Be quiet,' she commanded in a sulky tone and her cheeks reddened. She was standing in the pool, squelching the muddy bottom between her toes.

'You never stand up for me. You know you look pretty when you get mad.' He swam over to her. His smile made her nervous and she edged away from him.

'I don't know what you see in Taddeo. I mean, I'm faster, stronger and a lot smarter,' he boasted.

'Leave her be,' Taddeo said, as he watched Monte trap Daniela up against the wall of the crater.

'Get back from me,' she said, splashing Monte in the face.

He instantly splashed her back, filling her nostrils with water and leaving her snorting for breath.

'Leave my sister alone,' Francesca yelled and dive-bombed next to him, hoping to splash him in the face, but he turned away just in time. When she surfaced, Monte casually splashed water into her surprised face, causing her to swallow some.

With Francesca spluttering, Daniela climbed out of the pool and glared back at Monte.

'Why do you always have to wreck everything? We were having a fun swim and now it's all wrecked. I'm going back.'

'Me too,' said Francesca.

Marietta quickly hopped out with the other girls and they grabbed their clothes. Elmo and Taddeo also climbed out and went to fetch their clothing.

'That's right, run along with the girls,' Monte called to the boys. 'Seeing as you act like them.'

The group of children, dripping wet, stalked off, pulling on shirts and shorts and skirts. They did not look back. Monte had upset them and they wanted to distance themselves from him.

'We'll come back for another swim later,' Daniela said to the group. 'And we won't tell Monte.'

After lunch, true to their agreement, the children gathered at the camp's front gate. Nardo and the three-year-olds were not with them. They ran down the dirt path, eager to the reach 'the hill' before Monte could see them. Taddeo was the fastest and reached the waterhole first, but as soon as he arrived, he turned around to face the group behind him, holding up a hand to signal a halt.

'Don't come,' he called, trying desperately to stop them, but they found it hard to slow their pace and were upon him with a few more strides.

Daniela peered behind Taddeo and let out a startled scream of horror.

There, lying on the edge of the waterhole was a soppy clump of wet white fur. It took them a few seconds to realise that it was the mother cat they had re-housed in the barn. They peered around for her litter. The kittens had grown into playful, seven-month-old cats but they were nowhere to be seen.

Suddenly a sinister voice called out to them.

'I think the others are in a bag on the bottom,' Monte crowed. He was standing on the other side of the crater, looking at the water's murky surface, smiling with laughter in his eyes.

'And how would you know that?' Taddeo demanded.

'I saw a bag with a big rock in it tied up over there. It was meowing a lot before it got tossed in.'

'No. I don't believe it. You wouldn't ...' Daniela began, the colour draining from her face.

'Me? Who said I did it? I just happened to see it.'

'I don't believe you. I'm going to the barn to check.'

Teary-eyed, she ran. Francesca and Marietta went with her, running as fast as they could to keep up with the distressed older girl.

'You've gone too far,' Elmo said, moving towards Monte.

'Leave him,' Taddeo advised, not wanting a fight. He didn't like conflict and hated physical altercations.

'He drowned the cat and its kittens,' Elmo exploded. 'If it's a fight he wants, maybe we should give him one.'

'If we hit him, he'll run to his mama and we'll get in trouble. He's always been a tattle-tale. Let's just leave him and never talk to him again,' Taddeo suggested.

Frustrated, Elmo clenched his fists. 'Really? We're not going to hit him?'

'No,' Taddeo said. 'Let's just go.'

Taddeo started to walk off. Elmo remained, staring at Monte.

'Want to end up on the bottom of the pool too?' Monte asked him quietly. His smiled had disappeared and his shining eyes narrowed.

Elmo didn't reply. A shiver ran down his back. Slowly, he turned and hurried after Taddeo. He actually felt afraid.

'Goodbye scaredy cats. It's been a day for scaredy cats!' Monte shouted after them.

'I hate him,' seethed Elmo.

'He wants you to hate him,' Taddeo said. 'And it's best not to give him what he wants.'

'Why would anyone want to be hated?' Elmo couldn't understand it.

'Because he can't be loved.'

'By my sister, Daniela?' Elmo queried.

'By anyone. Monte's just a bad kid. Best we stay away from him.'

The boys made their way to the barn. They wanted to check on the girls and they were also curious as to whether any of the young cats had survived. With Monte, you could never tell whether he was telling the truth.

In the barn, they found the girls huddled around one scrawny black and white cat. She was alone and overwhelmed by the sudden attention. They stayed at the barn until dusk, but no other cats appeared. It seemed only one had escaped being drowned.

The girls cried together, missing the good-natured mother cat and the rest of the litter. The boys were sad too, but fought back tears.

That night, as the children climbed into their bunks for sleep, Marietta started to weep again.

'What's wrong?' Contessa asked, surprised at the abrupt bout of tears.

Ettore looked over, wondering what had brought it on. Husband and wife exchanged a confused glance and shrugged.

'I'm sad,' she whimpered at long last.

Contessa swept back the girl's black curls and kissed her on the cheek. 'Why are you so sad?'

'Monte killed the cats,' she blurted out. Taddeo and Nardo sat up in their bunks, stunned that she had told their parents. Isabella was already asleep, having gone to bed earlier, and so did not hear the news. The children had informed Nardo of the gruesome finding and he was sorry he hadn't been there with two strong arms to back up Elmo.

'Monte did what?' Ettore asked, coming closer to his daughter.

'He drowned them,' she sniffled and then, remembering the black kitten that had been her favourite, sobbed harder.

'Is this true, Taddeo? Did the boy drown some cats?' He was slightly alarmed by the accusation.

'We didn't see him, but ...'

'Did he or didn't he?'

'I think he did,' Taddeo answered his father.

'I see. And what did you do when you found out?'

'We ...' Taddeo started to feel heat in his cheeks. 'We walked away.'

'I wouldn't have,' Nardo grumbled.

'I see.'

'Should we tell his parents?' Contessa asked her husband.

'No,' Taddeo and Nardo said together.

'They'll never believe it,' Taddeo added.

'The boys are right there. Could create conflict within the camp. Best forget it, but ...'

'Yes, Papa?' Taddeo was eager for his advice, as he had not been sure how to react in the face of such a dreadful act.

'Be careful of the boy. If he can kill cats ...'

'Try not to play with him,' Contessa cut in. 'He's not very nice, is he?'

'No,' Marietta cried. 'He's the meanest boy ever.'

In the morning, Contessa sought out Lisa and told her about how her children believed that Monte had drowned some cats.

She wasn't as surprised as Contessa thought she'd be. After all, Lisa and Cappi were in the same room as the boy's family and knew him better. 'I've been watching him. He's different. He doesn't care about things in the right way.'

Contessa shuddered. 'Poor Marietta. She cried herself to sleep.'

'I think I have something to cheer them.'

Lisa had received a package from her daughter Lena. She had been getting regular mail from her for some time after discovering she was residing in a displaced persons camp in Napoli. However, the young family had been on the move again. The most recent letter had explained that Lena and Rico and their little girl Vittoria had been forced to leave Napoli when their camp had closed down. They had gone north to another camp in Cremona. There, Rico had been able to travel to Milano to find work, and had managed to obtain a low paying job. As a result, Lena was able to purchase a few extra things and, at the earliest opportunity, had sent a package of treats to her mother.

Lisa took out the package and showed it to Contessa. 'Shall we let the children see it?'

Contessa and Lisa went into the room where Martino, Taddeo, Nardo, Marietta and Isabella were stirring from their sleep. It was early in the morning and they were still in their bunks.

'What are you doing here before breakfast?' Marietta queried sleepily, staring at Lisa.

'Well, I've received a present and I need help opening it.' Lisa revealed the package she had been hiding behind her back.

'Oh wow!' Martino exclaimed.

The children hopped down from their beds and hurried over to it.

'Well, open it. It's too hard for me,' Lisa urged them.

The children tore into the brown paper and gasped when it revealed a tin of shortbread biscuits.

'Oh wow!' Contessa echoed her son as the shiny red tin came into view. 'Would you look at that!'

'Shall I open the tin?' Lisa asked.

'Yes, yes,' they cried in unison.

The tin was popped open and every child handed a lovely, delicate biscuit. Lisa then offered the sweets to Contessa, Nonna and Ettore who took one and thanked her repeatedly.

'That's a nice start to the day,' Martino said.

'A very good start,' Nonna agreed.

For the children, the day's luck kept flowing. They discovered that Monte had attached himself to some other Italian boys, who were older, around the ages of ten and eleven. It meant they no longer had to worry about avoiding him. It seemed Monte was in agreement and did not want to play with them either.

Spring passed without any more mishaps. The black and white cat became their mascot and they visited it regularly. They named it Milksha, in memory of Lisa and Dino's playful, white goat. Milksha came to expect their visits and would step out of the barn to meet them, meowing happily and rubbing up against their legs.

It wasn't until mid-summer that news started to circulate within the camp that sparked everyone's interest. Rumours and half-truths sprang up and spiralled out of control until no one knew what to believe. But when American emigration officials actually arrived at the camp and started holding interviews, they saw that the rumours were in fact based in truth. The excitement was tangible.

However, for many, the rush of joy caused by the arrival of the clean-shaven officials soon led to grave disappointment. If they wanted to migrate to America, they would need a sponsor, someone they knew living there to vouch for them, and provide support in settling in the United States. Even then, it could be several years before they would be taken in. Ettore and Contessa had no such connections in America and so had very little hope of being accepted for US settlement.

It was a deep blow. Ettore's spirits sagged under the weight of what he was facing—a bleak and wretched future. Italy's unemployment was one of the worst in Europe. Germany was badly destroyed, with many cities lying in ruins. Without any hope of going to America, he couldn't see any prospect of eking out a living and establishing a home. Misery drove him on long walks around the surrounding farms, hands in pockets that felt all too empty. Would he ever work and support his family again? A home—what he would give to have a home for them. He didn't like thinking of their house in Fiume, but when he did, it caused him deep sadness. It had been a fine house and they once had a good life, but looking back didn't serve him. He could only look forward—to what?

A few weeks later and another buzz of anticipation tore around the camp. Officers from Canada were coming to visit. Ettore made inquiries. Again, he learned that you needed to have kin in Canada willing to sponsor you in order to be accepted. They had no such family ties.

'We're stuck here,' Nonna moaned to Contessa and the other women in their group. 'Can't even go to the toilet in peace. I don't want to be here for another German winter. It will kill me before I get on a ship.'

'We don't have much choice,' Lisa said sadly. 'They say we can go to Argentina or Brazil.'

'Not stable. No place to take our young families. No. I'd rather stay in Italy and starve,' Nonna sighed, her jaw setting stubbornly.

'Roberto mentioned Australian officials are coming next month,' old Gilda said.

'Yes, he did. That's worth finding out about,' Bianca said.

'Australia!' Nonna gasped. 'Don't know a thing about it. Isn't it a wild country?'

'I don't know. I've heard of Sydney,' Contessa said. 'It's their capital city so it must have buildings.'

'Aren't they good at tennis? I think Edrico mentioned that,' Tazia piped up.

'Tennis … they play, do they?' Lisa asked, interested.

'Yes. That's true. They have some talented tennis players,' Nonna said suddenly recalling. 'Well, they must have a lot of space to play tennis.'

'If they can keep the kangaroos off the courts,' Tazia laughed.

The women were smiling. Australia didn't seem such a bad option. It was a peaceful country and developing … there would be jobs. When the Australian officials arrived, the Italians made appointments and had interviews.

Ettore entered the temporary office that had been set up by the Australian delegation at the camp. As he sat waiting for his interview, he stared at a huge poster they had hanging on the wall. It was of a strong, young man in a singlet, wearing a slouch hat, hard at work at a rail yard. His tanned, muscular arms were shining with sweat and he was smiling broadly, flashing white teeth. The caption beneath the poster read: 'Australia: a man's job awaits you.'

Ettore felt hope. He was not afraid of hard work. He held up his hands and turned them over, stretching them out. They were soft, his fingers pink and his arms scrawny. A prolonged diet of bland camp food that offered little nutrition and a long stretch of unemployment had sapped him of strength and hardiness. But he did have a trade. He used to be a mechanic before the war and was handy with tools. That might impress them. He dropped his hands to his trousers and wiped the sweat from them. No point showing them he was nervous.

His eyes were drawn again to the poster. The man had blue skies behind him and he appeared well fed and happy. He wanted to be that man ...

Afterwards, Ettore returned to the camp.

'Well?' Contessa asked, peering hopefully up at him.

'They want to meet you and the children tomorrow. But it seems there will be no problem if we want to go. Once we're accepted, we will go back to Trieste for political and medical screening and further processing but it seems they are looking for people in our situation.' He was starting to believe his own words. They would be accepted. He sat down on the low bunk bed and put his face in his hands to hide the tears. He had thought they would never get out.

'They'll give us jobs,' he said, lifting his face to reveal red eyes and flushed skin.

Contessa sat next to him and put her arm around him. 'A job is all you need. Perhaps I can work too. We'll be all right now.'

For the first time since their house had been bombed, they had a fleeting glimpse of a stable and independent future. And they would be able to go back to Trieste for the processing. When Ettore looked at his wife's face, he saw that she was smiling through her own tears.

'Wait until I tell Nonna!' she breathed.

Chapter sixteen

November 1947
Trieste, Italy

The only sorrow anyone had at saying goodbye to Germany was the children's grief in parting from their pet cat Milksha. Daniela sobbed for hours on the train as it rattled south, taking them back to their blessed Italy.

Before long, Ettore was once again walking the streets of Trieste alongside Roberto, Edrico and Cappi. They were smoking cigarettes and had a purpose in their steps. They had been told they could get some low-paid work at a security firm and were on their way to apply.

The Paris Peace Treaty, in placing it under the protection of the United Nations, had established the city as the Free Territory of Trieste. They also learned that Fiume was now officially Rijeka, a city of Yugoslavia.

As before, Trieste was still divided into two zones and they were residing in Zone A, ruled by the Allied Military Government. They had returned to the same displaced persons camp where Contessa and Bianca had first met, but since then there had been some improvements, as the authorities had time to address the logistical issues. They all wholeheartedly agreed that the food in Trieste was better than the fare served in Germany, especially as spaghetti was now on the menu, to the delight of both adults and children.

The men were pleased to pick up some night-shift work, as it helped supplement their personal supplies and allowed them to buy a few extra clothes for the winter. They were all hopeful that by the end of the cold season, they would be on a ship to sunny Australia and their new lives would be under way. Together they dreamed about their new lives in the vast, distant land—dreams that became more dazzling in each retelling. Surely, it would not be long now.

But it was.

Two more years went by. A further two years of sleeping on the floor upon scratchy mattresses. Two more years of queues for food, for water, for the toilet …

The one joy for Lisa was that Lena, Rico, Vittoria and newborn baby girl Elisa joined them in Trieste, transferring from the camp in Cremona. Having grandchildren to dote upon and her daughter to converse with had cheered her immensely, and while she remained frail and weak, her spirits lifted and some sparkle returned to her eyes. It was just what she needed.

'We will come with you to Australia,' Lena told her mother excitedly. 'Rico will get work and we'll be able to get our own house again. You and Cappi can live with us.'

'It will be wonderful,' she smiled, pressing down the pins in her hair. It was what Dino would have wanted, for the family to stay together.

'I hope Cappi will meet a girl soon,' Lisa confided to her daughter. 'He needs some happiness. Love will bring him that.'

'Cappi is handsome. He should find a girl easily, when he's ready.'

'He's twenty-four. He's ready,' Lisa stated. 'He just has to know it.'

Lena smiled. 'I'll let you know if I see any overly long glances.'

'Well, the girls are looking at him. I've seen them,' Lisa laughed. 'He can take his pick.'

'In that case, he should have a girlfriend soon enough. Maybe a shipboard romance.'

They both giggled. They couldn't wait to be on that ship. Australia was going to change everything for them.

In November 1949, Martino celebrated his sixth birthday in Trieste. He had never known his own home.

He and Gian were still close friends, as close as brothers, having grown up together in the camps. They now attended Italian primary schools, wearing the traditional grembiule, a black smock with wide white collar, worn over the top of their normal clothes. They were still the same height, with dark hair and eyes and skinny limbs. From the back, it was hard to tell them apart. But from the front, Martino had finer features, with bright eyes that sparkled with spirit. In contrast, Gian had heavy-lidded eyes that cast a relaxed gaze upon the world, and there was often a laid back curl to his lips. He seemed more interested in keeping the peace, whereas Martino sought excitement. Together, they had fun, with Martino making Gian laugh, and Gian knowing when the joke had gone too far, ensuring they stayed out trouble. After classes, the two junior pupils wandered around the portside town, following the American troops until they gave them pieces of gum or chocolate. They also regularly played soccer with Taddeo, Nardo, Elmo and some other boys in the camp.

Soccer was the game of choice and one of the nearby soccer clubs had donated an old ball to the camp to give the kids something to do—a strategy aimed at keeping them off the streets, looking for trouble. It worked. The club also let them use their field for one hour a week, the hour just before dusk on a Tuesday. This much-anticipated session had the children plotting, planning and training anywhere they could so that they could field two teams and hold a serious competition.

Taddeo, who had just turned twelve years old, headed up the Italian team, and he allowed boys of any age and even girls to participate. There were no rules on numbers. The more players the better. Nardo, back at full strength and despite being younger, was a formidable player, a natural striker who scored many of the team's goals. Elmo, with his big feet and solid build, was a strong and fast defender. Gian, lacking speed and power, relied on the element of surprise. Being small, they did not expect his craftiness, and he was often able to wrest the ball from the other team and turn the game back around in their direction.

Monte did not run with the Italian boys. He joined the other team, which mostly comprised anti-Communist Russian Whites, who had fled to Serbia after the 1917 Bolshevist Revolution and fled again in more recent times from the control of Yugoslav's Tito. Other players were a mix of Serbians, Bulgarians and Romanians, who were also seeking refuge from the Communist regime in Trieste.

Martino liked to keep near Nardo, running up front, passing the ball to his capable brother whenever he had the chance. He liked to watch Nardo in action, sidestepping the defensive players who would swarm towards him, and slotting the ball into the net, past a furious Monte, who was the opposition's goalkeeper. Monte would yell and abuse his own players for their failure to defend. He shouted until he was spitting, his anger explosive and, for the Italians, somewhat amusing. It made scoring goals that much more satisfying.

Daniela and Marietta preferred to watch the games and clapped and cheered loudly when the Italians scored. But eight-year-old Francesca took to the field. The tall, straight-hipped girl loved to run with the boys. Her tackling was gutsy. She was light on her feet and fast and contributed well in the mid-field. Nardo admired her zeal on the field, but off field, she was just another annoying girl.

The games were fiercely contested, with parents coming down to watch their sons or daughters compete. Nardo was regularly named Best Player for the Italian side, making Ettore proud.

'That's my boy,' he cried out, clapping and whistling whenever he scored.

'Where did you learn to play like that?' he asked his son after he came off having scored an impressive hat trick.

'I don't know,' Nardo replied. 'We've always played soccer.' It was true. The kids had always had something to kick around, even if it was just a tin can.

On the other hand, Monte was fuming and Edrico had to resort to yelling and threatening him to calm his irate temper. Monte was a terribly sore loser. Daniela had even seen him vandalising shopfronts on his way home from a match after his team had lost 5-1.

In Trieste, the Italians won more Tuesday games than they lost. Contessa, Nonna and Bianca smiled throughout, enjoying seeing their children having so much fun and displaying some obvious talent.

'I wonder if Australian children play soccer ...' Contessa mused, hoping that they did. Their children would do well if that were the case.

One afternoon, when the bigger boys were training and Martino was tired of missing out on getting a touch of the ball, he wandered up the street from the camp and began watching a street cleaner going about his chores. The cleaner looked up, saw the boy staring at him and gave him a wink.

Martino smiled, and regarding the wink as a friendly gesture, spoke up. 'That's a hard job,' he said, having observed the old man constantly stooping to pick up rubbish with a sharpened stick. 'Looks like you could do with some help.'

The old, grey-haired man, with a thick, lighter grey moustache ignored him, thinking he was just passing a comment, but after a few moments noticed the litter was being cleared in front of him. He stopped, straightened his back, and saw the kid had fashioned his own long stick and was hard at work stabbing litter and shoving it into a bag.

'Look at that. You're doing it!' The man smiled. In all the

fifty-two years he had been cleaning the streets of Trieste that had never happened before.

'What's your name boy?' he asked.

'Martino.'

'You're a good boy, Martino. But you know, I get paid to do this and you don't have to help me.'

'I don't mind helping. It's a big job for one person. Two people can do it,' Martino assured him. The boy was pale, much too thin, and his clothes were in need of mending, but he was smiling and serious and ever so keen.

'Well, I would never say no to a helper,' the man said, trying to make the kid feel happy.

'Good. Less talk and more work, I think. Or your boss will get mad.'

'That's true.' The old man nodded, his eyes sparkling above his moustache, which was twitching with amusement. 'I wouldn't want to upset my boss.'

The pair set to work, stabbing their sticks into the gutters, making their way down the street with casual ease.

Martino enjoyed the work so much that he went in search of the cleaner the next day, and the next. He always met the cleaning man at the top of their street and joined him in clearing litter around the block. Martino learned that the cleaner went by the name of Carlo. He had been cleaning the streets practically all his working life and knew every street, every building and their purpose. For him, the bombing of the city had been very traumatic, as his rounds brought him face to face with damaged and ruined buildings, those he loved and knew the history of— those he had passed every day for years on his rounds, but would never pass by again. He missed them. But for every loss there were many spared, and he looked upon them as grand survivors. He was very proud of his knowledge and enjoyed divulging it to Martino, pointing out buildings and telling him their age, what was happening behind their tall, stony facades, and what used to happen even before that.

'You know everything,' Martino said, wide-eyed with admiration.

'Not everything, but I know Trieste. She's a beautiful city.'

Soon the meetings became regular and grew longer, so that every weekday at four o'clock, Martino met Carlo and they worked together for about an hour. For the boy, it not only kept him out of trouble and gave him something to do, but it provided him with an agreeable friend who listened, smiled and nodded at his musings, and occasionally offered some fatherly advice. They worked through the winter, only rainy days preventing them from seeing to their chores.

Contessa became aware of her son's duties and felt a sense of pride. He was such a kind child. 'Why do you help the street cleaner every day?' she asked.

'Because he's my friend and needs a hand. He is getting old, like Nonna, and I am young and strong.'

'You are a big six-year-old,' Contessa agreed. 'Look at those arms. I think cleaning is making them stronger.'

'Do you think so?' He immediately examined his skinny arm, seeing only a stick-like bone.

'There's muscle in there,' Contessa told him. 'Let me feel.' She touched his arm and nodded. 'Oh yes, definitely stronger.'

That did it. Martino now had another reason to keep up his afternoon work. It would make him stronger.

The weeks turned into months. Carlo started looking forward to the leg of his rounds that included the little boy. Martino was never late and was ever so chatty. He fell into the habit of telling Carlo all about his school lunchtime soccer matches and about the Tuesday afternoon soccer games. Carlo grew to know so much about the Italian team that he even finished his cleaning early to turn up and watch a couple of matches.

'Your brother is a good player,' he told him the next day as they plucked litter from beneath some outdoor seating.

'Nardo? Yes. Everyone says so. I want to be just like him when I get bigger.'

'You could be. You're fast for your age.'

'Really?' Martino asked astounded. No one had ever commented on his play before. It was always Nardo that people raved about.

'Yes. You have a lot of skill. Your brother wouldn't score half the goals he does without you feeding the ball to him. You're always there at the right time. You're a thinking player. You don't just kick it. You pass it well.'

Martino straightened up and stared, gob smacked. He could not believe his ears. He was helping Nardo to score! A thinking player. Well, well, imagine that! Carlo had just made his day. He went back to cleaning with his chest puffed out. A thinking player, he kept saying to himself. He liked the sound of that!

Chapter seventeen

May 1950
Trieste, Italy

Despite gusty winds, Martino and Gian kicked a tin can back and forth to each other in front of the silos. Now and then the wind would sweep it away and Martino would kick thin air.

'Papa said our ship to Australia leaves in three more months,' Gian told his friend.

'Where's Australia?' Martino asked, not having given it much thought. His parents had been talking about moving there for years, but as it never seemed to eventuate, he had come to think it wouldn't happen.

'Don't know, but I heard it has kangaroos.'

'What … all over the place?'

'Guess so.'

The boys laughed.

'I'll have one as a pet then,' Martino said.

'Maybe we can ride them.'

'And race them.'

Martino gave the can a strong kick, and the wind caused it to sail high in the air, further than they anticipated. The boys laughed appreciatively. Gian ran over to it and, as the air stilled, kicked it back.

'Are you sure we're going in three months?'

'Yes.'

'How long is that anyway?' Martino said.

'Um … weeks. A lot of weeks.'

Martino stopped. He placed his foot on the can. 'You mean

we really are going? Leaving Italy? Leaving Trieste?'

'Yes. On a ship.'

Martino let that sink in and started to wonder what it would be like to be on a ship. He had seen many ships and boats in the harbour but had never stepped aboard one.

'Should be fun then.'

That night, Ettore and Contessa confirmed that they would be departing for Australia in just under three months, at the end of July, from the Italian port at Genoa. They would travel to the port by train.

It seemed their days as displaced persons were finally numbered. *Just in time too*, Contessa thought. The camp was becoming suffocatingly overcrowded, having swelled in the past few months from eight hundred to almost three thousand. A new wave of refugees were pouring out of the Julian region—many unhappy at Tito's dictatorial regime and fleeing to Trieste.

At the silos, conditions were rapidly worsening. It was becoming hard to sleep with so many tents pitched. The mattresses were practically butted up against each other and the thin blankets, strung up as walls around the family areas, no longer provided any privacy. It was noisy, stuffy communal living at its worst and most invasive. The food rations had been halved to accommodate the influx and the queues for everything had more than tripled. It was wearing down the patience of the long-term refugees, already tired of being cramped and uncomfortable and under fed. Now it was intolerable.

Two months went by, and the Saforo family became increasingly excited about their departure. They were already packed, not that they had much to take with them. It all fit into one old suitcase.

Getting carried away, Edrico traded in his cigarettes and a week's pay to purchase a second hand camera on the black market, saying it was important to take photos of their journey. For the Australia-bound Italians, it was as though they were going on an adventure, not unlike a holiday, with all them believing that once they had earned enough savings, they would return to Italy to buy a house.

As the final weeks approached, Martino thought it time to tell Carlo.

'We're going to Australia. It's real this time. Only three more weeks! Imagine that,' he announced to the old man, who was dressed in his usual work attire of grey trousers and navy blue shirt.

'You're leaving Italy?' the street cleaner asked, surprised. He paused to rub his grey eyebrows in disbelief.

'Yes, it's far, far away and even has kangaroos … I'm sorry I won't be able to help you anymore.'

Carlo smiled sadly. 'You've been good company for me,' he said as his kind eyes glistened. 'Who will tell me all about the latest soccer matches now, hey?'

'I don't know,' said Martino, trying to think. 'Oh well, we're not leaving right away. I can still come a few more times. I'm here today.'

Martino began to launch into an account of a match he had seen on the weekend, when his story was interrupted by the sound of his mother calling him.

'What does she want?' he wondered out loud.

'I don't know, but what I do know is that you should always run as fast as you can when your mother calls,' Carlo advised with a knowing wink.

'Sure thing. Sorry I have to go. I'll see you tomorrow.'

Martino hurried down the street into the camp and found his mother, father and Nonna waiting. His siblings Taddeo, Nardo, Isabella and Marietta had already been rounded up.

'What's going on?' Martino asked, surprised to see everyone gathered in the afternoon.

'I told you this morning. We have to go for our final medical check-up. They have to make sure we're healthy for our trip to Australia. Everything rests on this,' his mother explained, exasperated. 'Are you feeling well?'

'Yes.' Martino shrugged.

'Good, good. Just as well,' she breathed and gave a tight smile.

'Can I have a kangaroo as a pet?' Martino asked, reacting to her mention of Australia.

'God forbid!' Nonna exclaimed, rolling her eyes to the heavens.

'Quickly now, hold still. We have to comb your hair. We have to make ourselves as presentable as possible. We don't want to give them any reason whatsoever not to accept us.'

Martino winced as his mother dragged the comb vigorously through his thick hair, parting it neatly to one side, his fringe sweeping low across his forehead.

'Come on. We don't want to be late,' Ettore snapped, starting to walk out the door.

The family approached the registration building. They were directed to a floor where men and children had to line up with hundreds of others to have their heads shaven. The women also had their hair checked and crudely chopped short.

'Why did we have to comb our hair if it's going to be cut off?' Martino put to his mother as they waited in the queue.

'They're making sure you don't bring head lice on the ship,' she told him.

'Head lice—yuck!' Martino began to scratch at his head at the thought, earning a clip behind the ear from his Nonna.

'Stop that. We don't want to appear contaminated, even if we are!'

Afterwards, the men were separated from the women and children, as they were all required to strip naked for the medical examinations. Martino was stunned to see all the mothers taking off their clothes, including his Nonna. They looked embarrassed.

They were weighed, measured for height, X-rayed and checked over, then handed clean, army-issued clothing.

Nonna stared at the grey garments flung over her arms and as she moved away from the queue, she couldn't help remarking in a loud voice, 'It is like we're not human, just numbers.' Many of the women standing nearby, tired and miserable, agreed and nodded their heads.

'Quiet,' Contessa hissed at her mother. 'We want to go to Australia. I don't want to be sleeping on the floor forever.' She was nervous, more than she wanted to admit. To be refused entry to Australia now would be devastating.

'I know, I know … but there could be a nicer way. We're not criminals!'

'What are you talking about? They're not putting us in handcuffs! It's just a check-up and some clothes.' Contessa tried to make light of it, wishing her mother would just for once be compliant. This was their last hurdle to resettlement—it had to go smoothly.

'Listen, we may be displaced but we still have our dignity. We don't have to be checked over like animals.'

Many women, on hearing Nonna speak, murmured their assent. One woman even applauded.

'When we have a home, then we can feel proud,' Contessa asserted. 'First we must do as we are told. Please Mama, just put up with it. This is the way it has to be.'

'I know, I know,' the old woman muttered.

The following day after school, Martino walked up the street to meet Carlo as usual. He walked a little slower, as he was somewhat ashamed for the cleaner to see his head, practically bald after a rough shearing.

'At least I don't have lice,' he quipped to Carlo on approach.

'No, I dare say you don't,' the amiable cleaner agreed. 'They certainly make sure of that.'

Martino shuffled his feet, eager to get started.

'So, are you still going to Australia then?'

'Yes. We had our check-up. We are all clear to go.'

'Good. It's good. You will have a new life.'

'I don't really want a new life. This one is okay, but I do want to go on a ship.'

'You will enjoy the ship. But, before we begin, I have something for you,' Carlo announced, looking mysterious.

'For me?' Martino blinked, not sure if he'd heard correctly.

'I told the other cleaners you were leaving, and they agreed that you should be paid for all your hard work. I took this envelope around and everyone put in a note. So here you are, your very first wage. May it help you on your big journey to Australia.'

He took the envelope, ogling the money in awe. 'I didn't expect any pay. I just wanted to help.'

'And you have, more than you know,' the man told him with heartfelt sincerity.

'Thank you so very much. I'll give this to my mother; she'll spend it on something for the trip.'

'Wise decision,' Carlo said, smiling approvingly. 'Now best you run along. Spend your last weeks in Italy playing with the other kids, not cleaning with me.'

Martino studied the cleaner, wonderingly. 'But you have paid me to work. I have to help now! Don't you want me to?'

'Sure, sure I do. You can help if you want to ...'

'I'll keep working until I leave. I want to.'

Carlo watched the boy eagerly start picking up litter and scraps while he talked about his day at school and how he had scored a goal in a soccer match at lunchtime.

As he listened to his endless enthusiastic chatter, tears welled in his eyes. Hell, he was going to miss the kid.

* * *

The next three weeks slipped by quickly. It was Sunday, and they would catch the train to Genoa on Tuesday, with the ship due to set sail the following day. The families had already attended church and afterwards the Italian women—Contessa, Nonna, Bianca, Gilda, Tazia, Lisa and Lena - walked to the vast square fronting Trieste's harbour for the last time. They were beside themselves with excitement. They couldn't stop smiling, laughing and joking. They did their hair up and shared some make-up. Then off they went to say their goodbyes to the port. It was agreed that they would, at least, miss that.

While their mothers were at the square, Martino and Gian went to a nearby soccer field to watch one of the local derby games. They decided to stand behind the goal posts, as it was shady there and the day was very warm. During a stoppage in the match, while a player was being treated for an injury, the goalkeeper spun around and addressed the boys.

'Hey, you two kids!'

'You mean us?' Gian said, looking about.

'Yes, you kids. Do us a favour? Buy us a packet of cigarettes?'

'What with? Do we look rich to you?' Gian shouted back, thinking he was crazy.

The goalkeeper threw some money at them. 'Hurry back before the game ends.'

Now the boys knew he was crazy. Who just gives them money?

'Go on,' urged the goalie. 'Be quick.'

Not for a second did the boys consider buying cigarettes. No one just gave them anything. They could not believe their good fortune and hurried off into town with the easily acquired loot.

Their feet led them back to their camp.

'What should we spend it on?' Martino asked, looking about for ideas.

'Candy?' suggested Gian.

'Great idea!'

'Really? You've scored some money and you're going to blow it all on candy?' came a drawling voice behind them.

They turned to see Monte, leaning against a street lamp, watching them. His chin was tilted upward and his arms were folded casually against his chest.

'What would you spend it on?' Martino asked.

Monte shrugged. 'Fun. An adventure.'

'Like what?' Martino asked, obviously interested.

'Like ... going on a train or something.' Monte indicated the railway station behind them with a flick of his head.

'A train ride?' Gian turned and stared at the station, thinking hard. He loved trains. He knew their families had come to Trieste from Germany by train, but he couldn't really remember the trip, being so young at the time.

'Yeah. You could go somewhere ... like ... Milano.'

Martino knew his brothers didn't like Monte and they had often warned him about staying away from the boy. He felt guilty about talking to him and yet, he was intrigued by the idea of a train ride and couldn't help but throw in a quick question. 'What's Milano?'

'It's a big city in Italy,' Gian answered. 'I know because I have an aunt who lives there.'

'You could go visit your aunt,' Monte put to them and lowered his face to hide a mischievous smile twitching upon his lips.

'Is it far?' Martino asked, seriously considering it.

'Not that far. You could be there and back before dark. No one would even know you had gone,' Monte replied, looking up with a straight face and emotionless eyes.

The boys were sold. A short train journey to see a nice aunt who would probably give them biscuits, seeing it was such a rare visit. Yes. It was a grand way to spend some money. They hurried up the road to the railway station and bounded exuberantly up the steps.

'Have fun,' Monte muttered, resisting an urge to laugh out loud. He then ran away as fast as he could so that no one would ever know he had put the gullible little boys up to it.

Martino and Gian fronted the ticket seller, requesting passage for two to Milano. The seller, an old man with red, watery eyes, and stinking of tobacco, barely gave them a second look. He took their money and handed over the tickets.

'Platform two. One hour,' the man wheezed gruffly.

Scooting around the corner, the boys laughed together.

'That was easy,' Martino cried, delighted there actually was a train bound for Milano that day. They had enough money left over to buy a piece of candy each, so they went to the shop beside the station, settled on a packet of gum to share, then made their way to the correct platform to wait and chew.

Right on time, the train pulled in and the boys boarded, finding seats at the back of a middle carriage. They sat on proper, soft leather seats by a large window. It felt magnificent. The inspector checked their tickets, eyeing them warily, but said nothing. The whistle blew and they started to move. They had done it! They could barely sit still for excitement.

For the next half an hour, their faces were glued to the window, watching the fast passing scenery and Italian countryside. Though some hours later, the novelty had worn off, and they were wishing the trip would end.

'I thought Monte said it wouldn't take long!' Martino complained.

They struggled against their desire for sleep, as they were afraid to miss the stop, shifting in their seats. It began to occur to them that they would not be able to return to Trieste by dark, which would make their parents worry.

'We might get in trouble for this,' Martino stated. 'Big trouble. My papa will kill me if I'm not back for dinner.'

'Don't worry. My aunt can call them or something,' Gian said, though he shared Martino's concern. He started to realise that he wasn't really sure where exactly his aunt lived in Milano. He knew it was in an apartment block, but he had never been there before. He figured he could just ask the stationmaster if he knew of her. Surely he would know. What was her last name again?

* * *

Night fell on Trieste and at the silos.

When Martino didn't return as usual, Contessa grew anxious. She craned her neck looking out for him, and asked Nardo several times if he knew where his younger brother could be. After a while, her agitation compelled her to go search for him and she went tent by tent, calling his name. It was so unlike him. He always turned up for food and their usual dinnertime had come and gone without a trace of him. She ran into Taddeo who had eaten his dinner quickly and hurried off to join some other boys.

'I saw him with Gian heading to a soccer match,' Taddeo said, casting his mind back. 'That was ages ago. I haven't seen either of them since.'

It seemed Taddeo was the only one to have seen them that day and they had not been spotted again since. Contessa made a beeline for Bianca's tent, where she was lying down, talking to Daniela.

'Sorry to interrupt. Have you seen Gian or Martino? Martino hasn't come in for dinner and he doesn't seem to be anywhere.'

Bianca sat up. 'No. I thought Gian must be with Martino.'

'No one has seen them since this morning.'

Bianca was alarmed. 'Have you asked their friends, you know the boys they play soccer with?'

'Not all of them.'

'We should start there. Come. Let's go together.'

The women tracked down every boy they could find within the camp and asked them about Gian and Martino, but each boy in turn shook their head. Soon their husbands became aware the boys were missing and also started looking. By late evening, half the men from the refugee camp had joined the city police in searching for the two lost children.

For hours, they called the boys' names, walking up and down darkened streets, but there was not a trace of them.

Contessa returned to the camp where Nonna was waiting in case the boys came back of their own accord. The lights had long since been extinguished and hundreds of people were sleeping on their mattresses.

'They're not back,' Nonna whispered, answering the worried inquiry stamped on Contessa's face.

'Where are they then?' Contessa sighed wearily. Her frustration escalated with each passing hour.

'At least he is with Gian. The two of them should be safe together,' Nonna said softly, trying to calm her daughter.

'Can we help search?' Taddeo asked, sitting up. He was meant to be asleep, as it was close to midnight.

'Not now. The streets are dark. Don't worry, many are helping the police with the search. If they are not found by morning ...' Contessa became teary at the thought. 'If not found, you can search then, in the morning. Now go back to sleep.'

Taddeo reluctantly lay down, but found it hard to drift back to sleep. He was worried about his little brother. What could have happened to him? He knew the city well and would never willingly stay out all night. It wasn't like him at all. He feared something very bad had happened to him. After what seemed hours, sleep overcame his restless mind, but he awoke early with the sun. One glance around their sleeping quarters and he knew not only had Martino not come home but his papa too had spent the entire night away.

'Now can I go search?' he asked his mother, who sat red-eyed and exhausted on her mattress, her fingers interlaced on her lap.

'Yes,' she muttered.

'And me?' Nardo leapt to his feet as his brother rose.

'All right.'

Marietta sat up too. Her curls were tousled and her mouth opened in a wide yawn. 'And me?' she said sleepily.

'Taddeo and Nardo can go. Marietta, you should stay here with Nonna. If Martino returns, it would be best if you are here too.'

Marietta seemed to accept the arrangement and lay back down, her eyes closing immediately. It was very early, and she was too tired to argue. She said a quiet prayer for Martino to be brought home safe and slumped back into sleep.

'Put shoes on,' Contessa advised. 'And make sure you stay together and come back in one hour for breakfast. Hear me? One hour! I won't have three boys missing.'

'All right, Mama.'

It was eerily quiet in the street outside the camp. A tangerine-streaked sky cast a gentle light on the city, and the air was dewy with a salty tang.

'Where should we start?' Nardo asked, looking around as though half expecting to see Martino coming towards him.

'Maybe we should go to the soccer field. That's where they were last.'

'Good idea.'

Nardo stepped off the footpath on to the road, making to cross it, when he spied the figure of a boy lurking in the shadows of the railway building further up the street.

'Hey, who's that do you think?' Nardo asked, turning to Taddeo who had also spied the loitering body.

'Don't know. We should find out.'

They edged closer and were surprised and instantly wary to discover Monte.

'You're up early,' Taddeo threw at him.

'So are you.'

'We're looking for Martino and Gian. Seen them?' he asked, more out of a need to say something than expecting any useful information. Monte started smiling, a wicked, mischievous smile that hinted at some secret knowledge.

Taddeo's stomach tensed, and he felt Nardo lunge forward like a striking snake.

'What do you know?' Nardo thundered, striding towards him. 'Speak or I swear I'll …' His fists were balls of fury and he had them clenched in front of him, at the ready. The boy was not the small, insignificant child he once was; he was taller, stronger and capable of landing a solid punch.

Monte's smile vanished, and he held up a hand. 'Stop right there. I don't know anything.'

'You do,' Nardo insisted. 'Tell us what you know.'

Monte turned his head sideways and fixed his sights on the dark brick railway station. Nardo's eyes followed warily.

'What about it? Did you see them at the station? Did they go in?' Nardo demanded.

'Maybe.'

'They didn't have any money,' Taddeo pointed out.

'Whatever you reckon.'

'Listen, did they get on a train or not?'

Monte laughed. 'I think they did. They wanted an adventure.'

Nardo and Taddeo exchanged glances. What to believe?

'Where did they go then?' Taddeo asked, fishing for something more definite.

'I don't know,' Monte said casually. He smiled again, clearly enjoying having knowledge that they so desperately wanted.

'Tell us …' Nardo shouted, his fists clenching again.

'Why should I?'

'Because …' Nardo itched to slam him.

'Because we want our little brother back,' Taddeo cut in.

Monte's smile lingered and then straightened into a serious line. He stared at Taddeo. Then, suddenly feeling generous, he said, 'I think they said they were going to visit an aunt.'

'An aunt?' Taddeo's mind whirled. 'Not Aunt Maria in Bergamo?'

'In Milano, I think they said.'

'And you didn't think to tell anyone this?' Taddeo was appalled that Monte had held his silence and not told anyone. He had to have known there was a huge party searching all night for the boys.

'It was none of my business,' the boy said, grinning as though it was all some kind of joke.

'We're meant to be on a ship in two days. If we can't find Martino and Gian by then ...' Taddeo said, trying to explain the seriousness of the situation to the unconcerned Monte.

But the less tolerant, fiercer Nardo couldn't be bothered with tedious explanations. He wrenched back his fist and slammed it into Monte's face as hard as he could, splitting the boy's lip. Blood spouted in a small red shower, splattering on the ground. Monte screamed and his hands flew to his mouth where he was shocked to feel a clammy chin. He pulled back his fingers to see blood dripping from them.

Nardo was surprised to see him start crying but didn't care. 'If anything happens to my brother,' he dealt the warning unsympathetically, 'I'll hit you again.'

He stormed off, pausing only when Monte's ominous next words reached him.

'I hope you never find your stupid little brother and I hope your family never goes to Australia. I don't want you there. You'll pay for this!' His vitriolic tirade was mixed with a blubbering of tears, spit and blood.

Enraged, Nardo looked back.

'Leave him,' Taddeo commanded. 'Come on. We've got to tell Mama.'

The brothers hurried back inside the camp, hoping to catch their mother before she returned to the search. They needed to tell her what they had learned straight away. That is if they could even believe Monte. It occurred to them both that the boy could be lying just to throw them off the scent.

Contessa was shocked by the boys' report.

'Monte says they got on a train to Milano?' She couldn't understand how it was possible or what it would mean in terms of finding them. Milano was a huge city about six hours west by train. They could be anywhere! What if some men had noticed two innocent boys wandering around lost and grabbed them? Terrifying possibilities flashed through her mind. She gulped.

'I'll go tell the police,' she said, adopting a facade of calm. But she was far from it. They were meant to be catching a train to Genoa port tomorrow. What if the boys couldn't be found and brought back to Trieste in time? After all the assessments, paperwork, waiting … she didn't want to think about it. They couldn't miss that ship. If they did, well, the authorities had spelled it out. If you don't board, you go to the back of a very long queue. They would have to wait months, if not years to get another passage processed. She glanced about the overcrowded camp, hating everything about it. No. This was not happening. The boys would be found in time. They had to be.

Once the police were notified of the lead on the boys' whereabouts, they called off the search in Trieste and contacted the police in Milano.

Unaware of the new development, Ettore, Roberto, Edrico, Rico and Cappi continued looking, walking up and down every street. They even ventured close to Trieste's Zone B, which was under military administration of the Yugoslav People's Army. From certain streets, they could see down to heavily guarded crossover points—a scrum of Italian guards, a considerable gap, then a mass of Yugoslav guards.

Ettore was reminded of the guards at his prison and started thinking about the sinkhole and their callous treatment of Italians. He shuddered. Thoughts crept into his mind, dark thoughts that he did not want to acknowledge. Could two young boys somehow slip across the dividing line from Zone A to Zone B? Or, worse still, and yet more probable, could they have been snatched?

He had heard of men suddenly 'disappearing' from their camp. Some rumours put the disappearances down to spies living among them and then returning, but there was no concrete evidence as to why the men kept vanishing.

'Damn that child,' he cursed to himself, wanting to stop such ominous thoughts. He looked back at the Yugoslav checkpoints, anger rising from memories too young and raw. Not for the first time, he wished he and his family were thousands of miles away from the Communist zone. In fact, Australia would be just about the right distance. Australia! They had a ship to board. They had to find Martino by then.

The sun was high overhead. Ettore returned to camp, tired, cramped and fatigued. He half hoped he would return to Martino's smiling face, those happy, carefree eyes, his skinny legs and knobby knees … but only Nonna and Contessa awaited him.

'I'm sorry,' he said, collapsing down on the mattress.

'We've heard that the boys might be in Milano,' his wife informed him, wanting to break the news quickly.

'Milano?' He lifted his head. 'How?'

Contessa told him about Nardo's and Taddeo's run in with Monte.

'Monte knew and didn't tell anyone?'

'Seems so.'

'He's a bad, strange kid that one. Can't trust him. Who knows if they really are in Milano?'

'Well, the police have shifted their search there.'

Ettore remained quiet, lowered his head and closed his eyes. 'I'll get a couple of hours sleep then I'll start looking again. Just in case that Monte kid is lying!'

Hundreds of people from the camp joined in the late afternoon search after work or their afternoon siesta. Many children, worried about the boys who were well known for their enthusiasm on the soccer field, joined in the mass search. It was better to do something than sit around waiting to hear from the Milano police. And besides, no one could fully trust Monte. If Ettore said it was still worth searching in Trieste, then search they would.

That afternoon, Edrico approached his son. 'What happened to your lip?' he asked, noticing it was bruised and swollen.

'Nothing. I got knocked playing soccer.'

'So. You saw the boys get on train?' he asked bluntly.

'I heard them talking about going to Milano to visit Gian's aunt,' he said. 'I tried to talk them out of it, but they wouldn't listen to me. The other kids never listen to me. It's not fair. I try to help ...' Monte started to cry but his father was not having it.

'You heard them talking about catching a train and did nothing? You didn't try to stop them ... you didn't tell their mother? Why not? They are six-year-old boys!' Edrico was terribly disappointed in his son. 'You don't understand. If it weren't for Ettore and his friend Cappi, I wouldn't be standing here alive right now. I owe him so much and you ... you had a chance to help his son, to tell everyone where he'd gone and yet you chose not to—you didn't tell anyone.'

'I told you, Papa. They all hate me.'

'Right now, I don't blame them,' he said, averting his eyes from his son's astonished face.

At that moment, Tazia joined them. 'What is it? What's going on? What are you talking about?'

Edrico was too ashamed to answer, but his boy suddenly squeaked, 'Papa thinks it's all my fault the boys got on a train. I had nothing to do with it. I heard them talking about getting on a train to Milano. I didn't know they would really do it. I told them not to, but they mustn't have listened to me.' Monte was sobbing and his mother put her arms around him. She believed every word.

'You should have told us sooner what you knew, but it's not your fault. It's not like you bought them the tickets or anything,' Tazia said compassionately.

'He should have stopped them,' Edrico said darkly. There was something about his son's story that didn't up. He wasn't sure about him, didn't fully trust him. He had caught him lying on too many occasions.

'How was he supposed to do that? He couldn't very well follow them around all day, now could he?' posed Tazia.

'They hate me, Mama. They wouldn't let me be with them even if I wanted to.'

'I've heard enough,' Edrioc snapped. 'Mark my words, if those boys are not back to get on the ship, we're not going either. Roberto and Ettore are my friends. We go to Australia when they go!'

'But ...' Tazia began, looking horrified. 'We can't miss the ship.'

'That's something Monte should have thought about.' Edrico gave his son a piercing glare. 'Is there anything else you wish to tell us that could help find them? Anything at all?'

'They caught the train to Milano,' Monte said. 'I know it for sure. They did. They really did.'

Edrico nodded. 'I will go and tell hundreds of people that they are wasting their time searching in Trieste then.' Angry and mortified at his son's role in the affair, he marched off to find Ettore.

'You believe me, don't you, Mama?'

'Of course I do. Your father is just blind where his friends are concerned. I know you're a nice boy. You would never lead little kids astray.' She kissed him on the cheek and he smiled.

Carlo started work at the top of the street that led down to the displaced person's camp. He was surprised but not overly concerned when Martino did not show up at the usual time. *He must be late*, he thought. However, the minutes ticked by and he started to wonder what had happened to his little helper. He had never missed a day. Perhaps he was ill? He was due to leave Trieste for Genoa the next day and the boy had promised he would work one last time on the Monday. They had saved their goodbyes for the occasion but if he didn't show, he was unlikely to see him ever again. He felt sad, but he knew their family would be better off in another country. Italy was in great turmoil after the war.

As he cleaned his way down the street, he came to the camp where Martino and his family had resided for the past two years. He found his eyes searching among the children playing out front, hoping to catch sight of the boy to sing out a last farewell. However, he did not seem to be among them. A shame! Then suddenly he saw a girl, with thick, curly dark hair, whom he knew to be Martino's sister. He had seen her at the soccer game. Her wild curls and oddly shaped nose were hard to forget.

'Hello,' he called out to her. 'Martino ... he did not come cleaning today. Is he all right?' he asked her.

Marietta turned and saw the friendly, wiry cleaner with his bag of trash in one hand and his stick in the other. She had forgotten that Martino normally went to work at that time in the afternoon. It would have been his last cleaning session.

'I'm sorry. My brother has gone missing. They think he got on a train to Milano but they're not sure. He could still be in Trieste. No one can find him but the police are looking. Mama is worried we may not get to go to Australia if we don't find him by tomorrow.'

For a moment he didn't understand what she was saying, and then the full impact of her words hit him. The child had disappeared and they could not emigrate without him.

'Oh no ... no. This is terrible news. He didn't use the money I gave him to catch the train, did he?'

Marietta shrugged. 'No one knows how they could pay for tickets.'

'They?'

'He went with his friend.'

'I see. This is terrible. I feel bad. I shouldn't have given him the money. I should have given it to his mother.'

Marietta gawked at him, not sure what to say.

'Well,' he stood awkwardly, his stick scraping on the ground. 'I hope you find him. I really do. I'm sorry if somehow I've caused all this.'

'Don't worry, mister. Martino liked you. He liked cleaning.'

'Yes. Yes. I liked him cleaning too,' he smiled forlornly and shuffled away, still cleaning as he went, though absently, his shoulders forward, his smile gone.

Further down the street, in a musty, shadowy alleyway, Nardo found himself cornered by Monte. The boy had promised to tell Nardo more information about where Martino had gone and so he had willingly been led down the filthy, urine-soaked alley. Once out of view from the main street, Monte had slipped out a pocketknife that he grasped with deadly intent.

'Everyone hates me. They all think it's my fault the boys went missing. They all blame me—even my papa,' he seethed with malice gleaming in his eyes. 'All because of you and your brother.' He moved closer to Nardo, lifting the knife to be level with the boy's small, flat stomach.

'I just told them ...'

'I know what you told them. You should have kept your mouth shut.'

Monte flung himself on the smaller boy, who lifted his arms to defend himself. They both fell to the ground, the grime from the street smearing across their bare arms and legs. They rolled, the knife poised in Monte's hand, pushing forward, downward towards Nardo's throat.

My God. He's actually trying to kill me, Nardo thought, his mind chaotic with fear and confusion.

Desperately, he tried to force the hand with the knife away from his skin, but Monte's strength was fuelled by his rage.

I can't stop him, Nardo thought. Sweat made his hands slip from Monte's wrist. The knife tip was on his throat. The fight was draining his energy, making him weaker …

* * *

Outside the camp, a little way up the street, Bianca and Contessa sat together, watching the train station as though their boys might emerge from the building and walk down the steps at any moment.

'Of all the things to happen,' Bianca murmured.

'I don't know how they paid for tickets,' Contessa replied, shaking her head. 'When Martino got money from the cleaner, he gave it straight to me. It's not like him to spend money on such a thing.'

'Maybe they just snuck on the train without the guard seeing.'

'They might have done,' Contessa conceded. The boys had picked up so many bad habits from the camp in Germany.

Their sons had been playmates since the age of two, when the women used to watch over them carefully. And now they had wandered off, this time too far for them to follow. They felt guilty, as though somehow they were to blame. They should have kept a closer eye on them, should not have allowed them to go to the soccer matches on their own.

'They will get hungry and tired soon. Surely they will find a policeman and tell him what's happened. They are smart boys,' Contessa said.

'I've sent a telegram to my cousin in Milano. Gian calls her his aunt. You never know, they might find a way to her.'

'I hope so.'

They waited for hours. Ettore and Roberto brought them some food for lunch. They ate without tasting it, which was perhaps a good thing. The soup was particularly oily that day.

Many people from the camp came out and wished them luck. 'God speed on finding your boys,' they whispered. Everyone knew that they had disappeared.

The afternoon went by without any news. They were meant to catch a train to Genoa in another fifteen hours. If the boys weren't found soon, their dream, the heady dream that had nurtured their spirits for so long, would crumble away.

'Tomorrow, we should ask for assistance to go to Milano to join the search there,' Ettore said decisively. He was coming to accept that they would not be on the train to Genoa.

Roberto nodded, meekly. 'Yes. Good idea.'

Bianca put her head in her hands and wept. Her husband wrapped his arms around her. 'Come now. They'll figure it out. They'll come back.'

'Let's hope they do it soon,' Ettore added, voicing what they were all thinking.

* * *

Nardo felt the knife cutting against his skin. *Surely there should be blood by now*, he thought. *One more thrust and it will all be over …*

Monte, looking triumphant, mustered the last of his strength to bear down on the knife.

Nardo closed his eyes and braced for it. He thought about his parents and felt sorry for them losing two boys in one week. Images clouded together. The word 'sorry' was all that was left in his world of white fear. He had lost the fight.

And then … somehow, miraculously Monte was being pulled back from him. The knife was snatched from the boy's hand. Someone had come to his aid. Thank God!

Footsteps … Monte was retreating. A hand helped him stand.

'Thanks,' he mumbled, feeling giddy.

'Are you all right?'

'I think so.' His eyes focused. 'Do I know you?'

'My name's Carlo. I'm looking for a boy. I came down this alley because I heard a noise … for a moment, I thought you were him.'

'I know.'

'You know?'

'Yes. You are looking for my brother. I look a bit like him.'

'Your brother?'

'Yes. Martino.'

'Yes, yes,' the cleaner said, nodding, examining the boy's face closer in the dim light. 'You do look like him. I had to go looking for Martino. I feel it's partly my fault he's missing. People believe he got on a train to Milano but they're not sure.'

'Everyone seems to think it's their fault.'

Carlo was confused by his response and then, as Nardo rubbed at his pinpricked neck, he understood. 'That boy … the one with the knife. He blames himself for your brother's disappearance?'

'Sort of. But he probably had more to do with it than you.'

'He did? I don't understand. Why would he want Martino to be lost? Why was he trying to kill you? He was trying to kill you!'

'Yes,' Nardo agreed, still struggling to believe it. 'He would've if you hadn't turned up with that sharp stick.' He looked at the long stick in Carlo's hands.

'I'm a cleaner. Martino cleans with me.'

'Now I know you.'

'Why was the boy trying to kill you?'

Nardo considered the question, recalling the sheer hatred in Monte's eyes. 'Guilt seems to make people go crazy.'

Carlo looked at Nardo's serious face in the gloom of the alley. 'You are Martino's brother. That is for sure. Ah … you are the star soccer player.'

'How do you know?'

'I came to a game. Yes. You're a strong player. Martino is talented too. You wait and see.'

Nardo only hoped to see Martino return, let alone play soccer again.

Carlo read the boy's expression and felt a wave of sorrow and sympathy. 'I'm sorry. Forgive me. He's a smart boy, your brother. He'll figure it out. I don't accept he's not coming back.'

'Sometimes … it doesn't matter how smart or how strong or how good you are.'

'And sometimes … it does matter.'

Nardo hoped he was right.

'This boy with the knife … what is his name?'

'Why do you ask?' Nardo queried warily.

'Well, what he did was very wrong. He needs to be reported. The police should know about it.'

Nardo considered it and knew the old man was right, but if Monte was reported it could affect the plans to go to Australia. Edrico and Tazia were good people.

'I will tell my father about it. He will take care of it,' Nardo replied, but he doubted very much that he would. His father was a close friend of Monte's father … he couldn't put him in the awkward position of having to turn on his friend's son, not this close to boarding the ship. There was plenty of time to deal with Monte once they were in Australia. That's if they got to

Australia … with his brother still missing, who knew what was going to happen.

'I've got to get back. I don't want my parents worrying about me too,' Nardo said. He was suddenly eager to get back to see if they had found Martino.

'Of course. I'll walk with you.'

Back at the camp, Nardo was quick to learn that Martino and Gian were still missing. His parents were so distraught that even if he wanted to tell them about his dreadful altercation with Monte in the alleyway, he wouldn't have had the heart. Besides, a part of him was embarrassed for falling for Monte's trap. He should not have been so stupid as to let himself be lured alone in a dark place with that boy! Best to try and forget it and keep well away from him.

Around eight o'clock that night, the police visited the camp asking to see Ettore and Roberto. A camp official came to fetch them.

'The police want to speak with you in the office,' the weary official advised them.

Ettore and Roberto hurried to meet the police in the small, tattered looking room at the back of the camp.

'Any news?' they asked, all too hopeful as they burst into the lowly lit office.

The older police officer smiled. 'Yes. The two boys walked into a police station near Milano railway station about an hour ago. They are safe and well but hungry. The police have given them some food and water and they will be cared for until we can put them on a train tomorrow. An officer will accompany them.'

Ettore and Roberto breathed a huge sigh of relief and hugged each other.

'It is the best news ever,' Roberto said, wiping at tears. 'Fantastic.'

'I can't believe it. Just like that, they are found,' Ettore said. It sounded too good to be true.

'Yes. They did the right thing. They got lost and wandered around for a long time but somehow the lads remembered to retrace their steps to the train station and found our police station. All in all, they have had a big adventure; thank goodness it has ended well.'

'But officers ...' Ettore began, thinking ahead. 'We're due on a train tomorrow morning. It will take us to Genoa where we are going to board a ship to Australia. If we miss the train ... I don't know when we can catch another. We have waited years to emigrate.' His voice had grown thin, and he choked on his final words.

The senior policeman took in what he had said and mulled it over. He observed the men, noticing their old, thin clothes, closely cropped hair, yellowish complexions and scrawny builds. The scar from Roberto's bullet wound was prominent on the side of his head.

'I see,' said the policeman. 'Perhaps we can help. Wait here.'

The uniformed officer disappeared and returned a short while later. 'It is all arranged. Your sons will be driven down in a police car. That will give them a fast escort back to Trieste, with the sirens on and everything,' the officer smiled. 'They will be here by midnight.'

'Tonight?' Roberto gasped. He was light headed with relief and leaned on the office wall for support.

Ettore swallowed hard on a sob of relief. He shakily recovered and, looking at the officer, nodded his sincere thanks. 'They will love the siren,' he said and managed a lopsided smile. 'But they don't deserve such a homecoming!'

'You have a long ship voyage ahead—plenty of time to get mad at him then.'

Both fathers smiled.

'Yes. I've never been so happy to have someone to get mad at,' Ettore said.

'Well,' said Roberto. 'Let's go tell our wives the good news.'

'Very good news. It won't sink in yet. Thank you officers. You have made two families very happy.'

'We like happy endings,' the officer said. And before the men turned to leave, he said to them with gusto, 'Good luck to you in Australia!'

* * *

That morning, as the emigrating families crossed the road to the train station, Martino, whose hand was firmly in Contessa's grasp, looked back down the steps at the camp.

There, on the footpath was his friend, Carlo.

The cleaner, on seeing him glance his way, gave him a wink and a short wave. 'Goodbye Martino,' he called happily.

His mother was pulling him too sharply and quickly for Martino to have a chance to shout back, but he did manage a big grin and a flutter of his free hand, which served for a wave.

It was enough for Carlo. It was enough for him to know that the boy had been found and would get on the ship. And, as fate would have it, he would not mourn the loss of a fine, big brother. All was right with the world.

Chapter eighteen

July 31ˢᵗ, 1950
Genoa Port, Italy

A long queue of people shuffled aboard the one-chimney, 8000-tonne *Amarapoora*. Older women bowed their heads and wept as their feet left Italian soil, perhaps for the final time.

Among the 634 passengers boarding that day was a group of bedraggled Italians from Trieste, comprising the Saforo family and their friends. Ettore carried their one, worn out suitcase, as his family, bewildered and elated, inched along the ramp onto the sturdy ship. Beside him was Martino, sleepy and quiet, but joyously present. Contessa's cheeks were flushed with excitement and she kept nervously checking all their children were with them. When her sparkling eyes met those of her husband's, they shared a smile of renewed optimism. They were doing it. They were leaving behind a war-torn country and seeking out a new life. It was what they had been talking about and planning for so long, and it was happening at last.

Behind them were their friends, their smiles equally as broad. Edrico and Tazia waved goodbye to the crowds who had come to see people off. Edrico turned at the top of the ramp to take a photo, one last shot of their homeland. Their son Monte did not look back. He was quiet and sullen and showed little enthusiasm for the sea voyage ahead.

Bianca and Roberto shuffled along with their children, who were in awe of the crowds and the size of the ship.

Cappi was not smiling but his eyes held more hope than they had in a long time. His mother Lisa, his sister Lena, her husband

Rico and their two little girls were excited; however, their steps were slow and measured, given their mixture of nerves and cautious anticipation. Boarding that ship was a moment they would never forget.

On board, the Saforo family was assigned to one cabin, crammed full of bunk-style beds. They entered the small, white-walled room and the youngsters immediately wanted to try out their new bedding.

'Wait, wait,' Ettore called to his children, already clambering up on to the bunks.

'There is not enough for all of you. So, Martino and Nardo— you take that bed. Marietta and Isabella—you have that one.'

'I want a top one!' Isabella wailed, her wide eyes brimming with tears. Her black hair had been cut very short and she sported a straight fringe running across her forehead.

'No, my sweet. You might fall out in the middle of the night and look how high it is.'

Unconvinced, she stood sniffling until Marietta, who was twice her age, happily plunked herself down on the lower bunk. 'Come, Isabella. Sit here.'

The little girl, who had turned four only two weeks ago, bounded over and climbed up.

'Nonna, take your pick.'

She chose one near the door as she sometimes required the toilet in the middle of the night and didn't want to disturb everyone when she left the cabin. Taddeo took the one above it.

'Why does he get one of his own?' Isabella asked.

'Because he is the oldest and biggest,' Ettore replied. 'Now let's go up on deck and wave goodbye to Italy.'

'Will we ever come back?' Martino squeaked. He knew he was in trouble from his rail escapade, and had been trying to keep a low profile since his return, but he had to know. All eyes were on him.

'Back to Italy?' Ettore considered the question. 'We will give Australia a chance. If we don't like it and we have enough money, we will come back.'

Everyone nodded and thought that a fair arrangement.

'When will we come back?' Martino continued unsure of what his father's answer had actually meant.

'When and if we want to,' his papa replied.

'Promise?'

Ettore sighed. 'It will depend on what the whole family wants to do.'

'What if the whole family wants to stay but I want to come back?'

Contessa smiled and went over to the sad-eyed boy. 'We are all going to miss things in Italy, but now we're going on a big adventure. Who knows what we will find in Australia? Give it a chance. You still have all of us and that's all that matters.'

Martino gazed around the cabin and saw his family watching him. Marietta poked her tongue out at him. Taddeo smiled kindly. Nardo turned his head to gaze out the porthole.

'Let's go out on deck then,' he said firmly, and took his father by the hand.

Ettore loved the feel of the child's trusting hand in his. 'I hope you like Australia,' he said casually. 'I hope we all do.'

'We will. As soon as we find a soccer ball, we'll be all right,' Martino said, rather wisely.

'That's the way,' Ettore said. 'Come on. It's time to say good-bye.'

Contessa was elated to be up on deck, the ship pulling away from the dock, but as the pretty city grew smaller in her sights, she suddenly realised what it was they were leaving behind. Their country, their language, their way of life! Sure, they had been displaced and living in appalling cramped conditions, but they had been among Italians, and not just any Italians. The people

of Trieste were a proud and sophisticated people with independent women and broad ideals. She loved the harbour, the sea,
the square, the sense of belonging in a place that valued family
and the home … those were the things that had reminded her of
Fiume. Could she still feel that way in another land?

Ettore had said they could come back. As Contessa watched
the land slip from view, she felt her heart wrenching. Small,
unexpected tears cascaded down on to quivering lips.

Nonna was next to her. The rest of her family had long since
wandered from the rail to explore the rest of the ship. Nonna
gripped her arm so tight it hurt, but she did not pull away. She
understood. She wanted to hold on tight too. Around the ship
was water … everywhere they looked. They were at sea and
would remain so for longer than she could have envisaged. For
Australia was not like Italy and, for them, no matter how much
they longed for it, there would be no going back.

Acknowledgments

I sincerely thank my father for allowing me to interview him at length, sharing his family's story and their struggle to flee from their beloved Italian city of Fiume. I also thank his brother and sisters for their support.

I am grateful to my father for introducing me to other Italians who experienced similar plights and for serving as interpreter.

I wish to acknowledge the hundreds of thousands of people who were displaced throughout Europe during World War II and to the countries who took so many in. It is believed that up to 350,000 Italians fled the north-eastern region of Italy in a mass exodus at the end of World War II, and between 5,000 to as many as 15,000 were killed, known as the 'foibe'. About 58,000 of these exiles were from Fiume. *Port of No Return* is a fictional tale set against these historical events.

I feel tremendous gratitude towards Michelle Lovi at Odyssey Books for helping to bring this story to life. I also thank my editor Jenna O'Connell for her keen eye and thorough efforts in preparing the work for publication.

I thank my husband Rene for his patience, honesty and feedback in providing those first and valuable edits.

Without support, this work would not have come to fruition. I am forever grateful to all who contributed in any way.

About the Author

Michelle Saftich is a first time author who resides in Brisbane, Australia, with her husband and two children.

She holds a Bachelor of Business/Communications Degree, majoring in journalism, from the Queensland University of Technology (QUT).

For the past twenty years, she has worked in communications, including print journalism, sub-editing, communications management and media relations.

In 1999, she was named National Winner for Best News Story in the ASNA (Australian Suburban Newspaper Awards).

Born and raised in Brisbane, she spent ten years living in Sydney; and two years in Osaka, Japan, where she taught English.

Connect with Michelle at www.michellesaftich.com

Printed in Australia
AUOC02n0749240516
276138AU00001B/1/P